CW00402674

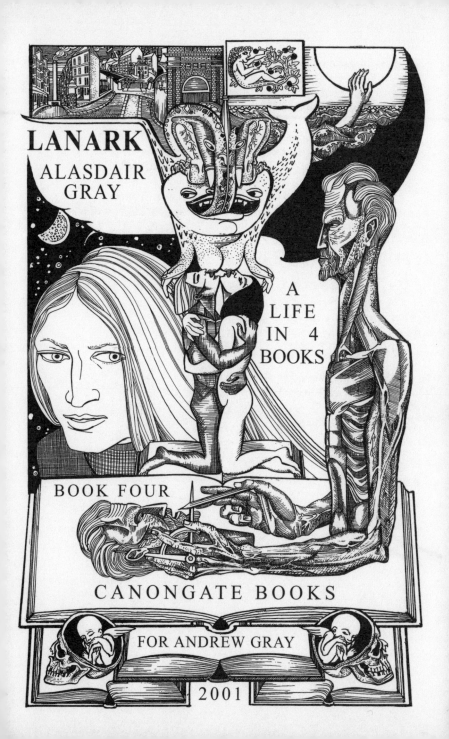

LANARK
ALASDAIR GRAY

A LIFE IN 4 BOOKS

BOOK FOUR

CANONGATE BOOKS

FOR ANDREW GRAY

2001

First published in Great Britain in 1981 by
Canongate Publishing Limited and re-published in 2001
as a four-volume limited edition of 2000 copies by
Canongate Books, 14 High Street, Edinburgh EH1 1TE.

Portions of this work originally appeared in *Scottish
International Review*, *Glasgow University Magazine*, and *Words
Magazine*.

British Library Cataloguing-in-Publication Data
A catalogue record for this book is available on
request from the British Library

ISBN 1 84195 120 X

Printed and bound in Great Britain
by Butler & Tanner Ltd, Frome

www.canongate.net

Who is all fire and wings and hearts and seed?
Has never ended, yet always starts
afresh when the wind changes?
Who gave and changes everything we need?

Who, with all water, weather, ground and spaces,
and many coloured eyes of stone, leaf, star,
won't let us rest in them, but instead
drops dead, stands attentive, raves and races?

Who makes all we joyfully, painfully love march away?
and will one day help us
out in a blink, before we are at last wise,
with a present too suddenly big to hold,
think of, or see, or say?

                                        —Anon

TABLE OF CONTENTS

By Arts is formed that great Mechanical Man called a State, foremost of the Beasts of the Earth for Pride

FORCE

BOOK FOUR

THE MATTER, FORM AND POWER OF A COMMONWEALTH

CHAPTER 31. Nan

Lanark opened his eyes and looked thoughtfully round the ward. The window was covered again by the Venetian blind and a bed in one corner was hidden by screens. Rima sat beside him eating figs from a brown paper bag. He said, "That was very unsatisfying. I can respect a man who commits suicide after killing someone (it's clearly the right thing to do) but not a man who drowns himself for a fantasy. Why did the oracle not make clear which of these happened?"
Rima said, "What are you talking about?"
"The oracle's account of my life before Unthank. He's just finished it."
Rima said firmly, "In the first place that oracle was a woman, not a man. In the second place her story was about me. You were so bored that you fell asleep and obviously dreamed something else."
He opened his mouth to argue but she popped a fig in, saying, "It's a pity you didn't stay awake because she told me a lot about you. You were a funny, embarrassing, not very sexy boy who kept chasing me when I was nineteen. I had the sense to marry someone else."
"And you!" cried Lanark, angrily swallowing, "were a frigid cock-teasing virgin who kept shoving me off with one hand and dragging me back with the other. I killed someone because I couldn't get you."
"We must have been listening to different oracles. I'm sure you imagined all that. Is there anything else to eat?"
"No. We used it all up."

With a clattering of purposeful feet a stretcher was pushed into the ward among a crowd of doctors and nurses. Munro marched in front; technicians followed dragging cylinders and apparatus. They went behind the screens in the corner and nothing could be heard but low hissing and some phrases which seemed to have drifted from the corridors.

". . . the conceived conceiving in mid conception . . ."

". . . . . inglorious Milton, guiltless Cromwell . . . . ."

"Why inglorious? Why not guilty?"

"She came naked. That helped."

Munro came over and stood at the bed's foot regarding them gravely. He said, "I've arranged a meeting with Lord Monboddo three hours from now to authorize your departure from the institute. I had meant you to wait here till then but we've had an unexpected delivery of human beings. They're in good condition, but feeble, and will die if someone puts them off their food. A nurse is bringing your clothes. You can dress and wait in the staff club."

"No need," said Lanark. "We wouldn't spread our opinions in a case like this."

Munro asked Rima, "Do you agree?"

"Of course, but I'd like to see the staff club."

"If I can trust you I'd like you to stay here. This is a lonely ward and company would help the woman feel at home."

Rima said brightly, "I'll be delighted to help you, Dr. Munro, but will you do something for us? Get Monsignor Noakes to send more of his lovely food. It will be easy to not mention food when we have some."

Munro walked away saying grimly, "I promise nothing, but I'll do what I can."

Lanark stared at her and said, "You are unscrupulous!"

She asked in a hurt voice, "Aren't you glad I'm not like you?"

"Very glad."

"Then show it, please."

They heard the technicians and their apparatus leave the ward. Only a few doctors were busy behind the screens when a nurse came to Rima and Lanark with an armful of clothes and a couple of fat rucksacks and said, "Dr. Munro wants you to dress now. He says the rucksacks are full of food for your journey and you can start eating it when you like."

Rima seized the female garments and stroked them with her fingertips. They were blond and velvety. A small excited smile curved her lips. She sprang naked from bed, saying, "I'll dress in the bathroom." She ran to the door at the end of the ward and Lanark examined the rucksacks. Each contained a rolled-up leather overcoat and hard little blocks of compressed fruit and meat wrapped in rice paper. One held a red thermos flask of coffee and a flat steel flask of brandy, the other a first-aid kit and an electric torch. Departure from this far too warm, too insulated place seemed disturbingly near. Lanark got up and carried his clothes to the bathroom.

Rima stood before a mirror, brushing her hair downward over a shoulder with slow, even strokes. She wore a short, amber-coloured, long-sleeved dress, and sandals of yellow leather, and Lanark stood half-hypnotized by her cool golden elegant figure. She murmured, "Well?"
He said, "Not bad," and started washing at a basin.
"Why don't you say I'm beautiful?"
"When I do you disparage me."
"Yes, but I feel lonely when you don't."
"All right. You're beautiful."
He dried himself and began putting on a grey tweed suit and pullover. She tied her hair carefully with a dark yellow ribbon, looking sad and thoughtful. He kissed her and said, "Cheer up! You're the light and I'm the shadow. Aren't you glad we're different?"
She pulled a face and went out, saying, "It's hard to shine without encouragement."

When he re-entered the ward, the doctors, nurses and screens had gone and Rima was talking to a woman in the corner bed. He joined them, noticing a small bald wrinkled head sticking from under a coverlet. The mother lay half sunk in a bank of pillows. Her body was slight, there were grey glints in her brown hair and youth and age were equally mingled in her gaunt little face. She smiled wanly and said, "It's strange seeing you again, mystery man."
He stared blankly. Rima said, "It's Nancy. Don't you remember Nan?"
He sat by the bed almost laughing with surprise. He said, "I'm glad you escaped from the Elite."
He could not stop grinning. Since entering the institute he had forgotten Sludden and his harem, and now these tangled love-lives seemed wonderfully funny. He pointed at the cot. "You've a nice-looking baby."
"Yes! Isn't she like her father?"
"Don't be silly," said Rima gently. "Babies aren't like people.

Who is the father anyway? Toal?"

"Of course not."

"Then who is he?"

"Sludden."

Rima peered at what was visible of the baby's face.

"Are you sure?"

Nan smiled sadly. "Oh, yes. I wasn't his fiancée, like Gay, or his vulgar mistress, like Frankie, or your clever mistress, like you. I was the poor little girl he had been kind to, but he loved me most, though I had to keep that a secret. Whenever I was tired of being neglected and tried to escape he would come to my lodgings and climb drainpipes and break in through windows. Sludden was tremendously athletic. He would hold me tight and tell me that though we'd slept together so often our lovemaking was still fresh and adventurous and it would be stupid to give it up because of the other girls. He said he needed all of you so that he could be lively with me. He was the first man I ever loved and I never really wanted anyone else, though I was always planning to leave him, before my illness got bad."

"What illness?"

"I began to grow mouths, not just in my face but in other places, and when I was alone they argued and shouted and screamed at me. Sludden was very good with them. He could always get them singing in tune, and when we slept together he even made me glad of them. He said he'd never known a girl who could be pierced in so many places."

Nan smiled in an almost motherly way and Lanark, with a pang of jealousy, saw the same soft, remembering look on Rima's face. Nan sighed and said, "But they drove even Sludden away in the end (the mouths did), because as I grew worse I needed him more and he didn't like that. He was going into politics and he had a lot to do."

Lanark and Rima cried out together, "Politics?" and Rima said, "He always made fun of people who went into politics."

"I know, but when you disappeared he replaced you with a protest girl, a big brassy blonde who played the guitar and kept telling us her father was a brigadier. I didn't like her at all. She said we should prepare to seize the reins of the economy, and it was very important to care for people, but she always talked too much to listen to anyone. While she was speaking Sludden would wink at us behind her back. A lot of the Elite crowd went protestant then. Hundreds of new cliques appeared with names and badges I can't even remember. Even criminals

wore badges. Suddenly Sludden came in wearing a badge
and laughing his head off. He'd gone with the blonde to a
protest meeting and been elected to a committee. He said we
should all become protestants because nobody had confidence
nowadays in Provost Dodd and we had a real chance of seizing
the city. None of that made sense to me. You see I was pregnant
and Sludden wouldn't allow me near enough to tell him. When
I managed it at last he grew very serious. He said it was a
crime to bring children into the world before it had been redeemed by revolution. He wanted the baby killed before it
was born but I wouldn't allow that. Pass her to me, please."
Rima lifted the baby into Nan's arms. It opened its eyes, gave
a small mew of complaint and returned to sleep against her
breast. She said, "He called me selfish, and he was right, I
suppose. I had never known anyone who wanted me before
I met Sludden, and now he didn't want me at all, and I needed
someone else, though the thought of the coming baby often
made me quite mad and sick. I felt I was being crushed under
a whole pile of women with Sludden jumping up and down
on top, wearing a crown and laughing. Then the baby would
move inside me and I would suddenly feel calm and complete.
I was sorry for Sludden then. He seemed a frantic greedy child
running everywhere looking for breasts to grab and mothers
to feed him and who would never, never have enough. Did
you feel that, Rima?"

Rima said shortly, "No."

"Why did you like him so much?"

"He was clever and amusing and kind. He was the only man
among us who hadn't a disease."

Lanark said, "He had no disease because he *was* a disease.
He was a cancer afflicting everyone who knew him."

Rima snorted. "Huh, you don't know who you're talking about.
Sludden liked you. He tried to help you, but you wouldn't
let him."

Nan smiled. "You're making Lanark jealous."

"Oh yes, she's making me jealous. But I can be jealous and
correct."

Rima said, "How did you get here, Nancy?"

"Well, I was in my lodgings when the pains began and I knew
my baby was coming. I asked the landlord to help but he was
frightened and ordered me out of the house, so I shut myself
in my room and managed (I can't remember how) to drag a
heavy wardrobe in front of the door. That nearly killed me.
The pains were so bad I fell down and couldn't move. I was

sure the baby had died after all. I felt I was nothing then, nothing and nobody, a nobody feeling nothing but horror, a piece of dirt as evil as the world. I suppose I screamed to get out because an opening appeared in the floor beside me."

Lanark shuddered and said, "Going through *that* nearly killed me. I knew a soldier who jumped in with his revolver and was gored to death by it. I don't see how a pregnant woman could survive at all."

"But it was easy. It was like sinking through warm dark water that could be breathed. Every bit of me was supported. I still felt the labour pains but they weren't sore, they were like bursts of music. I felt my little girl break free and float up to my breast and cling there. No, she must have drifted down for I was coming head first. I felt all kinds of muck flow out of me and vanish in the darkness. That darkness loved me. It was only when the light returned that the music became pain again and I fainted. That was a long time ago, and here I am, talking to you, in a lovely clean room."

Lanark said abruptly, "You'll be well cared for here."

He rose and walked through the nearest archway. Nan's story had recalled his own crushing descent in a way which made him long for sunlit landscapes of hill and water. Hopefully he raised the great Venetian blind, but the screen he had once thought a window was no longer there. In the centre of the wall, from floor to ceiling, was a double door of dark wood with panels of ornamental bronze. He pressed it but it was immovable, without handles or keyhole. He returned to the ward.

Nan breast-fed the baby and gossiped quietly to Rima. Lanark sat on his bed and tried to finish *The Holy War* but found it irritating. The writer was unable to imagine an honest enemy, and his only notion of virtue was total obedience to his strongest character. A nurse brought Nancy's lunch. She only ate part and a moment later Lanark was startled to see Rima eat the rest, glancing at him defiantly between forkfuls. He pretended not to notice and nibbled a block of dense black chocolate from the rucksack. The sour taste was so unwelcome that he lay down and tried to sleep, but his imagination projected cityscapes on the insides of his eyelids: sliding views of stadiums, factories, prisons, palaces, squares, boulevards and bridges. Nancy and Rima's conversation seemed like the murmur of distant crowds with fanfares sounding through it. He opened his eyes. The noise was not imaginary. An increasing

din of trumpets shook the air. Lanark stood up and so did
Rima. The trumpets grew deafening, then silent as a black
and silver figure entered and stood under the central arch. It
was a man in a black silver-buttoned coat, black knee breeches
and white stockings. He wore white lace at the throat and
wrists, silver-buckled shoes and a snowy periwig with a three-
cornered black hat on top. He held a portfolio in his left hand
and in his right an ebony staff tipped with a silver knob. His
face was the most surprising thing about him for it was Munro's.
Lanark said, "Dr. Munro!"
"At the moment I am not a doctor, I am a chamberlain. Bring
your rucksacks."
Lanark slung a rucksack on his shoulder and carried the other
in his hand. Rima said goodbye to Nan, who was comforting
her crying baby. Munro turned and rapped his staff against
the great doors, which clanged and swung inward. Munro led
them through, Rima pressing against Lanark's side. The doors
closed.

CHAPTER 32.
Council Corridors

They were in a wood-panelled, low-ceilinged, circular room, thickly carpeted and smelling like an old railway carriage. An upholstered bench went round the wall and a mahogany pillar in the centre supported a bald bronze head wearing a laurel wreath. Munro said loudly, "The northern lobby."

The head nodded and a faint rumbling began. Lanark realized they were in a carriage travelling sideways. Munro said, "The machinery joining the institute to the council chambers is rather antiquated. Take a seat, we'll be some minutes here."

They sat and Rima murmured, "Isn't this exciting?"

Lanark nodded. He felt strong and sure of himself and thought that a lord president director could have frightened him once, but not now. He was too old. Munro was pacing round the pedestal and Lanark called out, "Where do we go when we've seen Lord Monboddo?"

"We'll see what he says first."

"But these rucksacks have been packed for a particular kind of journey!"

"You're leaving at your own request, so you'll have to travel on foot. It's too late to discuss it now."

The doors opened and someone dressed like Munro led in two plump men in evening dress. Soon after the lift stopped again and another chamberlain brought in a group of worried men in crumpled suits. The three chamberlains talked quietly by the pedestal while the rest babbled in clusters on the bench.

". . . . not honouring us, it's the creature he's honouring . . ."

"His secretary is an algolagnics man."

". . . . . but he'll maintain the differential. . . . ."

"If he doesn't he's opening the floodgates to a free-for-all."
Munro approached Lanark and said grimly, "Bad luck! I expected to have the director to ourselves but he's receiving a deputation and conferring a couple of titles. He's available for ten minutes, I'll have to settle our business in three, so when we leave the lift stay close to me and say as little as possible."
"But this meeting will shape our whole future!"
"Don't worry, I, won't let you down."
The doors opened and the chamberlains led them out onto such a bright floor that Lanark's heart lurched, thinking he was in open daylight.

It was a floor of coloured marble inlaid in geometrical patterns. It was nearly a quarter of a mile across, but as the eye took in the height of the ceiling the width seemed insignificant. It was an octagonal hall where eight great corridors met below a dome, and looking down them was like looking down streets of renaissance palaces. The place seemed empty at first, but when his eyes got used to the scale Lanark noticed a great many people moving like insects about the corridor floors. The air was cool and, except for the remote sonorous echoes of distant footfalls, refreshingly quiet. Lanark looked around with open mouth. Rima sighed, slid her fingers out of his and stepped elegantly away across the marble floor. She seemed to grow taller and more graceful as she receded. Her figure and colouring blended perfectly with her surroundings. Lanark followed, saying, "This place suits you."
"I know."
She turned and walked past him, smoothing the amber velvet over her hips, her chin raised and face dreamy. Feeling excluded he stared around once more. Some benches upholstered in red leather lay about the floor and Munro sat on the nearest looking intently along a corridor, the staff and portfolio across his knees. Some distance behind stood a wooden medieval throne on top of three marble steps. The other chamberlains had brought their parties to it, and now the plump men in evening dress knelt side by side on the lowest step in an attitude of prayer. Close by, with folded arms, the deputation stood in a tight cluster. Their chamberlain was photographing them. Rima continued walking past Lanark in an aimless dreamy way till he said sharply, "It's impressive, of course, but not beautiful. Look, at those chandeliers! Hundreds of tons of brass and glass pretending to be gold and diamonds and they don't even light

the place. The real light comes from behind the columns
round the walls. I bet it's neon."
"You're jealous because you don't belong here."
He was hurt by the truth of this and said in a low voice, "Quite
right."
She laid a hand on his chest and stared excitedly into his eyes.
"But Lanark, we could live here if you wanted to! I'm sure
they'd give you a job, you can be very clever when you try!
Tell Munro you want to stay. I'm sure it's not too late!"
"You've forgotten there's no sunlight here and we don't like
the food."
Rima said wistfully, "Yes, I had forgotten that."
She walked away from him again.

He sat beside Munro and tried to keep calm by looking
up into the deep blue dome. It was painted with angels blowing
trumpets and scattering blossoms around figures on clouds. He
specially noted four ponderous horsemen on some puffs of cu-
mulus. They wore Roman armour, curly wigs and laurel wreaths
and managed the horses with their knees, for each held a sword
in the left hand and a mason's trowel in the right. On similar
clouds facing them stood four venerable men in togas holding
scrolls and queerly shaped walking sticks. Both groups were
gazing at the height of the dome where a massive man sat
upon a throne. His strong face looked benevolent, but something peering in it suggested he was shortsighted or deaf. The
painter had tried to distract from this by loading him with
impressive instruments. A globe lay in his lap and a sword
across his knees. He held scales in one hand and a trowel in
the other. An eagle with a thunderbolt in its beak hovered
over his head and an owl looked out from under the hem of
his robe. A turbaned Indian, a Red Indian, a Negro and a
Chinaman knelt before him with gifts of spice, tobacco, ivory
and silk. Lanark heard Munro ask, "Do you like it?"
"Not much. Who are these horsemen?"
"Nimrod, Imhotep, Tsin-Shi Hwang and Augustus, early presidents of the council. Of course the titles were different then."
"Why the wigs and armour?"
"An eighteenth-century convention—the mural was painted
then. The men facing them are former directors of the institute:
Prometheus, Pythagoras, Aquinas and Descartes. The figure
on the throne is the first Lord Monboddo. He was an insignificant legislator and an unimportant philosopher, but when council and institute combined he was a member of both, which

made him symbolically useful. He knew Adam Smith."

"But what is the institute? What is the council?

"The council is a political structure to lift men nearer Heaven. The institute is a conspiracy of thinkers to bring the light of Heaven down to mankind. They've sometimes been distinct organizations and have even quarrelled, though never for long. The last great reconciliation happened during the Age of Reason, and two world wars have only united us more firmly."

"But what is this heavenly light? If you mean the sun, why doesn't it shine here?"

"Oh, in recent years the heavenly light has never been confused with an actual *sun*. It is a metaphor, a symbol we no longer need. Since the collapse of feudalism we've left long-term goals to our enemies. They're misleading. Society develops faster without them. If you look closely into the dome, you'll see that though the artist painted a sun in the centre it's almost hidden by the first Monboddo's crown. Stand up, here comes the twenty-ninth."

A tall man in a pale grey suit was crossing the smooth marble floor accompanied by three men in dark suits. A herald in medieval tabard marched in front with a sword on a velvet cushion; another came behind carrying a coloured silk robe. The whole party was advancing briskly to the throne when Munro stepped into the path and bowed saying, "Hector Munro, my lord."

Monboddo had a long narrow face with a thin, high-bridged nose. His hair was pale yellow and his eyes grey behind gold-rimmed spectacles, yet his voice was richly, resonantly masculine. He said, "Yes, I know. I never forget a face. Well?"

"This man and woman have applied for relocation."

Munro handed his portfolio to someone at Monboddo's side, who pulled out a document and read it. Monboddo glanced from Lanark to Rima.

"Relocation? Extraordinary. Who's going to take them?"

"Unthank is keen."

"Well, if they understand the dangers, let them go. Let them go. Is that paper in order, Wilkins?"

"In perfect order, sir."

Wilkins held out the document at an angle supported by the portfolio. Monboddo glanced at it and made snatching movements with his right hand until Munro placed a pen between the fingers. He was going to sign when Lanark shouted, "Stop!"

Monboddo looked at him with raised eyebrows. Lanark turned on Munro and cried, "You know we don't want to return to Unthank! There's no sunlight in Unthank! I asked for a town with sunlight!"
"A man with your reputation can't be allowed to pick and choose."
Monboddo said, "Has his chief given him a poor report?"
"A very poor report."
There was a silence in which Lanark felt something vital being filched from him. He said fiercely, "If that report was written by Ozenfant it ought not to count. We dislike each other."
Munro murmured, "It is written by Ozenfant."
Monboddo touched his brow with a fingertip. Wilkins murmured, "The dragonmaster. A strong energy man."
"I know, I know. I never forget a name. An abominable musician but an excellent administrator. Here's your pen, Munro. Uxbridge, give me that cape, will you?"
A herald placed a heavy green cloak lined with crimson silk round Monboddo's shoulders and helped him adjust the folds. Monboddo said, "No, we won't go against Ozenfant. Look, Wilkins, sort this out while I attend to these other chaps. We haven't much time, you know."
Monboddo strode onward to the throne, the cape billowing behind him. Most of his retinue followed.

Wilkins was a dark, short, compact man. He said, "What seems to be the problem?"
Munro said crisply, "Mr. Lanark does not know what relocation involves. He has asked to leave. I have found a city whose government will take him in spite of his poor record. He refuses to go because of the climate."
Lanark said obstinately, "I want sunlight."
"Would Provan suit you?" asked Wilkins.
"I know nothing of Provan."
"It is an industrial centre surrounded by farming country but in easy distance of highlands and sea. The climate is mild and damp with a yearly average of twelve hours' sunlight per day. The inhabitants speak a kind of English."
"Yes, we'll go there gladly."
Munro said, "Provan won't take him. Provan was the first place I asked."
Wilkins said, "Provan will have to take him if he goes to Unthank first."
Munro rubbed his chin and began to smile. "Of course. I had forgotten."

Wilkins turned to Lanark and said smoothly, "Industrially speaking, you see, Unthank is no longer profitable, so it is going to be scrapped and swallowed. In a piecemeal way we've been doing that for years, but now we can take it *en bloc* and I don't mind telling you we're rather excited. We're used to eating towns and villages but this will be the first big city since Carthage and the energy gain will be enormous. Of course people like you who've joined us already won't need to go through that messy business again. You'll be moved to Provan, which has a lively expanding economy. So visit Unthank with a clear mind. Think of it as a stepping stone to the sun."

"But how long will we have to live there?"

Wilkins glanced at his wristwatch.

"In eight days a full meeting of council delegates will give the go-ahead. We start work two days after."

"Then Rima and I will be in Unthank for twelve days?"

"No longer. Only a revolution can change our programme now."

"But I've heard Unthank is a more political place nowadays. Are you sure a revolution can't happen?"

Wilkins smiled.

"I meant that only a revolution *here* can change our programme."

"But have I no other choices?"

"Stay with us if you like. We can find work for you. Or leave and just wander about. Space is infinite to men without destinations."

Lanark groaned and said, "Rima, what should we do?"

She shrugged impatiently.

"Oh, don't ask me! You know I like it here and that hasn't influenced you so far. But I refuse to wander about in space. If you want to do that you can do it alone."

Lanark said in a subdued voice, "Right. We'll return to Unthank."

Wilkins and Munro straightened their backs and spoke in louder voices. Wilkins slid the paper into the portfolio and said, "Leave this with me, Hector. Monboddo will sign it."

Munro said, "They'd better not go without visas."

"Give me the ink, I'll stamp them."

Munro unscrewed the silver knob from his staff (it was shaped like a pair of spread wings) and held it upside down. Wilkins stuck his thumb in the socket and drew it out with a glistening blue tip. Rima was leaning forward to watch and Wilkins dabbed his thumb at her forehead, making a mark between the brows

like a small blue bruise. She gave a little shriek of surprise.
Wilkins said, "That didn't hurt, did it? Now you, Lanark."
Lanark, too depressed to ask for explanations, received a similar
mark; then Wilkins put his thumb in the knob a second time
and brought it out clean. He said, "It's not a conspicuous sign
but it tells educated people that you've worked for the institute
and are protected by the council. They won't all like you for
that but they'll treat you with respect, and when Unthank falls
you'll have no trouble getting transport to Provan."
Rima said, "Will it wash off?"
"No, only strong sunlight can erase it, and you won't find
that till you reach Provan. Goodbye."
He walked away across the floor, diminishing toward the tiny
distant throne where Monboddo, like a green and scarlet doll,
was graciously receiving a paper from the leader of the pygmy
deputation. Munro screwed the knob onto his staff and beckoned Rima and Lanark in the opposite direction.

Beyond the northern lobby the corridor was crossed by
a wrought-iron screen ten feet high. A gate in the middle was
guarded by a policeman who saluted as Munro led them
through. The corridor grew busier. Black and silver chamberlains led past small groups of people, some of them negro and
oriental. From windows overhead came the applause of distant
assemblies, faint orchestras and fanfares, the rumble and hum
of machinery. Brisk, well-dressed men and women came and
went through doorways on either side, and Lanark's rucksacks
made him feel unnatural among so many people carrying brief-
cases and portfolios. If Rima had offered to carry hers he would
have felt he had an ally, but she moved along the corridor
like a swan down a stream. Even Munro seemed a servant
clearing the way for her, and Lanark felt he would be unkind
not to trudge alongside like a porter. After twenty minutes
they came to another high octagonal hall where corridors met.
The blue dome here was patterned with stars and a lamp in
the height cast a white beam down on a granite monument
in the centre of the floor, a rough block carved with giant
figures and with water trickling from it into ornamental pools.
Girls and boys lounged smoking and chatting on steps surrounding this, and on the smooth tiled floor older people ate and
drank at tables among orange-trees in tubs. Soft laughter and
music sounded from windows overhead and blended with the
conversation, clinking cutlery, splashing fountains and whistling
of canaries from cages in the little trees.

Munro halted and said, "What do you think of it?"

Lanark no longer trusted Munro. He said, "It's better than the staff club," but the leisurely air of the place made his heart swell and eyes water. He thought, 'Everyone should be allowed to enjoy this. In sunlight it would be perfect.'

Munro said, "Since we're beside the exit we may as well rest while I give you advice on your journey."

He stuck his staff into the soil of a tub, sat at a table and beckoned a waiter. Rima and Lanark sat down too. Munro said, "I suppose you won't refuse a light refreshment?"

Rima said, "I'd love it."

Lanark looked round for the exit. Munro said, "Lanark appears to be angry with me."

Rima laughed. "No wonder! I liked hearing him argue with you and Monboddo and that secretary. I thought 'Good! I'm being defended by a strong man!' But you were too clever for him, weren't you?"

"He won't lose by it."

As Munro ordered from the waiter Lanark had the feeling of being watched. At nearby tables sat a mother, her twelve-year-old son and an old couple playing chess. None of these seemed specially attentive, so he gazed up at the rows of windows above the doors where waiters ran in and out. They were curtained with white gauze and seemed empty, but overhead, not far below the dome, a balcony projected and a group of men and women in evening dress were leaning over the parapet. The distance was too great to distinguish faces but a stout man in the centre dominated the party with wide gestures of the hands and arms, and appeared to point in Lanark's direction. Something like a pair of binoculars was produced and clapped to the face of a woman at the stout man's side. Feeling exasperated Lanark seized a newspaper on a nearby chair, opened it and started reading, presenting the back of his head to the watchers above. The paper was called *The Western Lobby* and was soberly printed in neat columns without spreading headlines or large photographs. Lanark read:

ALABAMA JOINS
THE COUNCIL

By accepting the creature's help in constructing the continent's largest neuron energy bank, New Alabama becomes the fifth black state to be fully represented on the council. Inevitably this will strengthen the hand of Multan of Zimbabwe, leader of the council's black bloc. Asked last night if this would not lead to increased friction in the council's already unwieldy conferences, the president, Lord Monboddo, said, "All movement creates friction if it doesn't happen in a vacuum."

Farther down the page his eye was caught by a name he knew.

OZENFANT RAMPANT

When presenting the energy department's quinquennial audit yesterday, Professor Ozenfant roundly condemned the council's adoption of decimal time. The old duodecimal time scale (declared the fiery Professor) had been more than an arbitrary subdivision of the erratic and unstable solar day. The duodecimal second had allowed more accurate readings of the human heartbeat than decimal seconds. Predictions of deterioration on the decimal scale had a 1.063 greater liability to error, which accounted for the recent reduction in the energy surplus. Sabotage by a rogue element in the intake had also been responsible, but the main culprit was the new time scale. Professor Ozenfant insisted that his words must not be taken as a criticism of Lord Monboddo. In committing us to decimal time the lord president director had simply ratified the findings of the expansion project committee. It was unfortunate that nobody in that committee had first-hand experience of the lonely, difficult and dangerous work of sublimating dragons. The whole business was one more example of a council rule undermining an institute process.

Lanark folded the paper into his pocket and peered upward again. The party still leaned upon the balcony wall, and the gestures of the man in the centre had a familiar, mocking, flamboyant quality. Rima had accepted a cigarette from Munro who was holding a lighter to the tip. Lanark said sharply, "Is that Ozenfant watching us? There, on the balcony?"

Munro looked upward.

"Ozenfant? I don't know. It's hardly likely; he isn't popular on the eighth floor. It might be one of his imitators."

"Why do people imitate him if he isn't popular?"

"He's successful."

The waiter placed a full glass of wine before each of them and a plate of something like an omelette. Rima took her fork and began eating. After a gloomy pause Lanark was about to follow her example when there came a sound of booing, laughter and ironical cheers. Along the space between the tables and the monument marched a procession of shaggy young men and women holding placards with slogans:

EAT RICE, NOT PEOPLE

EATING PEOPLE IS WRONG

FUCK MONBODDO

MONBODDO CAN'T FUCK

A policeman marched on either side and behind them slid a platform loaded with men and filming equipment.

"Protestants," said Munro without looking up. "They march every day to the barrier about this time."

"Who are they?"

"Council employees or children of council employees."

"What do *they* eat?"

"The same as everyone else, though that doesn't stop their denouncing us. Their arguments are ludicrous, of course. We don't eat people. We eat the processed parts of certain life forms which can no longer claim to be people."

Lanark saw Rima push her plate away. There was a tearful look on her face, and when he reached out and grasped her hand she grasped his in turn. He said sternly, "You were going to give us advice about our journey."

Munro looked at them, sighed and laid down his fork. "Very well. You will walk to Unthank across the intercalendrical zone. This means the time you take is unpredictable. The road is fairly distinct, so keep to it and trust nothing you can't test with your own feet or hands. The light in this zone travels at different speeds, so all sizes and distances are deceptive. Even the gravity varies."

"Then the journey could take months?"

"I repeat, you will cross an intercalendrical zone. A month is as meaningless there as a minute or a century. The journey will simply be easy or strenuous or a combination of both."

"What if our supplies give out?"

"Some reports suggest that people who find the journey difficult reach the other side in the moment of final despair."

Rima said faintly, "Thank you. That's very encouraging."

"Better put your coats on. It's cold down there."

The coats were ankle-length with hoods and a thick fleecy lining. They pulled on their rucksacks, smiled anxiously at each other, kissed quickly, then followed Munro across the floor and up the steps to the monument. The giant rock overhung the steps like a boulder balanced on a pyramid. Shadows cast by the light defined figures brooding in crevices, declaiming from ledges and emerging from a cave in the centre. A figure on top seemed to represent the sculptor. His face looked up at the light but his fists drove a chisel with a mallet into the stone between his knees. Lanark touched Munro's shoulder and asked what this represented.

"The Hebrew pantheon: Moses, Isaiah, Christ, Marx, Freud and Einstein."

They passed through a group of young people who stared and murmured, "Where are they going?" "The emergency exit?" "Look at those crazy coats!" "Surely not the emergency exit!" Someone shouted, "What's the emergency, Granddad?"

Munro said, "No emergency, just relocation. A simple case of relocation."

There was silence then a voice said, "They're insane."

They reached the summit where water trickled down into gold-fish ponds. The great boulder was supported by a surprisingly small pedestal with an iron door in it. Munro struck the door with his staff. It opened. They stooped and passed through.

CHAPTER 33. A Zone

In watery green light, between narrow cement walls, they descended a metal staircase for many minutes. The air grew chilly and at length they came into a cavernous low-ceilinged place which gave a sense of width without spaciousness, for the floor was covered by pipes and tubes of every size from the height of a man to the thickness of a finger, while the ceiling was hidden by cables and ventilation ducts. They emerged from a door in a brick pillar onto a metal walkway leading across the pipes. Munro moved down this and Lanark and Rima followed, sometimes clambering over an unusually large pipe by an arched metal ladder. For a long time the only sound was a distant pulsing hum mingled with gurgles and clanking and their echoing footsteps. Rima said, "This bending hurts my back."

"I see a wall in the distance. We'll soon be out of here."

"Oh, Lanark, how dreary this is! I was excited when we went up to Monboddo. I expected a glamorous new life. Now I don't know what to expect, except horror and dullness."

Lanark felt that too. He said, "It's just a zone we've got to cross. Tomorrow, or the next day, we'll be in Unthank."

"I hope so. At least we've friends there."

"What friends?"

"Our friends at the Elite."

"I hope we can make better friends than those."

"You're a snob, Lanark. I knew you were insensitive, but I never thought you were a snob."

They forgot their misery in the heat of a small quarrel until the walkway reached a platform before an iron door in a wall of damp-streaked cement. It was the first door they had seen for many days with hinges and a key in the lock. It was stencilled with large red letters:

**EMERGENCY EXIT 3124
DANGER! DANGER! DANGER! DANGER!
YOU ARE ABOUT TO ENTER
AN INTERCALENDRICAL
ZONE**

Munro turned the key and opened the door. Lanark expected darkness but his eyes were dazzled by an amazingly bright white mist. A road began at the threshold with a yellow stripe down the middle, but it was only visible for five or six feet ahead. He stepped outside and a wave of coldness hit his face and hands making him draw deep breaths of freezing air. They exalted him. He cried, "It's good to be in the open at last! Surely the sun is up there!"

"Several suns are up there."

"There's only one sun, Munro."

"It's been shining a long time. The light of many days keeps returning to zones like this."

"Then it ought to be even brighter."

"No. When light rays meet at certain speeds and angles they negate each other."

"I'm not a scientist, that means nothing to me. Come on, Rima."

"Goodbye Lanark. Maybe you'll trust me when you're a little older."

Lanark didn't answer. The door slammed behind him.

They walked into the mist guided by the yellow line on the road between them. Lanark said, "I feel like singing. Do you know any marching songs?"

"No. This rucksack hurts my back and my hands are freezing." Lanark peered into the thick whiteness and sniffed the breeze. The landscape was invisible but he could smell sea air and hear waves in the distance. The road seemed to rise steeply for it became difficult to walk fast, so he was surprised to see Rima vanishing into the mist a few paces ahead. With an effort he came beside her. She didn't seem to be running, but her strides covered great distances. He caught her elbow and gasped, "How can . . . you go . . . so quickly?"

She stopped and stared.

"It's easy, downhill."

"We're going uphill."

"You're mad."

Each stared at the other's face for a sign that they were joking until Rima backed away saying fearfully, "Keep off! You're mad!"

He stepped after her and felt acutely dizzy. At the same time something shoved him sideways. He staggered but kept his feet and stood swaying a little. He said weakly, "Rima. The road slopes downhill on this side of the line and uphill on the other."

"That's impossible!"

"I know. But it does. Try it."

She came near, put a foot hesitantly across, then withdrew it saying, "All right, I believe you."

"But why not test it? Hold my hand."

"Since we're both on the downhill side we may as well keep to it. We'll travel faster."

She began walking and he followed.

He now had sensations of descending steeply. Each stride covered more and more ground until he shouted, "Rima! Stop! Stop!"

"I'll fall if I try to stop!"

"We'll fall if we don't. It's getting too steep. Give me your hand."

They grabbed hands, dug heels in, slithered to a standstill and stood precariously swaying. He said, "We'll have to take this slowly and carefully. I'll go first."

He released her hand, stepped slowly and carefully forward, his feet slid from under him, he grabbed her for support and pulled her heavily down. They rolled over each other then he was tumbling sideways with a rhythmical bumping each time the rucksack passed under his body. When he came to rest and managed to stand up the ground seemed level and he was alone in the mist. Not even the yellow line was visible. He yelled "Rima! Rima! Rima!" and listened, and heard the distant sea. For a moment he felt utterly lost. He took the torch from his rucksack, switched it on and found the yellow line a yard away from him; then he remembered that if Rima had fallen over the line she would have rolled the opposite way. This was a cheering thought for it made events seem logical. He turned and climbed the hill, torch in hand, and after a lot of effort reached a summit where he heard a sound of weeping. Ten steps farther he found her squatting on the far side of the line, her hands covering her face. He sat down and put an arm round her shoulders.

After a while she looked up and said, "I'm glad it's you."
"Who else could it have been?"
"I don't know."
Her knuckles were bleeding. He brought out the first-aid kit,
cleaned the grazes and put on sticking plaster. Then they sat
side by side, tired out and waiting for the other to suggest a
move. At last Rima said, "What if we walked on different sides
of the line but held hands across it? Then when one of us
went downhill we'd be steadied by the one going up."
Lanark stared at her and cried, "What a clever idea!"
She smiled and stood up. "Let's try it. Which way do we go?"
"To the left."
"Are you sure?"
"Yes. You slid over the line without noticing."
The new way of walking was a strain on the linking arm but
worked very well. Eventually the road grew level on both sides
and part of a huge rocky wall could be seen through the mists
ahead. The yellow line ran up to an iron door painted with
these words:

EMERGENCY EXIT 3124
NO ADMITTANCE

Lanark kicked the door moodily. It was like kicking rock. He
said "It was me who slid over the yellow line, not you."
They turned round and set off again.

They had not gone far when they heard a strange wavering
sound, a sound Lanark seemed to recognize. Rima said, "Someone's crying."
He took the torch from his pocket and shone it ahead and
Rima drew a sudden breath. A tall blond girl, wearing a black
coat and a knapsack, squatted on the road with her hands over
her face. Rima whispered, "Is it me?"
Lanark nodded, went to the girl and knelt beside her. Rima
gave a little hysterical giggle. "Aren't you forgetting? You've
done that already."
But the grief of the girl before him made him ignore the one
behind. He held her shoulders and said urgently, "I'm here,
Rima! It's all right. I'm here!"
She paid no attention. The upright Rima walked past him, saying coldly, "Stop living in the past."
"But I can't leave a bit of you sitting on the road like this."
"All right, drag her along. I suppose helpless women make

you feel strong and superior, but you'll find her a bore eventually."

Her voice throbbed with such scorn, helplessness and humour that it drew him to his feet. Since the crouching Rima seemed unable to notice him he followed the moving one.

They joined hands and silently travelled a great distance. Nothing was visible but the pallor of the mist, nothing audible but the sighing sea. The cold air stung their faces; shoulder, elbow and fingers grew sorely cramped and burning, especially in mid-gradient when one was straining downhill to drag the other steeply up. They passed into a stupor in which they knew nothing but the pain in their arms and the ache of their feet on the road. Sometimes they entered a real sleep from which they were wakened by a pang of vertigo as one or the other wandered onto the line. These pangs, as strong as electric shocks, at last conditioned them into sleepwalking straight forward because Lanark had been unconscious for a long time when something cut him hard on the knee. He blinked and saw a huge tilted shape in the whiteness ahead. He brought out the torch and shone it down. His knee had struck the rim of a rusty iron wheel, flat on its side and blocking the roadway. He helped Rima onto it, led the way along one of the spokes, climbed over the hub and shone the torch at the shape overhanging them. He expected to see something heavily industrial, like the tower above a derelict mine shaft, so the object confused him. It was made of timber bound with iron into a shape like a tub cut away on one side. Rima said, "It's a chariot."

"But there's room inside for twenty or thirty men! What beasts could ever pull it? The head of that bolt is bigger than *my* head."

"Maybe you've shrunk."

"And it's ancient—look at the rust! Yet it's lying on top of a modern road. We'll have to walk round."

He jumped down between the chariot and the severed wheel and sank to his knees in dry sand. Rima landed near him, dropped her rucksack and flopped beside it, saying, "Goodnight."

"You can't sleep here."

"Tell me when you find somewhere better."

He hesitated but the narrow space shielded them from the cold air and the sand was very soft. He dropped his own rucksack and lay beside Rima, saying, "Rest your head on my arm."

"Thanks. I will."

They wriggled to make the sand fit their bodies and lay still
for a while. Lanark said, "Last night I lay on a goosefeather
bed with the sheets turned down so bravely. Tonight I'll sleep
in a cold open field along with the raggle-taggle gypsy."
"What's that?"
"A song I remember. Are you sorry we left the institute?"
"I'm too exhausted to feel sorry about anything."
A little later her voice seemed to reach him from a distance.
"I'm glad I'm exhausted. I couldn't sleep here if I wasn't ex-
hausted."

He was wakened by musical whirring which came from
far away, passed overhead and faded into silence. Rima stirred
and sat up, spilling sand from her shoulders, then stretched
her arms and yawned. "Ooyah, how fat and sticky and stale I
feel."
"Fat?"
"Yes, my stomach's swollen."
"It must be wind. You'd better eat."
"I'm not hungry."
"Could you drink hot coffee? There's a flask of it in your rucksack."
"Oh, I could drink that, yes."
She unbuckled the rucksack, put her hand in and drew out,
with a disgusted look, the red thermos flask which tinkled and
shed a stream of brown droplets. She tossed it away and began
brushing sand from her hair with her hands. Lanark said, "You
must have smashed it when you fell. You'd better take your
food out, the damp will spoil it."
Nothing he said would persuade her to touch the food so he
removed it himself, peeled off the sodden wrappings and re-
packed it in his own rucksack along with the brandy flask. Then
they rose, walked around the chariot and saw the shadowy
prow of another chariot. The road was hidden by a wilderness
of broken chariots which loomed in the mist like a fleet of
sunk battleships, the shafts, axles, broken rims and naked spokes
sticking up between sand-logged hulls like masts, anchors and
titanic paddlewheels. It was impossible to climb through so
they trudged round, often stopping at first to pour sand from
their shoes but soon tiring of this and plodding uncomfortably
on. Many hours seemed to pass before they stepped onto asphalt
again. They sat and had a nip of brandy before emptying their
shoes for the last time, then they joined hands over the yellow
line and resumed walking.

New freshness filled them. There was little or no strain on their arms, the mist grew warm as if the sun was about to come through and they were soothed by pleasant sounds: first larksong overhead, then the crooning of pigeons and a swishing as if heavy rain were falling in a forest. Once they heard such a loud gurgling and creaking of oars that Lanark groped with his torch to the roadside, expecting to see the bank of a wide river, but though the water noise grew louder he saw nothing but sand. Farther on they were passed by footsteps and voices going the opposite way. The voices travelled in clusters of two and three and spoke quietly and indistinctly except for a couple who seemed to be arguing.

". . . a form of life like you or me."

". . . here's ferns and grass. . . ."

"What's wonderful about grass?"

As they passed through an invisible crowd of chattering children some real raindrops dashed in their faces and the mist turned golden and lifted. The straight road, embanked in places, ran without undulation across undulating sand to a mountain on the horizon. Tiny farms, fields and woodlands covered foothills which glittered in the rain as though dusted with silver: the summit was split into many snowy peaks with clouds drifting down between them, and all this was seen under a rainbow, a three-quarter violet blue green yellow orange red arc shining sweetly in a shining sky. Rima smiled at the distance and gripped both his hands. She said, "It was good of you to bring me out of that place. You're very wise sometimes."

They kissed and walked onward. The mist descended and the strange gravities of the road strained their arms once more. Again they avoided the strain by walking in a half-conscious daze. At last Rima said, "We're nearly there."

Lanark jerked awake and saw a rocky wall above them in the mist. He switched on the torch and an iron door appeared with these words on it:

EMERGENCY EXIT 3124
NO ADMITTANCE

Rima sat down with her back to the door and folded her arms. Lanark stood staring at the words, trying not to believe what he saw. Rima said, "Give me something to eat."

"But—but—but this is impossible! Impossible!"

"You led us right round these chariots and back along the road."

"I'm sure it's a different door. It's rustier."

"The same number's on it. Give me that rucksack."

"But Munro said the road was clearly marked!"

"Are you deaf? I'm starving! Pass the bloody rucksack!"

He sat down and laid the rucksack between them. She opened it and began eating with tears flowing down her cheeks. He laid a hand on her shoulder. She shook it off so he started eating too. Hunger and thirst hadn't troubled him much since entering the zone and now he found the food so taste-less that he returned it to the rucksack, but Rima chewed as fast and savagely as if eating were a sort of revenge. She devoured dates, figs, beef, oatmeal and chocolate and all the time the tears poured down her cheeks. Lanark stared in awe and at last said timidly, "You've eaten more than half the food."

"Well?"

"We've still a long way to travel."

She made a noise between a howl and a laugh and went on eating till nothing was left, then she uncorked the brandy flask, drank two mouthfuls and got up and staggered into the mist. He dimly saw her kneel at the roadside and heard vomiting sounds. She returned looking pale, lay down with her head in his lap and fell asleep at once.

The weight on his lap was comforting at first. Her face, childish in sleep, filled him with the tender, sad superiority we usually feel for the sleeping; but the road was hard, his position uncomfortable and he began to feel trapped. His thoughts kept exploring the road ahead, wondering how to escape from it. His muscles ached with the effort of keeping still. At last he kissed her eyelids until she raised them and asked "What's wrong?"

"Rima, we must get away from here."

She sat up and pressed her hair back with her hands.

"If you don't mind I'll just stay and wait for you to come wandering back."

"You may wait a long time. I refuse to die at the door of a place where I've acted wickedly."

"Wickedly? Wickedly? You use more meaningless words than anyone I've ever met."

He wondered how to be soothing and said experimentally, "I love you."

"Shut up."

His anger rose to the surface. "I love the reckless way you abandon courage and intelligence whenever things get really difficult."

"Shut up! Shut up!"

"Since we're determined to behave badly, please pass the brandy."

"No, I need it."

He got to his feet and said, "Are you coming, then?"

She folded her arms. He said sharply, "If you need the first-aid box, you'll find it in the rucksack."

She didn't move. He said humbly, "Please come with me."

She didn't move.

"If you knock the door hard enough, somebody might open it."

She didn't move. He laid the torch beside her, said quickly, "Goodbye," and walked away. He was descending the first hill in great strides when something punched his back. He turned and saw her, tearstained and breathless. She cried, "You'd have left me! You'd have left me alone in the fog!"

"I thought you wanted that."

"You're a cruel nasty idiot."

He said awkwardly, "Anyway, give me your hand."

They joined hands and all at once his body felt aching-feeble. He even lacked strength to hold her fingers. It was Rima who kept them together and moving along the road. He loathed her. He wanted to lie down and sleep so he disguised his staggers as a carefree way of walking and thought malignantly, 'She'll soon tire of dragging me along,' but Rima continued for a great distance without complaining. At last, feeling lightheaded, he pretended to hum a tune to himself. She stopped and cried, "Oh, Lanark, let's be friends! Please, please, why can't we be friends?"

"I'm too tired to be friendly. I want to sleep."

She stared at him, then her face relaxed into a smile. "I thought you hated me and wanted to get away."

"At the moment that is perfectly true."

She said cheerfully, "Let's sit down. I'm tired too," and sat on the road. He would have preferred the sand at the roadside but was too tired to say so. He lay beside her. She stroked his hair and he was almost sleeping when he felt something strange and sat up.

"Rima! This asphalt is cracked! It's covered with moss!"

"I thought it was more comfortable than usual."

He looked uneasily around and saw through the mist a thing which shocked him out of tiredness. A dark humped headless creature, about four feet high with many legs, stood perfectly

still in front of them. The feet were gathered together and
the legs bent as if to jump. Lanark felt Rima grip his shoulder
and whisper, "A spider."
His scalp tightened. There was a thudding in his ears. He stood
up and whispered, "Give me the torch."
"I haven't a torch. Come away."
"I'm going nowhere with that behind me."
He took a breath and stepped forward. The dark body became
a cluster of bodies, each with its own leg. He called happily,
"Rima, it's toadstools!"
A clump of big toadstools grew on the yellow line so that
half the domed heads tilted left and the other half to the right.
Lanark bent down and stared between the stems. They were
rooted in a heap of rotten cloth with rusty buckles and a blis-
tered blue cylinder in it. He pointed: "Look, the thermos flask!
That pile of old clothing must be your rucksack!"
"Don't touch! It's horrible!"
"How did they come here? We left them beside the chariots.
They can't have crawled along the road to meet us."
"Can any dreadful thing not happen here?"
"Be sensible, Rima. Strange things have happened here but
nothing dreadful. This fungus is a form of life, like you and
me."
"Like you, perhaps. Not like me."
Lanark was fascinated. Peering closely he moved round the
cluster and felt his ankles brushed by something light.
"And, Rima, here's ferns and grass."
"What's wonderful about grass?"
"It's better than a desert full of rusty wheels. Come on, there's
a slope. Let's climb it."
"Why? My back's sore, and you're supposed to be tired."
Beyond the toadstools the road vanished under an overgrown
embankment. Lanark scrambled upward and Rima, grumbling,
came after.

They climbed through gorse, brambles and bracken, feeling glad of the protective coats. The white mist faded until
they emerged into luminous darkness under an immense sky
of stars. They stood beside a ten-lane motorway which lay across
the mist like a causeway across an ocean of foam. Vehicles
were whizzing along too quickly to be recognized: tiny stars
in the distance would suddenly expand, pass in a blast of wind,

shrink to stars on the opposite horizon, and vanish. There was
a thirty-feet-high road sign on the grassy verge:

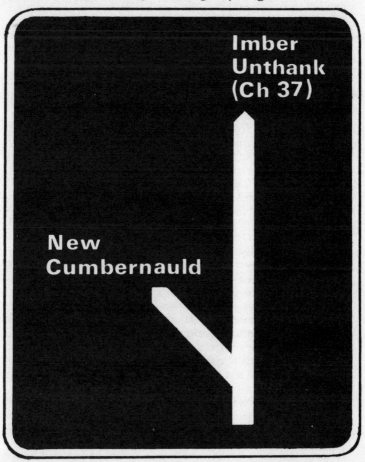

:"Good," said
Lanark happily. "We're on the right road at last. Come on."
"It seems a general rule that when I'm able to walk you feel
exhausted and when I need a rest you keep dragging me along."
"Are you really tired, Rima?"
"Oh, no. Not at all. Me tired? What a strange idea."
"Good. Come along, then."

As they started walking a glow appeared on the misty horizon
to their left and a globe of yellow light slid up into the sky
from behind a jagged black mountain. Rima said, "The moon!"
"It can't be the moon. It's going too fast."
The globe was certainly marked like the moon. It swung upward
across Orion, passed near the Pole Star and sunk down below
the horizon on the far side of the road. A little later, with a
piece of rim missing from one side, it rose again behind the
mountain on the left. Rima stood still and said desperately "I
can't go on. My back hurts, my stomach's swollen, and this
coat is far too tight."
She unbuttoned it frantically and Lanark stared in surprise. The
dress had hung loose from her shoulders, but now her stomach
was swollen almost to her breasts and the amber velvet was
as tight as the skin of a balloon. She gazed down as if struck
by something and said faintly, "Give me your hand."
She pressed his hand against the lower side of her belly, staring
wildly at his face. He had begun to say, "I feel nothing," when
his palm received, through the tense stomach wall, a queer
little pat. He said, "Somebody is in there."
She said hysterically, "I'm going to have a baby!"
He gaped at her and she glared accusingly back. He struggled
to keep serious and failed. His face was stretched by a huge
happy grin. She bared her teeth and shrieked, "You're *glad!*
You're *glad!*"
"I'm sorry, I can't help it."
In a low intense voice she said, "How you must hate me. . . ."
"I love you!"
". . . grinning when I'm going to have horrible pains and
will split open and maybe die . . ."
"You won't die!"
". . . beside a fucking motorway without a fucking doctor in
fucking sight."
"We'll get to Unthank before then."
"How do you know?"
"And if we don't I'll take care of you. Births are natural things,
usually."
She knelt on the grass, covered her face and wept hysterically
while Lanark started helplessly laughing, for he felt a burden
lifted from him, a burden he had carried all his life without
noticing. Then he grew ashamed and knelt and embraced her,
and she allowed him. They squatted a long time like that.

CHAPTER 34. Intersections

When he next looked at the sky a half-moon was sailing over it. He said, "Rima, I think we should try to keep moving." She got to her feet and they started walking arm in arm. She said miserably, "It was wrong of you to be glad."

"There's nothing to worry about, Rima. Listen, when Nan was pregnant she had nobody to help her, but she still wanted a baby and had one without any bother."

"Stop comparing me with other women. Nan's a fool. Anyway, she loved Sludden. That makes a difference."

Lanark stood still, stunned, and said, "Don't you love me?" She said impatiently, "I like you, Lanark, and of course I depend on you, but you aren't very inspiring, are you?"

He stared at the air, pressing a clenched fist to his chest and feeling utterly weak and hollow. An excited expression came on her face. She pointed past him and whispered, "Look!"

Fifty yards ahead a tanker stood on the verge with a man beside it, apparently pissing on the grass between the wheels. Rima said, "Ask him for a lift."

Lanark felt too feeble to move. He said, "I don't like begging favours from strangers."

"Don't you? Then I will."

She hurried past him, shouting, "Excuse me a minute!"

The driver turned and faced them, buttoning his fly. He wore jeans and a leather jacket. He was a young man with spiky red hair who regarded them blankly. Rima said, "Excuse me, could you give me a lift? I'm terribly tired."

Lanark said, "We're trying to get to Unthank."

The driver said, "I'm going to Imber."

He was staring at Rima. Her hood had fallen back and the

pale golden hair hung to her shoulders, partly curtaining her
ardently smiling face. The coat hung open and the bulging
stomach raised the short dress far above her knees. The driver
said, "Imber isn't all that far from Unthank, though."
Rima said, "Then you'll let us come?"
"Sure, if you like."
He walked to the cab, opened the door, climbed in and reached
down his hand. Lanark muttered, "I'll help you up," but she
took the driver's hand, set her foot on the hub of the front
wheel and was pulled inside before Lanark could touch her.
So he scrambled in after and shut the door behind him. The
cabin was hot, oil-smelling, dimly lit and divided in two by a
throbbing engine as thick as the body of a horse. A tartan
rug lay over this and the driver sat on the far side. Lanark
said, "I'll sit in the middle, Rima."
She settled astride the rug saying, "No, I'm supposed to sit
here."
"But won't the vibration . . . do something?"
She laughed.
"I'm sure it will do nothing nasty. It's a nice vibration."
The driver said, "I always sit the birds on the engine. It warms
them up."
He put two cigarettes in his mouth, lit them and gave one to
Rima. Lanark settled gloomily into the other seat. The driver
said, "Are you happy then?"
Rima said "Oh, yes. It's very kind of you."
The driver turned out the light and drove on.

    The noise of the engine made it hard to talk without shout-
ing. Lanark heard the driver yell, "In the pudding club, eh?"
"You're very observant."
"Queer how some birds can carry a stomach like that without
getting less sexy. Why you going to Unthank?"
"My boyfriend wants to work there."
"What does he do?"
"He's a painter—an artist."
Lanark yelled, "I'm not a painter!"
"An artist, eh? Does he paint nudes?"
"I'm *not* an artist!"
Rima laughed and said, "Oh, yes. He's very keen on nudes."
"I bet I know who his favourite model is."
Lanark stared glumly out of the window. Rima's hysterical de-
spair had changed to a gaiety he found even more disturbing
because he couldn't understand it. On the other hand, it was

good to feel that each moment saw them nearer Unthank. The speed of the lorry had changed his view of the moon; its thin crescent stood just above the horizon, apparently motionless, and gave a comforting sense that time was passing more slowly. He heard the driver say, "Go on, give it to him," and Rima pushed something plump into his hands. The driver shouted, "Count what's in it—go on count what's in it!"

The object was a wallet. Lanark thrust it violently back across Rima's thighs. The driver took it with one hand and yelled, "Two hundred quid. Four days' work. The overtime's chronic but the creature pays well for it. Half of it yours for a drawing of your girl here in the buff, right?"

"I'm not an artist and we're going to Unthank."

"No. Nothing much in Unthank. Imber's the place. Bright lights, strip clubs, Swedish massage, plenty of overtime for artists in Imber. Something for everybody. I'll show you round."

"I'm not an artist!"

"Have another fag, ducks, and light one for me."

Rima took the cigarette packet, crying, "Can you really afford it?"

"You saw the wallet. I can afford anything, right?"

"I wish my boyfriend were more like you!"

"Thing about me, if I want a thing, I don't care how much I pay. To heck with consequences. You only live once, right? You come to Imber."

Rima laughed and shouted, "I'm a bit like that too."

Lanark shouted, *"We're going to Unthank!"* but the others didn't seem to hear. He bit his knuckles and looked out again. They were deep among lanes of vast speeding vehicles and container trucks stencilled with cryptic names: QUANTUM, VOLSTAT, CORTEXIN, ALGOLAGNICS. The driver seemed keen to show his skill in overtaking them. Lanark wondered how soon they would reach the road leading off to Unthank, and how he could make the lorry stop there. Moreover, if the lorry did stop, he (being near the door) must get out before Rima. What if the driver drove off with her? Perhaps she would like that. She seemed perfectly happy. Lanark wondered if pregnancy and exhaustion had driven her mad. He felt exhausted himself. His last clear thought before falling asleep was that whatever happened he must not fall asleep.

He woke to a perplexing stillness and took a while understanding where he was. They were parked at the roadside and an argument was happening in the cabin to his right. The driver was saying angrily, "In that case you can clear out."

Rima said, "But why?"

"You changed your mind pretty sudden, didn't you?"

"Changed my mind about what?"

"Get out! I know a bitch when I see one."

Lanark quickly opened the door saying, "Yes, we'll leave now. Thanks for the lift."

"Take care of yourself, mate. You'll land in trouble if you stick with her."

Lanark climbed on the verge and helped Rima down after him. The door slammed and the tanker rumbled forward, becoming a light among other lights whizzing into the distance. Rima giggled and said, "What a funny man. He seemed really upset."

"No wonder."

"What do you mean?"

"You were flirting with him and he took it seriously."

"I wasn't flirting. I was being polite. He was a terrible driver."

"How does the baby feel?"

Rima flushed and said, "You'll never let me forget that, will you?"

She started rapidly walking.

The road ran between broad shallow embankments. Rima said suddenly, "Lanark, have you noticed something different about the traffic? There's none going the opposite way."

"Was there before?"

"Of course. It only stopped a minute ago. And what's that noise?"

They listened. Lanark said, "Thunder, I think. Or an aeroplane."

"No, it's a crowd cheering."

"If we walk on we may find out."

It became plain that something strange was happening ahead, for lights had begun clustering on the horizon. The embankment grew steeper until the road passed into a cutting. The verge was now a grassy strip below a dark black cliff with thick ivy on it. Wailing sirens sounded behind them and police cars sped past toward the light and thunder. The cutting ahead seemed blocked by glare, and vehicles slowed down as they neared it. Soon Rima and Lanark reached a great queue of trucks and tankers. The drivers stood on the verge talking in shouts and gestures, for the din increased with every step. They passed another road sign:

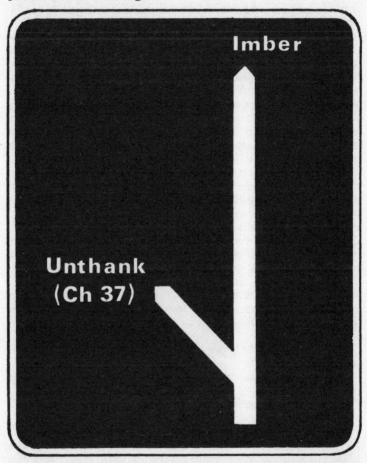

:and eventually Rima halted, pressed her hands over her ears, and by mouthings and headshakings made it clear she would go no farther. Lanark frowned angrily but the noise made thought impossible. There was something animal and even human in it, but only machinery could have sustained such a huge screeching, shrieking, yowling, growling, grinding, whining, yammering, stammering, trilling, chirping and yacacawing. It passed into the earth and jarred painfully on the soles of the feet. Still holding her ears Rima turned and hurried back and Lanark, after a moment of hesitation, was glad to follow.

Many more vehicles had joined the queue and drivers were standing on the road between them, for the backs of the trucks gave shelter from the sound. A young policeman with a torch was speaking to a group and Lanark gripped Rima's sleeve and drew her over to listen. He was saying, "A tanker hit an Algolagnics transporter at the Unthank intersection. I've never seen anything like it—nerve circuits spread across all the lanes like bloody burst footballs and screaming enough to crumble the road surface. The council's been alerted but God knows how long they'll take to deal with a mess like that. Days—weeks, perhaps. If you're going to Imber you'll need to go round by New Cumbernauld. If you're for Unthank, well, forget it."

Someone asked him about the drivers.

"How should I know? If they're lucky they were killed on impact. Without protective clothes you can't get within sixty metres of the place."

The policeman left the group and Lanark touched his shoulder saying, "Can I speak to you?"

He flashed his torch on their faces and said sharply, "What's that on your brows?"

"A thumb print."

"Well, how can I help you, sir? Be quick, we're busy at the moment."

"This lady and I are travelling to Unthank—"

"Out of the question sir. The road's impassable."

"But we're walking. We needn't keep to the road."

"Walking!"

The policeman rubbed his chin. At length he said, "There's the old pedestrian subway. It hasn't been used for years, but as far as I know it isn't *officially* derelict. I mean, it isn't boarded up."

He led them across the grass to a dark shape on the cutting wall. It was a square entrance, eight feet high and half hidden by a heavy swag of ivy. The policeman flashed his torch into it. A floor, under a drift of withered leaves, sloped down into blackness. Rima said firmly, "I'm not going in there."

Lanark said, "Do you know how long it is?"

"Can't say, sir. Wait a minute. . . ."

The policeman probed the wall near the entrance with his torch beam and revealed a faded inscription:

EDESTRIAN UNDER ASS
UNTHAN   00   ETRES

The policeman said, "A subway with an entrance like this can't be very long. A pity the lights are broken."

"Could you possibly lend me your torch? We mislaid ours and Rima—this lady—is pregnant, as you see."

"I'm sorry sir. No."

Rima said, "It's no use discussing it. I refuse to go in there."

The policeman said, "Then you'll have to hitch a lift back to New Cumbernauld."

He turned and walked away. Lanark said patiently, "Now listen, we must be sensible. If we use this tunnel we'll reach Unthank in fifteen minutes, perhaps less. It's unlit but there's a handrail on the wall so we can't lose our way. New Cumbernauld may be hours from here, and I want to get you into hospital as quickly as possible."

"I hate the dark, I hate hospitals and I'm not going!"

"There's nothing wrong with darkness. I've met several dreadful things in my life, and every one was in sunshine or a well-lit room."

"Yet you pretend to *want* sunshine!"

"I do, but not because I'm afraid of the opposite."

"How wise you are. How strong. How noble. How useless."

Bickering fiercely they had moved into the tunnel mouth to escape the blast of the din outside. Lanark abruptly paused, pointed into the dark and whispered, "Look, the end!"

Their eyes had grown used to the black and now they could see, in the greatest depth of it, a tiny, pale, glimmering square. Rima suddenly gripped the handrail and walked down the slope. He hurried after her and silently took her arm, afraid a wrong word would overturn her courage.

The roaring behind them sank into silence and the withered leaves stopped whispering under their feet. The ground levelled out. The air grew cold, then freezing. Lanark had kept his eyes fixed on the glimmering little square. He said, "Rima, have you let go the handrail?"

"Of course not."

"That's funny. When we entered the tunnel the light was straight ahead. Now it's on our left."

They halted. He said, "I think we're moving along the side of an open space, a hall of some kind."

She whispered, "What should we do?"

"Walk straight toward the light. Can't you button your coat?"

"No."

"We must get out of this cold as fast as we can. Come on. We'll go straight across the middle."

"What if . . . what if there's a pit?"

"People don't build pedestrian subways with pits in the middle. Let go of the rail."

They faced the light and stepped cautiously out, then Lanark felt himself slipping downward and released Rima's arm with a yell. Head and shoulder met a dense, metal-like surface with such stunning force that he lay on it for several seconds. The hurts of the fall were far less than the intense freezing cold. The chill on his hands and face actually had him weeping.

"Rima," he moaned, "Rima, I'm sorry . . . I'm sorry. Where are you, please?"

"Here."

He crawled in a circle, patting at the ground until his hand touched a foot. "Rima . . . ?"

"Yes."

"You're wearing thin sandals and you're standing on ice. I'm sorry, Rima, I've led you onto a frozen lake."

"I don't care."

He stood up, his teeth chattering, and peered about, saying, "Where's the light?"

"I don't know."

"I can't see it . . . I can't see it anywhere. We must find our way back to the handrail."

"You won't manage it. We're lost." Her body was beside him but her voice, low and dull, seemed to come from a distance. She said, "I'm a witch. I deserve this for killing him."

Lanark thought she had gone mad and felt terribly weary. He said patiently, "What are you talking about, Rima?"

After a moment she said, "Pregnant, silent, freezing, all dark, lost with you, feet that might fall off, an aching back, I deserve all this. He was driving badly to impress me. He wanted me, you see, and at first I found that fun; then I got tired of him, he was so smug and sure of himself. When he made us get out I wanted him to die, so he went on driving badly and crashed. No wonder you mean to lock me in a hospital. I'm a witch."

He realized she was weeping desperately and tried to embrace her, saying, "In the first place, the tanker that crashed may not be the one that gave us the lift. In the second place, a man's bad driving is nobody's fault but his own. And I'm not going to lock you up anywhere."

"Don't touch me."

"But I love you."

"Then promise not to leave when the baby comes. Promise you won't give me to other people and then run away."

"I promise. Don't worry."

"You're only saying that because we're freezing to death. If we get away from here you'll hand me over to a gang of bloody nurses."

"I won't! I won't!"

"You say that now, but you'll run away when the real pains begin. You won't be able to stand them."

"Why shouldn't I stand them? They'll be your pains, not mine."

She gasped and shrieked, "You're glad! You're glad! You evil beast, you're glad!"

He shouted, "Everything I say makes you think I'm evil!"

"You are evil! You can't make me happy. You *must* be evil!"

Lanark stood gasping dumbly. Every comforting phrase which struck him was accompanied by a knowledge of how she would twist it into a hurt. He raised a hand to hit her but she was with child; he turned to run away, but she needed him; he dropped down on his hands and knees and bellowed out a snarling yell which became a howl and then a roar. He heard her say in a cold little voice, "You won't frighten me that way."

He yelled out again and heard a distant voice shout, "Coming! Coming!"

He stood up, drawing breath with effort and feeling the chill of the ice on his hands and knees. A light was moving toward them over the ice and a voice could be heard saying, "Sorry I'm late."

As the light neared they saw it was carried by a dark figure with a strip of whiteness dividing head from shoulders. At last a clergyman stood before them. He may have been middle-aged but had an eager, smooth, young-looking face. He held up the lamp and seemed to peer less at Lanark's face than at the mark on his brow. There was a similar mark on his own. He said, "Lanark, is it? Excellent. I'm Ritchie-Smollet."

They shook hands. The clergyman looked down on Rima, who
had sunk down on her heels with her arms resting wearily
on her stomach. He said, "So this is your good lady."
"Lady," snarled Rima contemptuously.
Lanark said, "She's tired and a bit unwell. In fact she'll be
having a baby quite soon."
The clergyman smiled enthusiastically.
"Splendid. That's really glorious. We must get her into hospi-
tal."
Rima said violently, "No!"
"She doesn't want to go into hospital," explained Lanark.
"You must persuade her."
"But I think she ought to do what she likes."
The clergyman moved his feet and said, "It's rather chilly here.
Isn't it time we put our noses above ground?"
Lanark helped Rima to her feet and they followed Ritchie-
Smollet across the black ice.

It was hard to see anything of the cavern except that the
ceiling was a foot or two above their heads. Ritchie-Smollet
said, "What tremendous energy these Victorian chaps had. They
hollowed this place out as a burial vault when the ground upstairs was filled up. A later age put it to a more pedestrian
use, and it still is a remarkably handy short cut. . . . Please
ask any questions you like."
"Who are you?"
"A Christian. Or I try to be. I suppose you'd like to know
my precise church, but I don't think the sect is all that important,
do you? Christ, Buddha, Amon-Ra and Confucius had a great
deal in common. Actually I'm a Presbyterian but I work with
believers of every continent and colour."
Lanark felt too tired to speak. They had left the ice and were
climbing a flagged passage under an arching roof. Ritchie-Smollet said, "Mind you, I'm opposed to human sacrifice: unless
it's voluntary, as in the case of Christ. Did you have a nice
journey?"
"No."
"Never mind. You're still sound in wind and limb and you
can be sure of a hearty welcome. You'll be offered a seat on
the committee, of course. Sludden was definite about that and
so was I. My experience of institute and council affairs is rather
out of date—things were less tense in my time. We were delighted when we heard you had chosen to join us."

"I've chosen to join nobody. I know nothing about committee work and Sludden is no friend of mine."

"Now, now, don't get impatient. A wash and a clean bed will work wonders. I suspect you're more exhausted than you think."

The pale square of light appeared ahead and enlarged to a doorway. It opened into the foot of a metal staircase. Lanark and Rima climbed slowly and painfully in watery green light. Ritchie-Smollet came patiently behind, humming to himself. After many minutes they emerged into a narrow, dark, stone-built chamber with marble plaques on three walls and large wrought-iron gates in the fourth. These swung easily outward, and they stepped onto a gravel path beneath a huge black sky. Lanark saw he was on a hilltop among the obelisks of a familiar cemetery.

CHAPTER 35. Cathedral

After they had gone a little way Lanark stopped and declared, "This isn't Unthank!"

"You are mistaken. It is."

They looked down a slope of pinnacled monuments onto a squat black cathedral. The floodlit spire held a gilt weathercock above the level of their eyes, but Lanark was more perplexed by the view beyond. He remembered a stone-built city of dark tenements and ornate public buildings, a city with a square street plan and electric tramcars. Rumours from the council corridors had made him expect much the same place, only darker and more derelict, but below a starless sky this city was coldly blazing. Slim poles as tall as the spire cast white light upon the lanes and looping bridges of another vast motorway. On each side shone glass and concrete towers over twenty floors high with lights on top to warn off aeroplanes. Yet this was Unthank, though the old streets between towers and motorlanes had a half-erased look, and blank gables stood behind spaces cleared for carparks. After a pause Lanark said, "And Unthank is dying?"

"Dying? Oh I doubt it. The population has shrunk since they scrapped the Q39 project, but there's been a tremendous building boom."

"But if a place is losing people and industry how can it afford new buildings?"

"Ah, I know too little about chronology to say. I feel that what happens between *hearts* matters more than these big public ways of swapping energy. You tell me, no doubt, that this is a conservative attitude. On the other hand, radicals are the only people who'll work with me. Odd, isn't it?"

Lanark said irritably, "You seem to understand my questions, but your answers make no sense to me."

"That's typical of life, isn't it? But as long as you've a good heart and keep trying there's no need to despair. *Wer immer streband sich bemüht, den können wir erlösen.* Oh, you'll be a great deal of use to us."

Rima suddenly leaned on a stone and said quietly, without bitterness, "I can't go on."

Lanark, alarmed, clasped her waist though it worried him to be clasping two people instead of one.

Ritchie-Smollet said softly, "A giddy spell?" "No, my back hurts and I . . . I can hardly think."

"In my missionary phase I took a medical degree. Give me your pulse."

He held her wrist in one hand, beat time with the other, then said, "Eighty-two. Considering your condition that's quite good. Could you manage down to that building? A sleep is what you need most, but I'd better examine you first to make sure everything's in order."

He pointed to the cathedral. Rima stared at it. Lanark murmured, "Could we join hands and carry her?"

Rima pushed herself upright and said, "No, give me your arm. I'll walk."

The clergyman led them down dim weedy paths past the porticoes of mausoleums cut into the hillside. Gleams of light from below lit corners of inscriptions to the splendid dead:

> ". . . His victorious campaign . . ."
> ". . . . . whose unselfish devotion . . . . ."
> ". . . revered by his students . . ."
> ". . . . . esteemed by his colleagues . . . . ."
> ". . . beloved by all . . ."

They crossed a flat space and walked along a cobbled lane. Ritchie-Smollet said, "A tributary of the river once flowed under here."

Lanark saw that a low wall beside him was the parapet of a bridge and looked over onto a steeply embanked road. Cars sped up this to the motorway but there seemed to be a barrier: after slowing and stopping they turned and came back again. A tiny distinct throbbing in the air worked on the eardrum like the point of a drill on a tooth.

"What's that noise?"

"There appears to be a pile-up at the intersection: a burst transporter, one of these huge dangerous God-the-Father jobs. The council ought to ban them. The city looks like being sealed off for quite a while. However, we've adequate food stocks. Come through here, it's a short cut."

The parapet had given way to a wall screened by bushes. Ritchie-Smollet parted two of these uncovering a hole into brighter air. Lanark helped Rima through. They were in the grounds of the cathedral where gravestones lay flat like a pavement. Vans and private cars stood on them against the surrounding wall, and Rima sank down on the step of a mobile crane. Ritchie-Smollet thrust hands into trouser pockets and stared ahead with a small satisfied smile.

"There she stands!" he said. "Our centre of government once again."

Lanark looked at the cathedral. At first the floodlit spire seemed too solid for the flat black shape upholding it, a shape cut through by rows of dim yellow windows; then his eye made out the tower, roofs and buttresses of a sturdy Gothic ark, the sculpted waterspouts broken and rubbed by weather and the hammers of old iconoclasts.

"What do you mean, centre of government? Unthank has a city chambers."

"Ah, yes, we use it nowadays for property deals. Quite a lot of work is done there, but the *real* legislators come here. I know you're keen to meet them but first you'll have to sleep. I speak as a doctor now, not as a minister of the gospel, so you mustn't argue with me."

They walked over inscriptions more laconic than in the higher cemetery.

"William Skinner: 5½ feet North × 2¼ West."

"Harry Fleming, his wife Minnie, their son George, their daughter Amy: 6 feet West × 2½ North."

They reached a side entrance and crossed a shallow porch into the cathedral.

A long-haired young man wearing blue overalls sat reading a book on a lidded stone font near the door. He glanced up and said, "Where have you been, Arthur? Polyphemus is going berserk. He thinks he's discovered something."

"I'm in a hurry, Jack," said Ritchie-Smollet crisply. "These people need rest and attention. Will anywhere be clear for a while? I mean really clear?"

"Nothing scheduled for the arts lab."

"Then get blankets and pillows into it and clean sheets, really clean sheets, and make up a bed."

"Yes but" —the youth laid down his book and slid to the floor—"what will I tell Polyphemus?"

"Tell him politics is not man's chief end."

The youth hurried off between rows of rush-bottomed chairs covering the great flagged floor. The cathedral seemed vaster inside than out. The central pillars upholding the tower hid what lay beyond, but organ tones and blurred hymnal voices indicated a service there. At the same time the hard beat of wilder music sounded from somewhere below. Ritchie-Smollet said, "Not a bad God kennel, is it? The October Terminus are having a gig in the crypt. Some people don't approve of that, but I tell them that at the Reformation the building was used by three congregations simultaneously and in my father's house are many mansions. Do you need the lavatory?"

"No," muttered Rima, who had sunk into a chair. "No, no, no, no."

"Come on, then. Not far now."

They moved slowly down a side aisle and Lanark had time to notice that the cathedral had clearly been used in several ways since its foundation. Torn flags hung overhead; against the walls stood ornate memorials to soldiers killed while invading remote continents. Before the arches under the tower they turned left and went down some steps, then right and descended others into a small chapel. An orange light hung in the stone-ribbed ceiling but the stone was whitewashed and the effect was restful. The air was warmed and scented by paraffin heaters in the corners; a stack of plastic mattresses against a wall nearly touched the ceiling. Three of these were laid edge to edge and Jack was making a bed on the middle one. Rima lay down on it when he finished and Lanark helped remove her coat. "Don't go to sleep yet—I'll be back in a jiff," said Ritchie-Smollet and went out. Jack adjusted the wicks of the heaters and followed him. Lanark shed his own coat and sat with Rima's head on his lap. He was weary but couldn't relax because his clothes felt sticky and foul. He fingered the matted beard on his cheeks and chin and touched the thinning hair on his scalp. Clearly he had grown older. He looked down at Rima, whose eyes were closed. Her hair was black once more, and apart from the big belly her whole figure seemed slighter than in the council corridors. A small insulted frown between the brows suggested an angry little girl, but her lips had the beautiful repose of a mature, contented woman of thirty or forty. He gazed and gazed but couldn't decide her age at all. She sighed and murmured, "Where's Sludden?"

He overcame a pang of anger and said gently, "I don't know, Rima."

"You're nice to me, Lanark. I'll always trust you."

Ritchie-Smollet and Jack brought basins of hot water, towels, clean nightshirts, and went out again. Rima lay on the towels while Lanark sponged and dried her, taking special care of the great belly, which looked more normal naked than clothed. She slid between the sheets and Ritchie-Smollet returned with a black leather case. He knelt by the bed and took out thermometer, stethoscope and sterilized gloves in a transparent envelope. He slipped the thermometer below Rima's armpit and was tearing the envelope when she opened her eyes and said sharply, "Turn round Lanark."

"Why?"

"If you don't turn round I won't let him touch me."

Lanark turned round and walked to the far side of a pillar, his feet cold on the bare stone. He stopped and stared at the ceiling. The arching ribs came together in carved knops, and one showed a pair of tiny snakes twining across the brow of a very cheerful skull in the middle of a wreath of roses. Nearby on the vault someone had scribbled in pencil:

GOD = LOVE = MONEY = SHIT.

"Well, that seems all right," said Ritchie-Smollet loudly. Lanark turned and saw him repacking the case. "The little fellow seems the correct way up and round and so forth. If she insists on having it here I suppose we can manage."

"Here?" said Lanark, startled.

"Not in hospital, I mean. Anyway, I'll leave you to some well-earned rest."

He went out, pulling a red curtain across the door. Rima murmured, "Get in behind me."

He obeyed and she pressed her freezing soles greedily to his shins, but her back was familiar and cosy and soon they grew warm and slept.

He wakened among whispering and rustling. Chains of bright spots flowed zigzag over the dark vault and pillars and crowded floor. They were cast by a silver-faceted globe revolving where the orange lamp had hung, and now the only steady light shone on the steps to the entrance. These were the breadth of the wall. Young men in overalls were arranging electrical machines on them which sometimes filled the chapel with huge hoarse sighs. Three older men sat on the lower steps holding instruments joined by wires to the machinery, and a fourth was setting up a percussion kit with BROWN'S LUGWORM CASANOVAS printed on the big drum. Lanark saw he was part of an audience: the whole floor was paved with mattresses and covered with people squatting shoulder to shoulder. Beside him a delicate girl in a silver sari was leaning on a hairy, barechested man in a sheepskin waistcoat. Just in front a girl in the tartan trews and scarlet mess jacket of a highland regiment was whispering to a man with the braided hair, headband and fringed buckskin of an Indian squaw. People from every culture and century seemed gathered here in silk, canvas, fur, feathers, wool, gauze, nylon and leather. Hair was frizzed out like the African, crewcut like the Roman, piled high like Pompadour, straightened like the Sphinx or rippled over the shoulders like periwigs. There was every kind of ornament and an amount of nakedness. Lanark looked unsuccessfully for his clothes. He felt he had rested a long time but Rima was still sleeping, so he decided not to move. Other couples were reclining at length and even caressing in the shelter of sleeping bags.

There was applause and a small gloomy man with a heavy moustache stood with a microphone on the steps. He said, "Glad to be back, folks, in legendary Unthank where I've had so many legendary experiences. I'm going to lead off with a new thing, it bombed them in Troy and Trebizond, it sank like stone-cold turkey in Atlantis, let's see what happens here. 'Domestic Man.' "
He threw his head back and shouted:

"The cake she baked me bit me till I cried!"

The instruments and machines said BAWAM so loudly that hearing and thought were destroyed for a second.

"The bed she made me was so hard I nearly died!"
(BAWAM)

"The shirt she washed me folded its arms and tied
me up inside!"

(BAWAM)

"She's going domestic, she's got a great big domestic
plan, But *please* baby believe me lady I am
                    not a domestic man
                    not a domestic man
                    not a domestic man."
(BAWAM BAWAM BAWAM BAWAM BAWAM BAWAM
BAWAM BAWAM BAWAM)

Rima was sitting up, hands pressed over ears and tears pouring
down her cheeks. She spoke but the words were inaudible.
Lanark saw Ritchie-Smollet beckoning violently from the doorway behind the singer. He pulled Rima up and they stumbled
through the audience. The singer shouted:

"She cleans windows till they shine so I can't see!"
                    (BAWAM)
"She polishes floors till they suck my foot in up to
the knee!"
                           (BAWAM)
"She papers rooms till the walls start squeezing in on
me!"
                           (BAWAM)

As they passed the singer Rima waved so threateningly at a
bank of loudspeakers that someone grabbed her arm. Lanark
pulled him off and clumsy punches were exchanged on the
way to the door. Ritchie-Smollet separated them, his voice coming through the BAWAMing like a far-off whisper: ". . . entirely
my fault . . . delicate condition . . . failure of liaison. . . ."

It was quieter outside the door where Jack waited with
dressing-gown and slippers. Rima kept muttering "Bastards"
as she was helped into these.
"They dislike space, you see, and noise fills that up," said Ritchie-Smollet, leading them across the nave. "The fault is really
mine. I went out with a man who thought I could save his
marriage because I'd performed the ceremony. Illogical, really.
Didn't know him from Adam. I hadn't expected you to sleep
so long—if we had a clock it would be safe to say you snoozed
right round the bally thing. Contractions started yet?"
"No," said Rima.
"Good. In a brace of shakes you'll have a bed and a bite in

the triforium. I'd have put you there when you came but I feared you were too feeble to face the stairs.''

He opened a little door and they saw a stair hardly two feet wide spiralling upward in the thickness of the wall. Lanark said, "Excuse me, but can't we get a decent room in a decent house?''

"Rooms are hard to find just now. The house of God is the best I can offer.''

"When I was last here a quarter of the city stood empty.''

"Ah, that was before the new building programme started. Someone on the committee may offer you a spare room eventually. Anyway, we can wait for them in the triforium—your clothes are there.''

Ritchie-Smollet ducked through the doorway and climbed. Rima followed and Lanark came after. The stairs were laboriously steep. After several turns they passed through another door onto the inner sill of a huge window. Rima gasped and clutched a handrail. Far below a man moved like a beetle over the flagged floor and the echoing throbs of "Domestic Man" added to the insecurity. Ritchie-Smollet said, "That's Polyphemus on his way to the chapterhouse. My word, but the Lugworms are going it some.''

A few steps took them onto a walkway between rows of organ pipes, and a few more into the end of a very long low attic. The ceiling slanted from the floor to a wall of arches overlooking the nave. As they walked down it Lanark saw partitions dividing the loft on his left into cubicles, each containing a little furniture. In one a man in a dirty coat sat trying to mend an old boot. In another a haggard woman lay drinking from a flat-sided bottle. Ritchie-Smollet said, "Here we are," stepped into one and squatted on the carpet.

The cubicle had a homely look mitigated by a smell of disinfectant. It was lit by a pink silk-shaded lamp above a low bed that covered a third of the floor. The seats were stools and cushions but there was a low table, a chest of drawers and a tiny sink. The boards between the ceiling joists were covered by forget-me-not patterned paper, and on one of the two walls a hanger on a hook held Lanark's clothes, newly cleaned and pressed.

"Small but snug," said Ritchie-Smollet. "A regrettable lack of headroom but nobody will disturb us. I suggest Rima slip into bed (she'll find a hot-water bottle there) and you get dressed. Then Jack will bring us a meal, a companion will arrive for

your good lady, and we two can attend the meeting in the
chapterhouse. The provost should be there by now."
Lanark sank on a stool with elbows on knees and chin on hands.
He said, "You keep moving me about and I don't know why."
"Yes, it's difficult. In the present state of chronological confusion it's impossible to state things clearly. As secretary I can
only arrange meetings by keeping members here till the rest
arrive. But Gow's come, and poor Scougal and Mrs. Schtzngrm
and the ubiquitous Polyphemus. And chairman Sludden, praise
God."
Lanark looked at Rima. The sight soothed him. She lay smiling
against the pillows, a hand touching her full breast. There was
a soft calmness about her; the dimples at the corners of her
mouth were unusually deep. She said fondly, "It's all right,
Lanark. Don't worry."
He sighed and started dressing.

Jack entered with a loaded tray and Ritchie-Smollet poured
coffee into cups and passed plates around, chatting as he did
so.
"All out of tins, of course, but good of its kind. Easy to serve,
too, which is handy because there's only room for a very tiny
kitchen. There was amazing opposition when we set up this
little refuge—even more than to the arts lab in the lady chapel.
Yet these lofts have lain empty since the old monks marched
round them telling their beads. And what could better con-
form to the wishes of the founder? You know the poem, of
course:

> "If at the church they would give us some ale,
> and a pleasant fire our souls to regale,
> we'd sing and we'd pray all the livelong day,
> nor ever once wish from the church to stray,
>
> "And God, like a father, rejoicing to see,
> His children as pleasant and happy as He,
> would have no more quarrel with Devil or barrel,
> But kiss him and give him both drink and—"

"What the hell am I eating?" shouted Lanark.
"Enigma de Filets Congalés. Is it underdone? Try this pink
moist crumbly stuff. I can heartily recommend it."
Lanark groaned. A stink of burning rubber was fading from
his nostrils and his limbs were invaded by a familiar invigorating
warmth. He said, "This is institute food."

"Yes. The Quantum group delivers nothing else to us nowadays."

"We left the institute because we hate this food."

"I admire you for it!" cried Ritchie-Smollet enthusiastically. "And you've moved in the right direction! We have two or three millennialists on the committee and who's to blame them? Has not the prayer of humanity in all ages been for innocent and abundant food? Impossible, of course, but *wer immer strebend sich bemüht* et cetera. And one has to eat, unless one feels with Miss Weil that anorexia nervosa is a sacred duty."

"Yes I will eat!" cried Lanark savagely. "But please stop bombarding me with funny names and meaningless quotations!" He finished all the plates that Rima and Ritchie-Smollet left untouched and in the end felt bloated, drugged and horribly tricked. A voice cried, "Rima!" A plump woman of about forty wearing tarty clothes came in. Rima laughed and said, "Frankie!"

Frankie dropped a huge embroidered handbag on the floor, sat on the bed and said, "Sludden told me you were here— he's coming later. So the mystery man has put a bun in your oven, has he? Actually you don't look too bad—quite surprisingly winsome, really. Hullo, mystery man, I'm glad you've grown a beard. You look less vulnerable."

"Hullo," said Lanark ungraciously. He was not pleased to see Frankie.

CHAPTER 36. Chapterhouse

Ritchie-Smollet led them to the far end of the attic, through a small kitchen where Jack was washing dishes, and down another spiral stair in the thickness of the wall. They came into a square room with vaulted ceiling upheld by a great central pillar. A row of stone chairs with wooden backs were built into the length of each wall. Lanark thought this an awkward arrangement: if all the seats were occupied everyone would find the central pillar hiding three or four people opposite. A small, fit-looking man stood with feet apart and hands in pockets warming his back at an electric fire. Ritchie-Smollet spoke with less than usual enthusiasm.

"Ah, Grant. This is Lanark, who has news for us."

"Council news, no doubt," said Grant with a sarcastic emphasis, "I've been waiting over an hour."

"Remember the rest of us haven't got your knack of timing things. The provost may be in the crypt; I'll go and look."

Ritchie-Smollet left by a door in a corner. Grant and Lanark stared at each other. Grant seemed about thirty though there were some deep vertical wrinkles on his cheeks and brow. His short crisp hair was carefully combed and he wore a neat blue suit and red necktie. He said, "I know you. When I was a lad you used to hang around the old Elite with Sludden's mob."

"Not for long," said Lanark. "How do you time things? Have you a watch?"

"I've a pulse."

"You count your heartbeats?"

"I estimate them. We all developed that talent in the shops when the old timekeeping collapsed."

"You keep a shop?"

"I'm talking abut workshops. Machine shops. I'm a maker, not a salesman."

Lanark sat on a seat near the fire. Grant's voice offended him. It was loud, penetrating and clearly used to addressing crowds without help from the equipment which lets a man talk softly to millions. Lanark said, "Where's Polyphemus?"

"Eh?"

"I heard that someone called Polyphemus was here."

Grant grinned and said, "I'm here all right. Smollet calls me that."

"Why?"

"Polyphemus was a one-eyed ogre in an old story. I keep reminding the committee of a fact they want to forget, so they say I have only one way of seeing things."

"What fact is that?"

"None of them are makers."

"Do you mean workers?"

"No, I mean makers. Many hard workers make nothing but wealth. They don't produce food, fuel, shelter or helpful ideas; their work is just a way of tightening their grip on folk who do."

"What do you make?"

"Homes. I'm a shop steward with the Volstat Mohome group."

Lanark said thoughtfully, "These groups—Volstat, Algolagnics and so on—are they what people call the creature?"

"Some of us call it that. The council is financed by it. So is the institute. So it likes to call itself the foundation."

"I'm sick of these big vague names that power keeps hiding behind," said Lanark impatiently.

"So you prefer not to think of them," said Grant, nodding amiably. "That's typical of intellectuals. The institute has bought and sold you so often that you're ashamed to name your masters."

"I have no masters. I hate the institute. I don't even like the council."

"But it helped you come here, so it still has a use for you."

"Blethers!" cried Lanark. "People usually help each other if they can do it without troubling themselves much."

"Try a cigarette," said Grant, offering a packet. He had grown friendlier as Lanark grew angrier.

"Thank you, I don't smoke," said Lanark, cooling a little.

A while later Lanark said, "Would you tell me exactly what the creature is?"

"A conspiracy which owns and manipulates everything for profit."

"Are you talking about the wealthy?"

"Yes, but not the wealthy in coins and banknotes—that sort of wealth is only coloured beads to keep the makers servile. The owners and manipulators have smarter ways of banking energy. They pay themselves with time: time to think and plan, time to examine necessity from a distance."

An old man leaning on a stick and a dark young man with a turban entered and stood talking quietly by the pillar. Grant's loud voice had been even and passionless, but suddenly he said, "What I hate most is their conceit. Their institute breaks whole populations into winners and losers and calls itself *culture*. Their council destroys every way of life which doesn't bring them a profit and calls itself government. They pretend culture and government are supremely independent powers when they are nothing but gloves on the hands of Volstat and Quantum, Cortexin and Algolagnics. And they really think they are the foundation. They believe their greed holds up the continents. They don't call it greed, of course, they call it profit, or (among themselves, where they don't need to fool anyone) *killings*. They're sure that only their profit allows people to make and eat things."

"Maybe that's true."

"Yes, because they make it true. But it isn't necessary. Old men remember when the makers unexpectedly produced enough for everyone. No crop failed, no mine was exhausted, no machinery broke down, but the creature dumped mountains of food in the ocean because the hungry couldn't pay a *profitable* price for it, and the shoemaker's children went shoeless because their father had made too many shoes. And the makers accepted this as though it was an earthquake! They refused to see they could make what they needed for each other and to hell with profit. They would have seen in the end, they would have had to see, if the council had not gone to war."

"How did that help?"

"As the creature couldn't stay rich by selling necessary things to the folk who made them it sold destructive things to the council. Then the war started and the destructive things were used to wreck the necessary things. The creature profited by replacing both."

"Who did the council fight?"

"It split in two and fought itself."

"That's suicide!"

"No, ordinary behaviour. The efficient half eats the less efficient half and grows stronger. War is just a violent way of doing what half the people do calmly in peacetime: using the other half for food, heat, machinery and sexual pleasure. Man is the pie that bakes and eats himself, and the recipe is separation."

"I refuse to believe men kill each other just to make their enemies rich."

"How can men recognize their real enemies when their family, schools and work teach them to struggle with each other and to believe law and decency come from the teachers?"

"My son won't be taught that," said Lanark firmly.

"You have a son?"

"Not yet."

The chapterhouse had filled with chattering groups and Ritchie-Smollet moved among them collecting signatures in a book. There were many young people in bright clothing, old eccentric men in tweeds and a large confusion of in-between people. Lanark decided that if this was the new government of Unthank he was not impressed. Their manners were shrill and vehement or languid and bored. Some had the mark of the council on their brow but nobody displayed the calm, well-contained strength of men like Monboddo, Ozenfant and Munro. Lanark said, "Could you tell me about this committee?"

"I'm getting round to it. The war ended with the creature and its organs more dominant than ever. Naturally there was a lot of damage to repair, but that only took half our time and energy. If industry and government had been commanding us for the common good (as they pretend to do), the continents would have become gardens, gardens of space and light where everyone had time to care for their lovers, children and neighbours without crowding and tormenting them. But these vast bodies only cooperate to kill or crush. Once again the council began feeding the creature by splitting the world in two and preparing a war. But it ran into unexpected trouble—"

"Stop! You're simplifying," said Lanark. "You talk as if all government was one thing, but there are many kinds of government, and some are crueller than others."

"Oh, yes," said Grant, nodding. "An organization which encloses a globe must split into departments. But you're a very

ordinary victim of council advertising if you think the world
is neatly split between good governments and bad."

"What was the council's unexpected trouble?"

"The creature supplied it with such vast new weapons that a
few of them could poison the world. Most folk are dour and
uncomplaining about their own deaths, but the death of their
children depresses them. The council tried to pretend the new
weapons weren't weapons at all but homes where everyone
could live safely, but for all that an air of protest spread even
to the council corridors. Many who had never dreamed of governing themselves began complaining loudly. This committee
is made of complainers."

"Has complaint done any good?"

"Some, perhaps. The creature still puts time and energy into
vast weapons and sells them to the council, but recent wars
have been fought with smaller weapons and kept to the less
industrial continents. Meanwhile the creature has invented
peaceful ways of taking our time and energy. It employs us to
make essential things badly, so they decay fast and have to be replaced. It bribes the council to destroy cheap things which don't
bring it a profit and replaces them with new expensive things
which do. It pays us to make useless things and employs scien-
tists, doctors and artists to persuade us that these are essential."

"Can you give me examples?"

"Yes, but our provost wants to speak to you."

Lanark stood up. A lean, well-dressed man with bushy
grey hair came through the crowd and shook his hand, saying
briskly, "Sorry I missed you upstairs, Lanark—you were too
quick for me. Don't worry—she's all right."

The voice was familiar. Lanark stared into the strange, haggard,
bright-eyed face. The provost said reassuringly, "It's all right—
she's in excellent spirits. I'm glad there was someone dependa-
ble like you with her. Frankie will tell us when the contractions
start."

Lanark said, "Sludden."

"You didn't recognize me?" asked the provost, chuckling.
"Well, none of us are the men we were."

Lanark said harshly, "How's your fiancée?"

"Gay?" said Sludden ruefully. "I hoped *you* could tell me about
Gay. The marriage didn't work. My fault, I'm afraid; politics
puts strain on a marriage. She joined the institute. The last I
heard of her was that she had gone to work for the council.
If you didn't see her in the corridors she's probably with a

foundation group, Cortexin perhaps. She had a talent for communications."

Lanark felt baffled and feeble. He wanted to hate Sludden but couldn't think of a reason for doing it. He said accusingly, "I saw Nan and her baby."

"Rima told me. I'm glad they're well," said Sludden, smiling and nodding.

"The committee is convened," said Ritchie-Smollet. "Please be seated."

People moved to the walls and sat down. Sludden took a chair with a high carved back and armrests; Ritchie-Smollet led Lanark to a seat on Sludden's right and himself sat on his left. Grant sat beside Lanark. Ritchie-Smollet said, "Silence, please. The internal secretary has failed to make an appearance, so once again we must take the minutes of the last meeting as read. Never mind. The reason for the present meeting is . . . but I call on our chairman, provost Sludden, to explain that."

"We are privileged to have among us," said Sludden, "a former citizen of Unthank who till recently worked for the institute under the famous—perhaps I should say infamous—Ozenfant. Lanark—here he is beside me—has elected to return here of his own free will, which is no doubt a testimonial to the charm and friendliness of Unthank but proves also the strength of his own patriotic spirit."

Sludden paused. Ritchie-Smollet cried, "Oh, jolly good!" and clapped his hands. Sludden said, "I understand he has had personal consultations with Monboddo."

A voice behind the pillar shouted, "Shame!"

"Monboddo certainly has no friends here, but information about where Unthank stands in the council is hard to obtain, so we welcome any source of light on the subject. Also with me is Grant, sufficiently known to us all."

A voice behind the pillar shouted, "Up the makers, Poly!"

"Grant feels he has important news for us. I don't know what it is, but I suppose it will keep till we have heard our guest speaker?"

Sludden looked at Grant, who shrugged.

"So I will call on Lanark to take the floor."

Lanark rose confusedly to his feet. He said, "I'm not sure what to say. I'm not patriotic. I don't like Unthank, I like sunshine. I came here because I was told Unthank would be scrapped and swallowed in a few days, and anybody here with a council passport would be transferred to a sunnier city." He sat down. There was silence, then Ritchie-Smollet said, "Monboddo told you this?"

"No, one of his secretaries did. A man called Wilkins."

"I strongly object to the tone of the last speaker's remarks," cried a bulky, thick-necked man in a voice twice as penetrating as Grant's.

"Though he openly boasts of being no friend to Unthank, our provost has introduced him as if he was some sort of ambassador, and what news does the ambassador bring? Gossip. Nothing but gossip. The mountain has laboured and given birth to a small obnoxious rodent. But what is the *tendency* of the speech by this self-proclaimed enemy of the city which nurtured him? He tells us that after some vague but imminent doomsday those who carry a council passport will be transferred to a happier land while the majority are *swallowed*, whatever that means. I will, however, say this. *I* have a council passport, like several others on the committee, and like the speaker himself. His statements are clearly devised to spread distrust among our brothers and dismay and dissension in our rank and file. Let me assure this messianic double agent that he will not succeed. Nobody is better able to fight the council than men like Scougal and me. We love our people. We will sink or swim with Unthank. Meanwhile I propose that the committee combat the demoralizing tendency of the guest speaker's tirade by pretending we never heard it."

"Oh, not a tirade, Gow!" said Ritchie-Smollet mildly. "Lanark spoke four short sentences. I counted them. We ought to hear a little more before dismissing him totally. Wilkins said Unthank would be scrapped and swallowed. Did he indicate why?"

"Yes," said Lanark. "He said you were no longer profitable, and scrapping you would bring some kind of energy gain. He said his people were used to eating towns and villages, but Unthank would be their first city since Carthage."

A howl of laughter went up from different parts of the room. A voice behind the pillar cried, "Carthage? What about Coventry?" and others shouted "Leningrad!" "Berlin!" "Warsaw!" "Dresden!" "Hiroshima!"

"I would like also to menshun," said a slow-voiced, white-haired lady, "Münster in 1535, Gonstantinoble in 1453 and 1204, ant Hierusalem more vrequently than vun cares to rememper."

"Please, please! A little more moderation!" cried Ritchie-Smollet. "These unhappy rationalizations took place when the council was split in two or menaced by sectarian extremists. I am sure Lanark is not lying when he tells us what he heard. I do suggest his informant misled him."

"The peaceful destruction of a modern city would be something new," said Sludden thoughtfully. "It would have to be a city with no effective government. And the creature would have to provide a lot of powerful new machinery. And the destruction would have to be approved by a full meeting of the council, a meeting where Unthank was represented."

"Wilkins said a meeting of council delegates would approve the action in eight days," said Lanark. "That was a while ago. The creature has delivered large suction delvers to something called the expansion project. I saw one. As for your government, you know it better than I do."

"Utter nonsense!" cried Gow. "The council has no heartier opponent in Unthank than myself. As the oldest and most active member of the committee I have wrestled with it since the last world war, and never till recently have we obtained from it such enormous concessions. A short while ago our roads and buildings were a century out of date. Now look at them! Modern motorways. High-rise housing. A city centre full of towering office blocks. We could have done none of this without council aid. Yet you suggest the council plans to smash us!"

"These new developments do not greatly veigh with me," said the slow-voiced lady. "The profits of this building vork haf gone to the creature. A city lives by its industry ant ours still declines. But ve cannot, on the vort of von man, assume the vorst. Ve neet documentary corroboration."

Gow said, "I have no wish to stoop to personal invective but—"

"Excuse me, Gow, Jack would like a chance to speak," said Sludden, indicating Ritchie-Smollet's helper who was waving from a corner.

"I was cleaning the guest speaker's suit," said Jack, "and I noticed a council paper in the pocket. Maybe that could tell us something."

Lanark pulled out the newspaper he had lifted in the council café. Sludden took it and started reading. Gow said, "I don't like using insulting language, but the welfare of the community drives me to it. This guest speaker of ours, this would-be plenipotentiary, is no stranger to *me*. On a recent delegation to the council *I* saw this so-called Lanark sniffing around Monboddo's throne with his long-haired girlfriend and his shabby little rucksack. He made no very creditable impression on the powers that be, I don't mind telling you. Is it likely, if there *was* a plot to dismantle this city, that they would trust the details to someone like *this?*"

"Give him laldy, Gow!" yelled a voice behind the pillar. Lanark gaped and stood up. He heard Grant at his side murmuring, "Careful now!" but a growing unease in his stomach had nothing to do with the debate. He said sharply, "Nobody trusted me with details. Wilkins would have told anybody these plans; he said only a revolution could change them. I don't care if you believe me or not."

He walked toward the door he had entered by.

Before he reached it Sludden cried, "Wait, everyone should hear this!" so he paused by the pillar. Sludden said, "This is from the chronology section of the *Western Lobby*:

> Nobody but a fanatic would suggest that the material of time is moral, but on occasions like the present, when the boundaries of the most stable continents seem melting into intercalendrical mist, it appears probable that a working timescale needs a higher proportion of common decency than the science of chronology has hitherto assumed. Decency is a vague term, and at present we suggest no more by it than a little more brotherhood between colleagues of equal or nearly equal standing.
>
> The authority of the council has always depended on the support of the creature, and until recently it was widely felt that Monboddo's connections with the Algolagnics–Cortexin group merely ratified his standing as a strong president. Recent disclosures, however, by the fiery energy chief Ozenfant show that recent loans of creature energy have been absorbed by the lord president's office to the almost total exclusion of the normal power corridor network.
>
> Although respect for the president director and respect for the decimal hour are not connected in logic, they seem to feed irrationally on each other in a state of collapsing

confidence. There is deep alarm in
council corridors that speculation
against the new timescale has now
exceeded the boundaries of reason
and may no longer be susceptible
to rational remedy. Only one thing
is certain. The swift dismantling of
a certain darkened district, which
once seemed a daring and debatable
act of rationalization, has become
a matter of urgent necessity."

"What's that supposed to mean?" asked Gow. "There are hundreds of darkened districts. What conceivable reason have you
for thinking they've chosen Unthank?"
"I came here to tell you that," said Grant. "Nearly two days
ago a Cortexin tanker and an Algolagnics transporter collided
at the intersection. All incoming traffic is diverted to Imber.
We have food supplies for three more days. By 'day' I mean
the old fashioned solar day of twenty-four hours, with roughly
seventeen hundred heartbeats an hour."
"Pull yourself together, Grant!" said Ritchie-Smollet. "Do you
suggest these vehicles were smashed in a criminal plot between
Algolagnics and the council? That is pure paranoia. The council
is sending experts to deal with the damage."
"You don't need a plot to cause crashes on a motorway," said
Grant. "They happen all the time. When they happen on the
council's doorstep they're cleared at once. Why the delay with
us?"
"Because we are not on the council's doorstep. From the council's viewpoint we are a remote and unimportant province, but
that does not mean they are out for our blood. The council
traffic commissioner has talked to me on the phone. His clear-
ance teams are fighting an imbalance at the Cortexin cloning
plant. Half West Atlantis will sink if that isn't stabilized first.
But he's moving heaven and earth to get the right men quickly
here too. He said so. I know him. He is an honest man."
"Haven't you seen how the council works in peacetime?" asked
Grant. "It never behaves badly. It never destroys a country
of peasant villages, for example, but it lets the creature turn
whole forests into paper so there are no roots to hold the
water back. And when an accidental storm arises (as they always
will), half a million people drown or die in the following famine,
and the council helps the survivors, and the helpers organize
the country's industry in ways the creature finds profitable. I'm
sure your traffic commissioner honestly wants to clear the inter-

section. I'm sure his honest experts have more urgent work
to do. And I'm sure that three days from now, when our administration crumbles and the city is a horde of starving rioters,
the council will introduce an honest emergency-aid programme
and honestly evacuate Unthank down whatever gullet the creature offers."

There was a long silence.

"It is true," said the slow-voiced lady softly, "that with efery
passing moment a broken nerf circuit of the new Algolagnics
model becomes a more dangerous object. Virst ve haf only
the fibrations, but after two days, on the old timescale, sublima-
tion produces radioactive fumes of an unusually lethal ant vide-
spreading type."

"Why not clear up the mess yourselves?" said Lanark impatiently.

"We lack protective clothing. Vithout it nothing is able to lif
vithin sixty metres of these objects."

"Are they heavy?" asked Lanark. "Could you flood the road
and float them off it?"

"Powerhoses," said Grant to Sludden. "Open a storm drain
and order the fire brigade to flush the mess down it with powerhoses."

"Impossible!" bellowed Gow. "Even if Unthank *is* menaced
in the way you suggest, which I do *not* for one moment admit,
the forcing of unqualified firemen to do the dangerous work
of trained nerve-circuit experts is in flagrant defiance of all
normal and democratic procedure. I am sure our provost is
not going to be led astray by the jeremiads of the guest speaker
and the rantings of brother Grant. Once again we see extremists
of the right and left combining in an unholy alliance against
all that is most stable in—"

"Blood will have to flow," said a loud dull voice behind the
pillar. "I'm sorry, I see no other way."

"Whose blood will have to flow, Scougal?" asked Ritchie-Smollet gently, "and when, and where, and why will it flow, Scougal?"

"I'm sorry if my remarks upset people" said the dull voice,
"I apologize. But blood will have to flow, I see no other way."

Lanark walked over to the little door, opened it, ducked under
the lintel and closed it behind him.

CHAPTER 37.
Alexander Comes

Finding no light-switch he climbed the narrow steep spiral in blackness, patting the wall as he neared the level of the attic. At last his hand touched a clumsy wooden bolt. He slid it back, shoved hard and stepped out into fresh air with a few stars overhead. Either he had left the chapterhouse by the wrong stairs or the stairs by the wrong door for he now stood in a gutter between two dim slopes of roof. He could hear muffled kitchen noises of water and clinking dishes, so the attic was nearby. The gutter was clearly a walkway too, so he moved along it toward the noise and came to a stone parapet overlooking a city square. It was a quiet square with a couple of tiny figures walking across. The houses on the far side were the old tenement kind with shops on the ground floor and some upper windows curtained and lit from inside. These seemed so pleasantly familiar that he stared, perplexed. Unthank was the only city he remembered, but he had always wanted a brighter place: why should he like the look of it now? The yattering noise from the intersection was very audible. So were the kitchen sounds which came from a door in a gable behind him. He knocked on this, and a moment later Frankie opened it. He was so delighted that he seized her waist and kissed her surprised mouth. She pushed him away after a while, laughing and saying, "Passionate, eh?"

"How is she?"

"She was sleeping when I left, but I sent for the nurse to be on the safe side."

"Thanks, Frankie, you're a good girl."

He walked beside the arches along the attic and softly entered the bright little cubicle. Rima smiled at him softly from her pillow. He said "Hullo" and squatted on a cushion by the bed. She whispered, "The contractions have begun."
"Good. A nurse is coming."
He held her hand under the bedclothes. A stout lady came busily in and frowned at him, then bent over Rima with a very wide smile.
"So you're going to have a wee baby!" she said in the loud slow voice some people use when speaking to idiots. "A wee baby just like your *mummy* had when *you* were born! Isn't that nice?"
"I'm not going to speak to her," said Rima to Lanark, then drew a sharp breath and seemed to concentrate on something.
"That's right!" said the nurse consolingly. "It doesn't *really* hurt now, does it?"
"Tell her my back's sore!" said Rima sharply.
"Her back's sore," said Lanark.
"And do you really want your husband to stay here? Some men find it very, very difficult to take."
"Tell her to shut up!" said Rima and a moment later added bitterly, "Tell her I've wet the bed."
"It isn't what you think," said the nurse. "It's perfectly natural." She turned the mattress and changed the sheets while Rima sat on a cushion wrapped in a blanket. Rima said, "I'm having a girl."
"Oh," said Lanark.
"I don't want a boy."
"Then I do."
"Why?"
"So that one of us will welcome it, whoever comes."
"You must always put me in the wrong, mustn't you?"
"Sorry."
She returned to bed, scowled, ground her teeth and worked hard for a while, holding his hand tight; then she relaxed and cried desperately, "Tell her to stop this pain in my back!"
"Things must get worse before they get better," said the nurse soothingly. She was drinking tea from a thermos flask.
"Ha!" snarled Rima. She thrust Lanark's hand away, clenched her fists outside the covers and started working again, sweating hard. For a long time spells of fretful repose were followed by spells of silent, urgent, determined labour.

At last she raised her knees high, spread them wide and said sharply, "What's happening?"

The nurse folded back the covers. Lanark leaned against the wall by the bed foot and stared into the red widening gash between Rima's thighs. She gasped and cried, "My back! My back! What's happening?"

"He's coming. I can see the face," said Lanark, for in the depth of the gash he seemed to see a squeezed-thin face emerging, six inches high and less than half an inch wide, the nose thin as a string and ending in an absurd little flap, the eyes on each side sunk in vertical creases. The mouth was a tight-pursed hole and the nurse kept sticking her finger in it, presumably to help it breathe. Then the mouth opened into an oval with something flat inside, and the oval grew and filled the whole gash, and the flatness was a dome coming out, and the dome was a head gripped by the nurse's hand. Then the universe seemed to go slow and silent. In slow silence a small, pale-lavender, enraged little person was lifted up, dragging after him a meaty cable. He had a penis, and his elbows and knees were bent, and his fists and eyes clenched tight, and his aghast mouth was yelling a soundless scream of fury. Rima, whose face seemed to have been scrubbed by a storm, turned on him a slow smile of loving recognition. The small person flushed red, opened an eye, then another, and after some hiccups his scream wavered out into angry sound. The universe returned to the usual speed. The nurse gave the baby to Rima and told Lanark sternly, "Go and get two soup plates from the kitchen."

"Why?"

"Do what you're told."

He ran along by the arches hearing sounds of a service from the cathedral floor. A remote ministerial voice was chanting, "My buird thou hast hanselled in face o' my faes; thou drookest my heid wi' ile, my bicker is fou an' skailin. . . ." Jack sat in the kitchen listening to Ritchie-Smollet, who was leaning on a table. "I would have advised more caution, but we've burned our boats and must abide the issue. Ah, Lanark! How are things with you?"

"Fine. Can I have two soup plates, please?"

"Congratulations! Boy or girl? How's the mother?" asked Ritchie-Smollet, handing over plates from a pile.

"Thank you. A boy. She seems all right."

"One has become two: the first and best miracle of all, eh? I hope you'll allow me the privilege of christening the little chap."

"I'll mention it to his mother but she isn't religious," said Lanark going to the door.

"Are you sure of that? Never mind. Come back when you can and we'll drink their health. I believe we've some cooking sherry in the larder."

The cubicle seemed full of women. Rima suckled the baby, Frankie poured water from a kettle into a basin, the nurse seized the plates and said, "That's fine, you can go now."
"But—"
"We can hardly move as it is, there's no room for you."
He watched his son enviously for a moment then went slowly away, but not toward the kitchen, for he didn't want company. He suddenly wanted to use himself vigorously, to run fast or climb high. He found a spiral stair near the organ loft and climbed quickly to another open walkway under the stars. It led through a chilling wind to another little door. He opened this and entered a large, dim, square, dusty room lit by hurricane lamps on the floor. A steep iron ladder slanted upward near the centre, and six Lugworm Casanovas lay smoking in sleeping bags along a wall. One of them said, "Shut it, man, nobody's too hot in here."
Lanark said, "Sorry," closed the door and crossed to the ladder. Its rungs were cold and gritty with rust, it shuddered at each step. When the upper shadows hid him from the eyes below he climbed more slowly, not lifting a foot until both hands gripped a rung, not raising a hand till both feet were firmly placed. He came to a floor of narrow planks set an inch apart. Light shining up between them showed the foot of a steeper ladder. He climbed this more slowly than ever. In the wall before, to each side, and behind him, were huge windows barred by horizontal stone slats. He looked down through them onto the black cathedral roof edged with city lights. He stood on thin rungs high up in an old stone cage and listened to the faintly whistling breeze. With each extra step he tried to remember that the ladder was solid, and braced by an occasional rod against a wall that had stood for many centuries, and would probably not collapse suddenly without warning. At last he reached, not a floor, but a narrow metal bridge. Black machinery overhung it. He made out timber beams, a big wheel and a bell whose rim, when he stepped underneath, came down to his shoulders. He raised a hand to the massive clapper and carefully pushed it forward, meaning gently to touch the side, but the weight increased with the angle, he had to use unexpected force and the shock of contact bathed him in a sudden sonorous *Dong*. Half deafened, half intoxicated by the sound,

he laughed aloud, let the clapper fall back and shoved it at
the rim with both hands, ducked as it swung back again and
then reached up again to hurl it forward. The detonation of
the strokes grew inaudible. He felt only a great droning rever-
berating the bell, the bridge, his bones, the tower, the air.
His arms were tired. He ducked out from under the bell and
gripped a handrail for support, though at first the sound in it
hurt his palms like an electric current.

The droning faded. He seemed to hear protesting cries
from below and, ashamed of the noise he had made, climbed
a ladder away from them. He came to a higher floor of wooden
slats where the blackness was total, except for a chink of light
below a door. He groped toward it, slid the bolt and went
out onto a windy platform at the foot of the floodlit steeple.
The racket from the intersection was audible again, sometimes
louder, sometimes fainter. He wondered if this was caused by
the blustering wind and stepped to the parapet facing the Necropolis, for the din seemed to come from behind it. The highest
monuments were silhouetted against a pulsing glow in the sky.
Wedges of shadow moved over this like the arms of a windmill.
The yattering noise sank to a dull stutter, hesitated, coughed
and stopped. The majestic beams of shadow swept the sky in
silence for a while, then suddenly widened as the glow faded.
The main light now was cast by the great lamp standards on
the motorway. A remote mechanical braying began and came
swiftly nearer. A line of red fire engines with braying sirens
appeared round a curving bridge from the intersection and
sped down the gorge between Necropolis and cathedral. The
air began filling with traffic sounds. Lanark walked round the
platform to the far side of the tower and looked down onto
the square. A couple of trucks rumbled across it pulling trailers
with metal wreckage on them; then a trickle of cars began
flowing in the opposite direction. A mobile crane drove through
a gateway to the cathedral grounds, crossed the stones of the
old graveyard and parked against a wall. Lanark suddenly felt
his chilled ears, hands and body and returned to the door in
the spire.

Coming down on the ladders he found the light from below
much stronger than before. The room where the Lugworms
had lain was lit by bulbs hung from improvised brackets. Two
electricians were working near the door and one of them said,
"A bloke was looking for you, Jimmy."

"Who was he?"

"A young bloke. Long hair."

"What did he want?"

"He didnae say."

Near the cubicle he heard a strange, steady little song. Sludden lay on the bed singing "Dadadada" and dandling a robust little boy in a blue woollen suit. Rima, in a blouse and skirt, sat knitting beside them. The sight filled Lanark with a large cold rage. Rima gave him an unfriendly glance and Sludden said brightly, "The wanderer returns!"

Lanark went to the tiny sink, washed his hands, then turned to Sludden and said, "Give him to me."

He took the child, who started wailing. "Oh, put him down!" said Rima impatiently. "He needs a rest and so do I."

Lanark sat on the bed foot and sang quietly, "Dadadada." The boy stopped complaining and settled in his arms. The small compact body was warm and comforting and gave such a pleasant feeling of peace that Lanark wondered uneasily if this was a right thing for a father to feel. He laid the boy in a pram by the bed and tucked a soft blanket round him.

Sludden stood up and stretched his arms, saying, "Great! That's really great. I came here for several reasons, of course, but one is to congratulate you on your performance. Don't sneer at him, Rima, he's a good committee man when he accepts discipline. He jostled Gow, and that allowed us to act. The committee is in permanent session now. I don't mean we're all in the chapterhouse all the time, but some of us are in the chapterhouse all the time."

Lanark said, "Listen, Sludden, I want the company of my wife and child. Do you understand me?"

"Of course!" said Sludden cheerily. "I'm just leaving. I'll come back for you all later."

"What do you mean?"

"Sludden has offered us room in his house," said Rima.

"We're not taking it."

"I don't want to force anything on you," said Sludden. "But this seems a strange place to bring up a child."

"Unthank is dead and done for, don't you realize that?" cried Lanark. "The boy and Rima and I are leaving for a much brighter city. Wilkins promised us."

"Don't trust your council friends too far," said Sludden gravely. "We've cleared the motorway, the food trucks are rolling in again. And even if Wilkins did tell the truth, you're forgetting

differences in timescale. The decimal calendar hasn't been introduced here and what the council calls days can be months—years, where we're concerned. And remember, Alexander was born here. You have a council passport. He hasn't."
"Who is Alexander?"
Sludden pointed to the pram. Rima said, "Ritchie-Smollet christened him that."
Lanark jumped up shouting, *"Christened?"*
Alexander started crying. "Shushush," whispered Rima, reaching for the pram handle and gently rocking it. "Shushushush."
"Why Alexander?" whispered Lanark furiously. "Why couldn't you wait for me? Why the bloody hurry?"
"We waited as long as we could—why didn't you come when we called?"
"You never called me!"
"We did. Jack went to the tower when you started your row and shouted up the ladder, but you wouldn't come down."
"I didn't know that was Jack shouting," said Lanark, confused.
"Were you drunk?" asked Rima.
"Of course not. You've never seen me drunk."
"Perhaps, but you often act that way. And Ritchie-Smollet says a bottle of cooking sherry has vanished from the kitchen."
"I'm leaving," said Sludden with a chuckle. "Outsiders should never mix in a lovers' quarrel. I'll see you later."
"Thank you," said Lanark. "We'll manage by ourselves."
Sludden shrugged and left. Alexander gradually fell asleep.

Rima sat with tight-shut lips, knitting hard. Lanark lay on the bed with hands behind his head and said gloomily, "I didn't want to leave you. And I didn't think I was long."
"You were away for hours—ages, it seemed to me. You've no sense of time. None at all."
"Alexander is quite a good name. We can shorten it to Alex. Or Sandy."
"He's called *Alexander.*"
"What are you knitting?"
"Clothes. Children need clothes, hadn't you noticed? We can't always live on Ritchie-Smollet's charity."
"If Sludden is right about calendars," Lanark mused, "we'll be a long time in this place. I'll have to look for work."
"So you're going to leave me alone again. I see. Why did you ring that bell? Are you sure you weren't drunk?"
"I rang it because I was happy then. Why are you attacking me?"

"To defend myself."

"I'm sorry I shouted at you, Rima. I was surprised and angry. I'm very glad to be back with you."

"Yes, it's easy for you to live in a box, you can run off to your towers and committee meetings whenever you like. When will I get some freedom?"

"Whenever you need it."

"And you'll stay here and look after Alex?"

"Of course. That's only fair."

Rima sighed and then smiled and rolled up her knitting. She came to the bed, kissed him quickly on the brow, then went to the chest of drawers and peered at her face in a mirror.

Lanark said, "Are you leaving already?"

"Yes, Lanark. I really do need a change."

She made up her mouth with lipstick. Lanark said, "Who gave you that?"

"Frankie. We're going dancing. We're going to get ourselves picked up by a couple of young young young boys. You don't mind, do you?"

"Not if you only dance with them."

"Oh, but we'll flirt with them too. We'll madden them with desire. Middle-aged women need to madden somebody some times."

"You aren't middle-aged."

"I'm no chicken, anyway. When Alex wakens you can change his nappy—there's a clean one in the top drawer. Put the dirty one in the plastic bag under the bed. If he cries you must heat some milk in the kitchen—not too hot, mind. Test it with your finger."

"Aren't you breastfeeding him?"

"Yes, but he has to learn to drink like an ordinary human being. But I'll probably be back before he wakens. How do I look?"

She posed before him, hands on hips. He said, "Very young. Very beautiful."

She kissed him warmly and left. He lay back on the bed, missing her, and fell asleep.

He was wakened by Alexander crying so he changed his nappy and carried him to the kitchen. Jack and Frankie were eating a meal at a table there. Frankie said, "Hullo, passionate man. How's Rima?"

He stared at her, confused, and blushed hotly. He muttered, "Gone for a walk. The boy needs milk."

"I'll make him a bottle."

Lanark strayed round the kitchen murmuring nonsense to Alexander, for there was a strange appalling pain in his chest and he didn't want to talk to adults. Frankie handed him a warm bottle with teat folded in a white napkin. He muttered some thanks and went back to the cubicle. He sat on the bed and held the teat to Alexander's mouth but Alexander twisted aside, screaming, "NonononononoMumumumum!"

"She'll be back soon, Sandy."

"NononononononononononoMumumumumumumumumum!"

Alexander kept screaming and Lanark walked the floor with him. He felt he was carrying a dwarf who kept hitting him on the head with a stick, a dwarf he could neither disarm nor put down. People in neighbouring cubicles began banging their walls, then a man came in and said, "There are folk trying to sleep in this building, Jimmy."

"I can't help that, and I'm not called Jimmy."

The man was tall and bald with white stubble on his cheeks, a single black tooth in his upper jaw, and wore a dirty grey raincoat. He stared at Lanark for a while then pulled a brown bottle from his pocket and said, "Milk's no use. Give him a slug of this—it's a great quietener."

"No."

"Then take a slug yourself."

"No."

The man sighed, squatted on a stool and said, "Tell me your woes."

"I have no woes!" yelled Lanark who was too plagued to think. Alexander was screaming "Mumumumumumumumum!"

"If it's woman trouble," said the man, "I can advise you because I was married once. I had a wife who did terrible things, things I cannae mention in the presence of a wean. You see, women are different from us. They're seventy-five percent water. You can read that in Pavlov."

Alexander fastened his gums on the teat and started sucking. Lanark sighed with relief. After a moment he said, "Men are mostly water too."

"Yes, but only seventy percent. The extra five percent makes the difference. Women have notions and feelings like us but they've got tides too, tides that keep floating the bits of a human being together inside them and washing it apart again. They're governed by lunar gravity; you can read that in Newton. How can they follow ordinary notions of decency when they're driven by the moon?"

Lanark laid Alexander in the pram with the bottle beside him
and gently rocked the handle.

The man said, "I was ignorant when I was married. I hadnae
read Newton, I hadnae read Pavlov, so I kicked the bitch out—
pardon the language, I am referring to my wife. I wish now
that I'd cut my throat instead. Do me a favour, pal. Give yourself
a holiday. Have a drink."

Lanark glanced at the brown bottle held toward him, then took
it and swigged. The taste was horrible. He passed it back, trying
to say thank you, but there were tears in his eyes and he could
only gulp and pull faces. A warm stupidity began to spread
softly through him. He heard the man say, "You have to like
women but not care for them: not care what they do, I mean.
Nobody can help what they do. We do as things do with us."

"What is for us," said Lanark, with a feeling of profound understanding, "will not go past us."

"A hundred years from now," said the man, "it'll all be the
same."

Lanark heard Alexander asking sadly, "When will she come?"

"Soon, son. Very soon."

"When is soon?"

"Near to now but not now."

"I need her now."

"Then you need her badly. You must try to need her properly."

"What is proply?"

"Silently. Silence is always proper. When I understand this
better I'll stop talking. You won't be able to hear me for miles.
I will radiate silence like a dark star shining in the gaps between
syllables and conversation."

"You're ignoring politics," said the man aggressively. "Politics
depend on noise. All parties subscribe to *that* opinion, if to
no other."

Alexander screamed, "They're biting me!"

"Who's biting you?" said Lanark leaning unsteadily over the
pram.

"My teeth."

Lanark put a finger in the small mouth and felt a tiny bone
edge coming through the gum. He said uneasily, "We age
quickly in this world."

"You must remember one important thing," said the man,
"You've emptied the bottle. I'm not complaining. I know where
to get another, but it costs a coupla dollars. A dollar a skull.
Right?"

"I'm sorry. I've no money."

"What's happening here?" asked Rima, coming angrily in.

"Sandy is teething," said Lanark.

"I'm just leaving, missus," said the man, and left.

Rima changed Alexander's nappy, saying grimly, "I can't trust you to do a thing."

"But I've fed him. I've cared for him."

"Huh!"

Lanark lay on the bed watching her. He was sober now and some of the ache had returned to his chest, but he was also thankful and relieved. After a while he said, "Did you enjoy the dancing?"

"Dancing?"

"You said you were going dancing with Frankie."

"Did I? Maybe I did. Anyway I missed Frankie and went house-hunting with what's-his-name. The fat soldier. McPake."

"McPake?"

"He used to hang around the old Elite with us. The Elite has vanished under a motorway now. Nothing there but a great concrete trench. They really are making a mess of this place."

"Did you find any houses?"

"Hundreds of them, all furnished and all beautiful. But we've no money so I was wasting my time. Is that what you're going to say?"

"Of course not!"

She had settled Alexander in the pram and was sitting despondently with drooping head and arms folded under breasts. He was pricked by tenderness and desire and went to her with arms outstretched, whispering, "Oh, Rima dear, let's love each other a little. . . ."

She smiled, jumped up and danced toward him with hands outstretched and nipping. "Oh, Rima dear!" she moaned through pursed-out lips. "Oh, lovey-dovey earie-dearie Rima, let's lovey-dovey an itsy-bitsy little. . . ."

Her nips were painful and he fended them off, laughing until they both fell side by side and breathless on the bed. A moment later he asked sadly, "Do I really seem like that?"

"I'm afraid you do. You're too nervous and pathetic."

She sighed, then unfastened her blouse, saying, "However, since you want it, let's love each other a little."

He stared, astonished, and said, "I can't make love when you've made me feel small and absurd."

"I've made you fell absurd, have I? I'm glad. I'm delighted. You make me feel small all the time. You've never paid

attention to my feelings, never once. You dragged us here
from a perfectly comfortable place because you disliked the
food, and what good did it do? We still eat the same food.
You laughed when I gave you a son and you can't even give
him a home. You use use use me all the time, and you're so
smugly sure you're right all the time. You're heavy and dismal
and humourless, yet you want me to pet you and make you
feel big and important. I'm sorry, I can't do it. I'm too tired."
She went to the seat by the pram and resumed knitting.

    Lanark sat on the bed with his face in his hands. He said,
"This is Hell."
"Yes. I know."
"I wish you could love me."
"You take me for granted, so I can't. You don't know how
to make me love you. Some men can do it."
He looked up and said, "Which men?"
She continued to knit. He stood up and cried, *"Which men?"*
"I might tell you if you wouldn't get hysterical."
Alexander sat up and asked in an interested voice, "Is Dad
going to get hysterical?"
Lanark shook his head dumbly then whispered, "I must get
out of here."
"Yes, I think you should," said Rima. "Look for a job. You
need one."
He went to the entrance and turned, hoping for a look of
friendship or recognition, but her face was so full of stony
pain that he could only shake his head.
"Goodbye Dad," said Alexander casually. Lanark waved to
him, hesitated, then left.

CHAPTER 38.
Greater Unthank

The shadowy nave seemed vast and empty till he neared the door and saw Jack sitting on the font. Lanark meant to pass him with a slight nod but Jack was watching with such a frank stare that he stopped and said tensely, "Could you please direct me to a labour exchange?"

"They're not called labour exchanges now, they're called job centres," said Jack, springing down. "I'll take you to one."

"Can Ritchie-Smollet spare you?"

"Maybe not, but I can spare him. I change bosses when I like."

Jack led him through the cathedral grounds to a bus stop on the edge of the square. Lanark said, "I can't afford a bus fare."

"Don't worry, I've got cash. What do you want at a job centre?"

"An unskilled job doing something useful exactly the way I'm told."

"Not many jobs like that in Unthank nowadays. Except in cleansing, perhaps. And cleansing workers have to be young and healthy."

"How old do you think I am?"

"Past the halfway mark, at least."

Lanark looked down at the prominent veins on the back of his hands and muttered after a while, "No dragonhide, anyway."

"What did you say?"

"I may not be young but I don't have dragonhide."

"Of course you don't. We aren't living in the dark ages."

Lanark felt like the victim of a sudden horrible accident. He thought, 'Over halfway through life and what have I achieved? What have I made? Only a son, and he was mostly his mother's work. Who have I ever helped? Nobody but Rima, and I've only helped her out of messes she'd have missed if she had been with someone else. All I have is a wife and child. I must make them a home, a secure comfortable home.'

As if answering the thought a bus crossed a corner of the square with a painting on the side of a mother and child. Printed over it were the words **A HOME IS MONEY. MONEY IS TIME. BUY TIME FOR YOUR FAMILY FROM THE QUANTUM CHRONOLOGICAL. (THEY'LL LOVE YOU FOR IT.)**

"I need a lot of money," said Lanark. "If I can't get work I'll have to beg from the security people."

"The name's changed," said Jack. "They're called social stability now. And they don't give money, they give three-in-one."

"What's that?"

"A special kind of bread. It nourishes and tranquillizes and stops your feeling cold, which is useful if you're homeless. But I don't think you should eat any."

"Why?"

"A little does no harm, but after a while it damages the intelligence. Of course the unemployment problem would be a catastrophe without it. Here comes our bus."

"This *is* Hell," said Lanark.

"There are worse hells," said Jack.

The bus was painted to look like a block of Enigma de Filets Congalés. On the side it said **NOW EVERYONE CAN TASTE THE RICH HUMAN GOODNESS IN FROZEN SECRETS, THE FOOD OF PRESIDENTS.**

Jack led Lanark to a seat on the top deck and brought out a cigarette packet labelled POISON. He said, "Like one?"

"No thanks," said Lanark and stared as Jack lit a white cylinder with DON'T SMOKE THIS printed along it.

"Yes, they're dangerous," said Jack, inhaling. "That's why the council insisted on the warning."

"Why doesn't it stop them being made?"

"Half the population is hooked on them," said Jack. "And the council gets half the money spent on them. They're an Algolagnics product. There are less dangerous drugs, of course, but they wouldn't be so profitable if they were legalized."

A bus going the other way carried a sentence past the window: **QUICK MONEY IS TIME IN YOUR POCKET—BUY**

MONEY FASTER FROM THE QUANTUM EXPONEN-TIAL.

Jack said, "You were being sarcastic—weren't you?—when you asked if Ritchie-Smollet could spare me?"

"I'm sorry."

"I don't mind. Yes, he depends on me, does old Smollet. So does Sludden. I choose my bosses carefully. *That* bloke was my boss once."

Jack pointed through the window at a tattered poster covering the end of a derelict tenement. It showed a friendly-looking man behind a desk with telephones on it. The words below said **ARE YOU LOOKING FOR A FACTORY SITE, A FAC-TORY OR A LABOUR FORCE? PHONE 777-7777 AND SPEAK TO TOM TALLENTYRE, CHAIRMAN OF THE WORK FOR UNTHANK BOARD.**

"Tallentyre was a very big man after they scrapped the Q39 project," said Jack. "In fact he was provost for a while. But Sludden did for him in the end. Sludden pointed out that the posters were put up in parts of Unthank where the unemployed lived, and folk with power to start new factories didn't live in Unthank anyway. So the action shifted to Sludden and Smol-let, and so did I. I enjoy being where the action is. That's why I'm with you, just now."

"Why are you with me?"

"You aren't what you pretend, are you? I agree with Gow. You're some sort of agent or investigator. Why ask about cleans-ing and social stability when you work for Ozenfant and carry a council passport?"

"I don't work for Ozenfant. And what use is a council passport to me?"

"It could get you a very well-paid job."

"I want that!" said Lanark excitedly. "How do I get one? I want that!"

"Ask the employment centre to put you on the professional register," said Jack sulkily. He seemed disappointed.

Lanark looked out of the window, feeling more hopeful. The bus was passing busy new shops whose fronts spread along whole blocks and showed brightly packaged food and drugs and records and clothes. He noticed many restaurants with oriental names and many kinds of gambling shops. In some he glimpsed people sitting with bags and baskets at counters, apparently gambling for food. The gaps left by demolished buildings were crammed with parked cars and surrounded by

fences with wild threats scrawled on them in bright paint.
CRAZY MAC KILLS, they said and **MAD TOAD RULES,**
and **THE WEE MALCIES ARE COMING,** but they didn't
distract from the larger message of the posters. These showed
pictures of family life, sex, food and money, and their words
were more puzzling.
**BOOST YOUR THERMS WITH NULLITY GREEN—BAG
HER IN YOUR BLOCKAL BLOOPER-MARKET.
GRIND YOUR SPECTACLES WITH METAL TEA, THE
SEX CHAMP ON THE CHILIASM.
THE SWEETEST DREAMERS INHALE BLUE FUME,
THE POISON WITH THE WARNING.
WISE BUYERS ARE THE BEST SEXERS—BUY HER A
LONG LIFE, AN EASY DEATH FROM QUANTUM
PROVIDENTIAL. (SHE'LL LOVE YOU FOR IT.)**
Lanark said, "What a lot of instructions."
"Don't you like advertisements?"
"No."
"The city would look pretty dead without them—they add to
the action. Read that."
Jack pointed to a small poster on the bus window which said:

**ADVERTISING OVERSTIMULATES,
MISINFORMS,
CORRUPTS.**
**If *you* feel this, send your name and address
to the Council Advertising Commission and
receive your free booklet explaining why we
can't do without it.**

They got off the bus in a large square Lanark knew well,
though it was brighter and busier than he remembered. He
gazed at the statues on their massive Victorian pedestals and
reflected that he had seen them before he saw Rima. The square
was still enclosed by ornate stone buildings except where he
and Jack stood before a glass wall of shining doors. Above
this great horizontal strips of concrete and glass alternated to
a height of twenty or thirty floors. Jack said, "The job centre."
"It's big."
"All the central job centres are housed here, and it's the central
centre of stability and surroundings too. I'll leave you now,
right?"
Lanark felt he was reliving something which had happened
once before, perhaps with Gloopy. He said awkwardly, "I'm

sorry I'm not what you thought—not a man of action, I mean."
Jack shrugged and said, "Not your fault. I'll give you a bit
of advice—"
He was interrupted by sudden siren blasts and a rattling like
thin thunder. The traffic halted round the square. Pedestrians
stood staring as an open truck sped past full of khaki-clad men
wearing black berets and holding guns. It had caterpillar treads
of a sort Lanark had seen rolling slowly over rough ground
in films, but ǫn the smooth road it raced so swiftly that it
was past as soon as recognized.
"The army!" cried Jack with a smile of pure appetite. "Now
we'll see some action. Hoi! Hoi! Hoi!"
He ran along the pavement shouting and waving to a taxi in
the resuming traffic. It came to the kerb and he leaped in.
Lanark watched it turn a corner, then stood awhile feeling sickened and uneasy. He was thinking about Alex, Rima and the
soldiers. He had never seen armed soldiers in a street before.
At last he turned and entered the building.

To a uniformed man in the entrance hall he said, "I'm
looking for work."
"Where do you live?"
"The cathedral."
"The cathedral's in the fifth district. Take lift eleven to floor
twenty."
The lift was like a metal wardrobe and packed with poorly
dressed people. When Lanark got out he had another feeling
of entering the past. He saw a dingy expanse tiled with grey
rubber and covered by men of all ages crowded together on
benches. A counter divided into cubicles by partitions ran along
one wall, and the cubicle facing the lift contained a chair and
a sign saying INQUIRIES. As Lanark walked toward this he felt
the air of the place resisting him like transparent jelly. The
men on the benches had a statuesque, entranced look as though
congealed there. All movement was exhausting—it would have
been equally tiring to go back. He reached the chair, slumped
onto it and sat, upright but dozing, until someone seemed to
be shouting at him. He opened his eyes and said thickly, "I
. . . am not . . . an animal."
An old clerk with bristling eyebrows behind the counter said,
"Then you ought to be on the professional register."
"Eh? . . . How?"
"Go down to the second floor."

Lanark got back to the lift and only wakened properly inside it. He wondered if all offices in that building had the same deadening influence.

But the second floor was different. It was covered by a soft green carpet. Low easy chairs clustered round glass tables with magazines on them, but nobody was waiting. There were no counters. Men and women too elegant to be thought of as clerks chatted to clients across widely spaced desks divided from each other by stands of potted plants. A girl receptionist showed him to the desk of a slightly older woman. She pushed a packet labelled BLUE FUME toward him, saying, "Please sit down. Do you inhale this particular poison?"

"No thank you."

"How very wise. Tell me about yourself."

He talked for a while. She opened her eyes wide and said, "You've actually worked with Ozenfant? How exciting! Tell me, what kind of man is he? In private life, I mean."

"He overeats and he's a bad musician."

The woman chuckled as if he had said something clever and shocking, then said, "I'm going to leave you for a moment. I've just had rather a good idea."

She came back saying, "We're in luck—Mr. Gilchrist can see you right away."

As they walked between the other desks she murmured, "Strictly between ourselves, I think Mr. Gilchrist is very keen to meet you. So is Mr. Pettigrew, though he doesn't show it, of course. You'll enjoy Mr. Pettigrew, he's a *tremendous* cynic." She led him to a door but didn't follow him through.

Lanark entered an office with two desks and a secretary typing at a table in the corner. A tall bald man sat telephoning on the edge of the nearest desk. He smiled at Lanark and pointed to an easy chair, saying, "He must be suffering from *folie de grandeur*. Provosts are buffers between us and the voters; they aren't supposed to *do* things. But nobody wants a riot, of course."

At the desk behind him a stout man leaned back smoking a pipe. Lanark sat looking through the window at the floodlit roof of a building across the square. A dome at one end had a glittering wind-vane shaped like a galleon. The tall man put the receiver down, saying, "That's that. My name is Gilchrist—I'm very pleased to meet you."

They shook hands and Lanark saw the council mark on Gilchrist's brow. They sat down in chairs beside a coffee table and Gilchrist said, "We want coffee, I think. Black or white, Lanark? See to that, Miss Maheen. I hear you are looking for professional employment, Lanark."

"Yes."

"But you've no definite idea of the kind of work you want."

"Correct. I'm more concerned about the salary."

"Would you like to work here?"

Lanark looked round the room. The secretary was attending to an electric percolator on top of a filing cabinet. The man behind the other desk had a large, dolorous, clownish face and winked at Lanark with no change of expression. Lanark said, "I'm very willing to consider it."

"Good. You mentioned salary. Unluckily salaries are a vexed question with us. It's impossible to pay a monthly or yearly sum when we can't even measure the minutes and hours. Until the council sends us the decimal clocks it's been promising for so long Unthank is virtually part of the intercalendrical zone. At present the city is kept going by force of habit. Not by rules, not by plans, but by habit. Nobody can rule with an elastic tape measure, can they?"

Lanark shook his head impatiently and said, "I've a family to feed. What can you offer me?"

"Credit. Members of our staff receive a Quantum credit card. That's much more useful than money."

"Will it let me rent a comfortable home for three people?"

"Easily. You could even buy a home. The energy to pay for it would be deducted from your future."

"Then I'll be glad to work here."

"I should explain the range of our activities."

"No need. I'll do whatever I'm told."

Gilchrist smiled and shook his head, saying "Social ignorance is only a virtue in the manufacturing classes. We professionals must understand the organism as a whole. That is our burden and our pride. It justifies our bigger incomes."

"Blethers!" said the stout man at the other desk. "Who in this building understands the organism as a whole? You and me and an old woman upstairs, perhaps, but the rest have forgotten. They were told, but they've forgotten."

"Pettigrew is a cynic," said Gilchrist, laughing.

"A *lovable* cynic," muttered Pettigrew. "Remember that. Pettigrew is everybody's lovable cynic."

The secretary laid a tray of coffee things on the table. Gilchrist carried his cup to the window, sat on the ledge and said oracularly, "Employment. Stability. Surroundings. Three offices, yet properly understood they are the same. Employment ensures stability. Stability lets us reshape our surroundings. The improved surroundings become a new condition of employment. The snake eats its tail. Nothing has precedence. This great building—this centre of all centres, this tower of welfare— exists to maintain full employment, reasonable stability and decent surroundings."

"Animals," said Pettigrew. "We deal with animals here. The scruff. The scum. The lowest of the low."

"Pettigrew is referring to the fact that there are not enough jobs and houses for everyone. Naturally—as in all freely competing societies—the unemployed and homeless tend to be less clever, or less healthy, or less energetic than the rest of us."

"They're a horde of stupid, dirty layabouts," said Pettigrew. "I know them, I grew up among them. You middle-class liberals like to pet them, but I wouldn't even let them breed. What we need is an X-ray device under the turnstiles at the football stadiums. Each man going through gets a blast of 900 roentgens right on the testicles. It would be perfectly painless. They wouldn't know what had happened till they got a wee printed card along with their entrance ticket. 'Dear Sir,' it would say. 'You may now ride your wife in perfect safety.' "

Gilchrist laughed until his coffee spilled into the saucer. "Pettigrew, you're incorrigible!" he said. "You talk as if a man's misery was all his own fault. You must admit that poverty, insanity and crime have multiplied since our major industry shut down. That isn't coincidence."

"Blame the unions!" said Pettigrew. "Prosperity is made by the bosses struggling with each other for more wealth. If they have to struggle with their workers too, then everybody loses. No wonder the big groups are shifting their factories to the coolie continents. I'm only thankful that the folk who lose most in the end are the envious sods who own the least. Greed isn't a pretty thing but envy is far, far worse."

"You're talking politics. It's time you shut up for a while," said Gilchrist amicably. He put down his cup on the window ledge, sat beside Lanark and said quietly, "Don't let his rough tongue upset you. Pettigrew is something of a saint. He's helped more widows and orphans than we've had good breakfasts."

"There's no need for excuses," said Lanark. "I realize now that nobody does well in this world if they don't belong to a big strong group. Your group handles the people who don't have one. I want to be with you, not under you, so tell me what to do."

"You're very abrupt," said Gilchrist. "Please remember we are here to help the unfortunate, and we *do* help them, as far as we can. Our problem is lack of funds. The recent Greater Unthank reorganization has given us a much larger staff to deal with the increasing number of unfortunates, so we have thousands of experts—planners, architects, engineers, artists, renovators, conservers, blood doctors, bowel doctors, brain doctors—all sitting on their bottoms praying for funds to start working with."

"So what can *I* do?"

"You can start as a grade D inquiry clerk. You will sit behind a desk hearing people complain. You must note their names and addresses and tell them they'll hear from us through the post."

"That's easy."

"It's the hardest job we have. You must give an appearance of listening closely. You must prod them with questions to keep the words flowing if they look like drying up. You must keep each one talking till they're exhausted—longer, if possible."

"And I write a report on what they tell me?"

"No. Just note their name and address and tell them they'll hear from us through the post."

"Why?"

"I was afraid you would ask that," said Gilchrist, sighing slightly. "As I already indicated, there are many whom we cannot help through lack of funds. A lot of these are still strong and vigorous, and it is a dangerous thing to suddenly deprive a man of hope—he can turn violent. It is important to kill hope *slowly,* so that the loser has time to adjust unconsciously to the loss. We try to keep hope alive till it has burned out the vitality feeding it. Only then is the man allowed to face the truth."

"So a grade D inquiry clerk does nothing but postpone."

"Yes."

Lanark said loudly, "I don't want—" then hesitated. He thought of the credit card, and a home with three or four rooms, perhaps in walking distance of this great building. Perhaps he would be able to go home for lunch and eat it with Sandy and Rima.

He said feebly, "I don't *want* this job."

"Nobody wants it. As I said, it's the hardest job we have. But will you take it?"

After a moment Lanark said, "Yes."

"Excellent. Miss Maheen, come over here. I want you to smile at our new colleague. He's called Lanark."

The secretary sat down facing Lanark and looked into his eyes. She had a smooth, vacant, fashionably pretty face and her hair was so golden and perfectly brushed that it looked like a nylon wig. For a split second her mouth widened in a smile, and Lanark was disconcerted by a click inside her head. Gilchrist said, "Show her your profile." Lanark stared at him and heard another click. Miss Maheen slid two fingers inside a pocket of her crisp white blouse above her left breast and drew out a plastic strip. She handed it to Lanark. There were two clear little pictures of him at one end, a disconcerted full face and a perplexed profile. The rest was covered by fine blue parallel lines with LANARK printed on top and a long number with about twelve digits.

"She's a reliable piece," said Gilchrist, patting Miss Maheen's bottom as she returned to her table. "She issues credit cards, makes coffee, types, looks pretty and her hobby is oriental martial arts. She's a Quantum-Cortexin product."

Lanark said bitterly, "Can't Quantum-Cortexin make something to work as a grade D inquiry clerk?"

"Oh, yes, they can. They did. We tried it out at a stability sub-centre and it provoked a riot. The clients found its responses too mechanical. Most people have a quite irrational faith in human beings."

"Roll on, Provan," said Pettigrew.

"Amen, Pettigrew. Roll on, Provan," said Gilchrist.

"What do you mean?" said Lanark.

"Roll on is a colloquialism whereby an anticipated event is conjured to occur more quickly. We're looking forward to our transfer to Provan. You know about that, of course?"

"I was told I could go there because I'd a council passport."

"Yes indeed. We'll manage things much better from Provan. I'm afraid this big expensive building has been a great big expensive mistake. Even the air conditioning doesn't work very well. But let's go to the twentieth floor."

They went through the desks of the outer office to a large and quiet lift. It brought them to a long narrow office containing about thirty desks. Half were occupied by people typing or

phoning; many were empty, and the rest surrounded by talk-
ative groups. Gilchrist led Lanark to one of these and said,
"Here is our new inquiry clerk."

"Thank God!" said a man who was carefully folding a paper
form into a dart. "I've just faced six of the animals, six in a
row. I'm not going out there again for a long, long time."
He launched the dart which drifted sweetly down the length
of the office. There was scattered applause.

"Good luck!" said Gilchrist, shaking Lanark's hand. "I promise
you'll be promoted out of here as soon as we find a replacement
for you. Pettigrew and I drink in the Vascular Cavity. It's a
vulgar pub but handy for the office and one always gets a good
eyeful." (He winked.) "So if you call there later we'll have a
jar together."

He went out quickly. The dart thrower led Lanark to the last
of a long row of doors in one wall. He softly opened it a
little way, peeked through the crack and whispered, "He seems
quiet. I don't think there's anything to worry about. You know
what to do?"

"Yes."

Lanark stepped through the door into a cubicle behind a counter
with an inquiries sign on it.

A thin, youngish man sat facing him. He had short ruffled
hair, a clean suit of cheap cloth, his eyes were closed and he
seemed barely able to avoid falling sideways. Lanark took the
knob of the door he had just come through, slammed it hard
and sat down. The man opened his eyes and said, "No no
no no . . . no no, you've got me wrong."

As his eyes focused on Lanark's face his own face began to
change. Vitality flooded into it. He smiled and whispered, "Lanark!"

"Yes," said Lanark, wondering.

The man almost laughed with relief. "Thank Christ it's you!"
He leaned over the counter and shook Lanark's hand, saying,
"Don't you know me? Of course not, I was a kid at the time.
I'm Jimmy Macfee. Granny Fleck's wee Macfee. You remember
the old Ashfield Street days when me and my sisters played
at sailing ships on your bed? My, but you've put on the beef.
You were thin then. You had pockets full of seashells and
pebbles, remember?"

"Were you that boy?" said Lanark, shaking his head. "How's
Mrs. Fleck? Have you seen her lately?"

"Not lately, no. She hardly goes out these days. Arthritis. It's her age. But thank Christ it's you. I've seen six of these clerks, and every one of them has tried to put me off by sending me to another. The problem is, see, that I'm married, see, and me and the wife have a mohome. *And* we've two weans, six years and seven years, boy and girl. Now I'm not criticizing mohomes—I *make* the bloody things—but there's not much room in them, right? And when we took this one the housing department definitely said that if I paid my rent prompt and kept my nose clean we'd get a proper house when we needed it. Well we've had an accident. The wife's pregnant again. So what can we do? Four of us and a screaming wean in a mohome? And having to use a public lavatory when we need a wash or a you-know-what? So what can we do?"

Lanark stared down at a pen and a heap of forms on the counter. He picked up the pen and said hesitantly, "What's your address?" Then he dropped the pen and said firmly, "Don't tell me. It's no use. This place isn't going to help you at all."

"What?"

"You'll get no help here. If you need a new house you'll have to find a way of getting it yourself."

"But that needs money. Are you advising me . . . to steal?"

"Perhaps. I don't know. But whatever you do please be careful. I haven't met the police yet, but I imagine they're fairly efficient when dealing with lonely criminals. If you decide to do something, do it with a lot of other people who feel the same way. Perhaps you should organize a strike, but don't go on strike for more money. Your enemies understand money better than you do. Go on strike for things. Strike for bigger houses."

Macfee screwed his face up incredulously and shouted, "Me? Organize a . . . ? Thanks for bloody nothing!"

He sprang up, turned and went toward the lift.

"Wait!" cried Lanark, climbing over the counter. "Wait! I've another idea!"

He forced his way through the dead air of the floor and managed to press into the lift before the doors shut. He was pushed against Macfee's shoulder in a mass of older men and younger women.

"Listen, Macfee," he whispered. "My family and I are shifting into a new place soon—you could get the old one."

"Where is it?"

"In the cathedral."

"I'm not a bloody squatter!"

"But this is legal—it's run by a very helpful minister of religion."

"How big is it?"

"About six feet by nine. The ceiling slopes a bit."

"Christ, my mohome's nearly that size. *And* it has a flat roof and two rooms."

"But it would suit us fine, mister!" said a haggard woman holding a baby. "Six feet by nine? My man and his brother and me *need* a place like that."

"Tell me one thing," said Macfee belligerently. "What do they pay you for working here?"

"Enough to buy my own house."

"Why do they pay you anything?"

"I think they employ a lot of well-educated people to keep us comfortable," said Lanark. "And because they're afraid we'd be dangerous if we had no work at all."

"Fucking wonderful!" said Macfee.

"Honest, mister, that room you're leaving sounds very, very nice. Where did you say it was?"

The door opened and they hurried across the entrance hall, Lanark keeping close to Macfee's shoulder. As they came onto the pavement three armoured trucks full of soldiers thundered past. "What's happening?" cried Lanark. "Why all these soldiers?"

"How do I know?" shouted Macfee. "I'm pig-ignorant, all I hear is the news on television and funny noises in the street. They were ringing the cathedral bell like madmen a short while back. How do I know what's going on?"

They walked in silence till they reached a corner where a sign projected above a door. It was a fat red heart with pink neon tubes running into it and *The Vascular Cavity* underneath. Lanark said, "At least let me buy you a drink."

"Can you afford it?" said Macfee sarcastically. Lanark fingered the credit card in his pocket, nodded and pushed the door open.

The room was lit by a dim red glow with some zones of gaudy brightness. Most of the tables and chairs were partitioned off by luminous grilles shaped and coloured like pink veins and purple arteries. A revolving ball cast a flow of red and white corpuscular spots across the ceiling, and the music was a low, steady, protracted throbbing like a lame giant limping up a thickly carpeted stair.

"What kind of boozer is this?" said Macfee.

Lanark stood and stared. He would have turned and walked out if it hadn't been for women. They filled the place with laughing, alert, indifferent young faces and throats, breasts, midriffs and legs in all kinds of clothing. He felt he had never seen so many girls in his life. Looking closely he saw there were as many men but they made a less distinct impression. For all he cared they were duplicates of the same confident long-haired youth and Lanark hated him. He stood transfixed between fascination and envy until someone shouted his name from a corner. He looked across and saw Gilchrist, Pettigrew and Miss Maheen standing at a bar quilted with red plastic. "Listen," he told Macfee. "That tall man is my boss. If anyone can help you it's him. Let's try anyway."

He led the way to the bar, and said "Mr. Gilchrist, this is an old friend of mine—Jimmy Macfee—I knew him as a boy. He's a client of mine, a really deserving case, and—"

"Now, now, now!" said Gilchrist cheerfully. "We're here on pleasure, not business. What would you both like?"

"A whisky as big as yours," said Macfee.

"The same, please," said Lanark.

Gilchrist gave the order. Macfee was clearly attracted by Miss Maheen who turned her head at regular intervals, smiling at each of them in turn.

"Why are you not drinking?" he asked when her split-second smile reached him.

"She doesn't drink," said Pettigrew dourly.

"Can't she speak for herself?" said Macfee.

"She doesn't need to."

"Are you her husband or something?" said Macfee.

Pettigrew coolly emptied his whisky glass and said, "What do you do?"

"I'm a maker. I make mohomes," said Macfee boldly. *"And I live in one."*

"Mohome makers aren't real makers," said Pettigrew. "My father was a real maker. I respect real makers. You're in the luxury trade."

"So you think a mohome is a luxury?"

"Yes. I bet yours has colour television."

"Why shouldn't it have?"

"I suppose you came to us because you wanted a house you could stand up in, with an inside lavatory, and separate bedrooms, and wooden window frames, and maybe a fireplace?"

"Why shouldn't I have a house like that?"

"I'll tell you. When mohome users get a house like that they crowd into one room and sublet the others, and rip out the plumbing to sell as scrap metal, and rip out the window frames and chop up the doors and burn them. A mohome user isn't fit for a decent house."

"I'm not that sort! You know nothing about me!" cried Macfee.

"I knew all about you as soon as I clapped eyes on you," said Pettigrew softly. *"You,* are an obnoxious, little, bastard."

Macfee stared at him, clenching his fists and inhaling loudly. His shoulders swelled and he seemed to grow taller.

"Miss Maheen!" said Pettigrew loudly. "If he threatens me, chop him."

Miss Maheen stepped between Macfee and Pettigrew and raised her right hand to throat level, holding it flat and horizontal with the small finger outward. Her smile widened and remained. Gilchrist said hastily, "Oh, there's no need for violence, Miss Maheen. Just *look* at him."

Lanark heard a snapping sound inside Miss Maheen's head. He couldn't see her face but he saw Macfee's. His mouth fell open, the lower lip trembled, he clapped his hands over his eyes. Gilchrist said quietly, "Lead him out, Lanark. This isn't his kind of pub."

Lanark gripped Macfee's arm and led him through the crowd.

Outside the door Macfee leaned against the wall, dropped his hands and shuddered. "Wee black holes," he whispered. "Her eyes turned into wee black holes."

"She's not a real woman, you see," said Lanark. "She's a tool, an instrument *shaped* like a woman."

Macfee bent forward and was sick on the pavement; then he said, "I'm going home."

"I'll take you there."

"Better not. I'm going to hit someone tonight. I *need* to hit someone tonight. If you don't keep away it'll probably be you."

He sounded so feeble that Lanark took his arm and walked with him along several busy streets, then several quiet ones. They passed a parked truck beside three workmen cementing a concrete block over a sewer grating. A soldier with a gun stood smoking nearby. Lanark asked the foreman, "What are you doing?"

"Cementing a block over this stank."

"Why?"

"Just don't interfere," said the soldier.

"I'm not interfering, but couldn't you tell us what's happening?"

"There's going to be an announcement. Just go to your homes and wait for the announcement."

Lanark noticed that every drain they passed was blocked up. A hollow shouting began in the distance and drew nearer. It came from a loudspeaker on top of a slow-moving van. It said, "SPECIAL EMERGENCY ANNOUNCEMENT. IN FIFTEEN MIN- UTES NORMAL HEARTBEAT TIME, PROVOST SLUDDEN WILL MAKE A SPECIAL EMERGENCY ANNOUNCEMENT. IF YOU HAVE NEIGHBOURS WITHOUT TELEVISION OR WIRELESS, CALL THEM IN TO HEAR PROVOST SLUDDEN'S SPECIAL EMERGENCY ANNOUNCEMENT IN FIFTEEN MINUTES NORMAL HEARTBEAT TIME. ALL SHOPS, OFFICES, FACT- ORIES, DANCEHALLS, CINEMAS, RESTAURANTS, CAFÉS, SPORT CENTRES, SCHOOLS AND PUBLIC HOUSES ARE ASKED TO RELAY PROVOST SLUDDEN'S EMERGENCY ANNOUNCE- MENT OVER THEIR LOUDSPEAKER SYSTEMS IN FOURTEEN AND A HALF MINUTES NORMAL HEARTBEAT TIME. THIS IS URGENT. . . ."

"What's *happening* to this city?" asked Macfee, shaking his arm free. They passed a long queue of people outside a public lavatory, then a wall of gigantic posters. Macfee said "Here" and they stepped through a gap between two posters onto a great area of gravel covered by rows of parked cars. He stopped beside one and opened the door. Lanark opened the door on the other side.

The front seat of the car extended the whole width and a plump young woman with a thin face sat in the middle. She said, "Come in. Sit down. Shut the door and shut up, both of you. Excuse my manners. I'll make tea in a minute but I don't want to miss my garden."

Lanark shut the door and leaned back with a feeling of relief. Sunlight streamed in through the windows and the car seemed to be thrusting slowly forward through a shrubbery of rose- bushes. Green leaves and heavy white blossoms brushed across the windscreen and past the windows of the doors. He saw golden-brown bees working in the hearts of the roses and heard their drowsy humming, the rustle of leaves, some distant bird calls. Mrs. Macfee took a small can from a shelf and pressed the top. A fine mist smelling like roses came out. She sighed and leaned back with closed eyes saying, "I don't need to see it. The sound and scent are good enough for me."

The car had no clutch or steering column, and the seat was the sort that could slide forward while the back flattened to form a bed. A glass panel and a blind shut out the back seat where the children were probably sleeping. Under the wind-

screen was a set of drawers, shelves and compartments. One
compartment held an electric plate, another a plastic basin with
a small tap above it. Macfee opened a tiny refrigerator door,
took out two cans of beer and passed one to Lanark.

The roses parted before the windscreen and the car, with
a sound of gurgling water, floated like a yacht onto a circular
lake surrounded by hills sloping up from the water's edge and
clothed from base to summit in a drapery of the most gorgeous
flower blossoms, scarcely a green leaf visible among the sea
of odorous and fluctuating colour. The lake was of great depth
but so transparent that the bottom, which seemed to be a mass
of small round pearly pebbles, was distinctly visible whenever
the eye allowed itself *not* to see, far down in the inverted heaven,
the duplicate blooming of the hills. The whole impression was
of richness, warmth, colour, quietness, softness and delicacy,
and as the eye traced upward the myriad-tinted slope, from
its sharp junction with the water to its vague termination in
the cloudless blue, it was difficult not to fancy a wide cataract
of rubies, sapphires, opals and golden onyxes rolling silently
out of the sky. Mrs. Macfee took another little can and sprayed
the interior with a scent of pansies. Macfee shouted "Sentimental rot!" and violently twisted a switch.
The interior became part of a sharp red convertible speeding
down a multi-lane freeway under a dazzling sun. A swarm of
dots grew visible in the heat haze ahead. The dots became a
pack of motorcyclists. The car accelerated, moving in sideways
toward the bikes.
"Jimmy!" said Mrs. Macfee. "You know I don't like this."
"You're unlucky, aren't you?" said Macfee. She pressed her
lips together, pulled open a drawer in the dashboard, took
out a sock and needle and started darning. Looking past her
profile Lanark saw the car drawing level with the leader of
the pack. He wore leather clothes with skull and swastika
badges. A girl like Miss Maheen dressed in leather clung behind
him. Then *froom!*—a glittering barbed dart shot out from
Macfee's side of the car and entered the cyclist's body under
the armpit. With a great screech the car swung round sideways
and ploughed into the pack. The scene outside went suddenly
slow. Slowly crashing and screaming cyclists were tossed into
the air or fell and clung in agony to the car bonnet until they
slid slowly off. Lanark shoved open the door beside him and
stared with relief at the dingy gravel park and a row of quiet
mohomes.

"Shut the door, we're freezing," yelled Macfee. Lanark reluctantly closed it. Bodies still spun ballet-like through swirling clouds of dust. Two bikes crashed with a tremendous explosion; then the scene was replaced by the head and shoulders of a man with a vividly patterned necktie. He said, "We are sorry to interrupt this programme but here is an emergency announcement by Provost Sludden, the chief executive officer of Greater Unthank. As this announcement contains a warning of serious health hazards for inhabitants of the Greater Unthank region, it is vital that everyone—especially those with children—gives it very special attention. Provost Sludden."

Sludden appeared, sitting on a leather sofa under a huge map of the city. His hands were clasped between his knees, and he looked gravely at the camera a while before speaking.

> "Hullo. Not many of you have seen me face to face like this, and I promise you I regret having to appear. A provost is a public servant, and a good servant should never march into the living room when the family is enjoying an evening of television and complain about the difficulties of his job. Good servants work quietly behind the scenes, providing their employers with what the employers need. But sometimes an unforeseen accident occurs. Perhaps a bath falls through the kitchen ceiling, and then no matter how competent a servant is, he must tell the boss and the boss's wife what has happened, because the household routine is going to be upset and everyone has a right to know why. Something unexpected has happened to the plumbing of the Unthank region, and as chief executive officer I am going to take you into my confidence and explain why.
>
> "But first I must tell you how your elected servants recently defeated a much greater problem: starvation. Yes. Starvation. The council was allowing a heap of poisonous muck from a burst transporter to isolate the city. Our foodstocks were nearly exhausted. We might have intro-

duced severe rationing in the hope that
the council would intervene to save us at
the last minute, but we decided not to risk
that. We decided to act ourselves. We told
our heroic fire brigade to sweep the poison
into the sewers—there was nowhere else
for it to go. They did. Unthank was saved.
We didn't publicize this triumph. It was
enough reward for us that nobody would
go hungry.

"Now for the bad news. The poison
from the motorway is creeping backward
through the sewage system in the form
of a very lethal and corrosive gas. It is
undermining our streets, our public buildings and our houses."

Sludden stood up and pointed to an area of the map outlined
in red.

"Here is the danger area: central Unthank inside the ring road and the district
east of the cathedral."

"That's us, all right," said Macfee.

"To prevent loss of life we must stop
the gas from spreading. Every drain and
sewer-opening in the danger area must
be blocked. This work is proceeding in
the streets and will soon start in houses
and other buildings. Sanitary workers
will call in to seal up every sink, urinal
and lavatory pan. Naturally this takes time,
so we invite your cooperation. Tubes of
plastic cement will soon be obtainable, on
demand, from your local police station and
post office. The homes of householders
who block their own drains will receive
nothing more than a routine inspection.
Meanwhile everyone should immediately
plug their sinks and fill them with water.
Lavatory pans will also stay safe for a while
if they are not actually employed. I will
now pause for three minutes to let everyone attend to their sink."

Three sentences appeared on the screen:

PLUG YOUR SINK.
FILL IT WITH WATER.
DON'T FLUSH YOUR LAVATORY PAN.

"Have another beer," said Macfee, passing a can across. "You too, Helen,"

She said, "I'm frightened, Jimmy."

"Frightened? Why? We're in luck at last. Mohomes don't have lavatories. Our sink isn't connected to the sewage system."

"But what will we do if we cannae use the public toilet?"

"I think the provost will announce plans for that," said Lanark. The speech had greatly impressed him. He thought, 'I'm glad Rima and Sandy are in the cathedral. Ritchie-Smollet will have taken the necessary precautions by now.' He sipped from the can. The inscription vanished and Sludden appeared once more.

> "There is one question I am sure you are all asking yourselves: How are we to get rid of our bodily waste? Well, you know, that question is as old as humanity itself. We tend to forget that interior flush lavatories are comparatively recent inventions, and three quarters of the world doesn't have them. For a while we must be content to use one of these, as our great-grandparents did."

He held up a chamberpot.

> "Those of you with small children probably have one already. New stocks are being rushed to the shops from the Cortexin Adhoc Sanitation plant at New Cumbernauld. Large orders have been placed with a small factory in Unthank which still makes the old-fashioned earthenware article, thus giving a much-needed boost to a neglected part of the city's economy. And though many will have to manage without one for a short period, I am sure they will be able to improvise with some other domestic utensil. As to the removal of the waste, you will receive through the post, if you have not received it already, a packet of these."

He held up a black plastic bag.

> "This is large enough to comfortably hold the contents of one full chamberpot. When tied at the neck it is both damp proof and odour proof. These should be stacked *beside,* not *inside,* your usual midden or dustbin. To speed collection, the cleansing workers will be helped by the army. That is why you have seen so many soldiers on the street lately."

"Soldiers don't need guns to shift shit," said Macfee.

> "Washing, if kept to a minimum, will present no problem. Once your sink is blocked it can be used in the usual way, except that the dirty water (which should be employed more than once) should be ladled into a pail and emptied into a gutter or convenient piece of ground. The same goes for urine. Fortunately a spell of mild weather is forecast, and our liquid waste will either evaporate or flow into districts where the drains still work."

"What if it rains?" said Macfee.

> "But we must also tackle the *causes* of this dangerous annoyance. We have already demanded action from the council, whose slowness caused this disaster in the first place. We have appealed to the Cortexin Group, who manufactured the poison. Both reply that experts are being consulted, the matter will be considered, that in due course we will hear from them. This is not good enough. So Professor Eva Schtzngrm has been made leader of a team who are working to gain the technology to clear the gas themselves, and we are choosing a delegate to speak up boldly for Unthank at the general assembly of council states soon to be held in Provan. The fact is that the council has treated Unthank badly. It is a long time since they

introduced their decimal calendar based on the twenty-five-hour day. They promised us new clocks, so we rashly scrapped the old ones, and the new clocks failed to arrive. I was a young man then and I confess that, like most people, I didn't care. Everyone likes to feel they have plenty of time; nobody likes seeing how fast it passes. But we can't cope with a public emergency without clocks, so we have created a new department, our own department of chronometry. This department has commandeered a television channel—this television channel—and I will show you what it is going to transmit."

Sludden walked over to a clock hanging on a wall, a pendulum clock with a case shaped like a small log cabin.

"Fucking miraculous," said Macfee, opening another beer can. Helen said, "Don't you think you've had enough?"

"This is one of many clocks recently unearthed from museums, lumber-rooms and antique shops. It may not look very impressive, but it is the first to be restored to perfect working order. When the others have been repaired they will be installed in the head offices of our essential services, and each one of them will be synchronized with this."

Sludden pointed to a weight shaped like a fir cone.

"Notice that the weight has been wound up and placed on a small shelf immediately under the case. At the end of this announcement, I will suspend it, and the clock will strike the hours of midnight: the time when an old day dies and a new day begins. The sound will be reinforced by a long blast upon police and factory sirens, who will repeat the noise at noon tomorrow. Employees of the chronometry department have also taken over ninety-two church towers with bells in them, and from now on they too will broadcast the message of this little clock.

"I know that quiet-minded people
will find this a rude intrusion on their pri-
vacy; that intellectuals will say that a return
to a solar timescale, when we don't have
sunlight, is putting clocks backward, not
forward; and that manual workers, who
time themselves by their pulses, will find
the whole business irrelevant. Never
mind. This clock allows me to make definite promises. By eight o'clock tomorrow
every house, mohome, office and factory
will have received an envelope of plastic
wastebags. By ten o'clock the first free
tubes of plastic cement will be available
at your local post office. And at every hour
I or some other corporation representative
will appear on this channel to tell you how
things are going. And now—"

Said Sludden taking the weight in his hand—

"I wish you all a very good night.
Eternity, for Greater Unthank, is drawing
to an end. *Time* is about to begin."

He suspended the weight. The pendulum swung left with
a tick, then right with a tock. The clock face grew till it nearly
filled the windscreen. Both hands pointed straight upright to
a small door above the dial, which flapped open. A fat wooden
bird popped out and in shouting "Cuckoo! Cuckoo! Cuck—"
Macfee turned a switch and the windscreen went transparent. The three of them sat in a row and stared through it at
the darkened carpark. Sirens, hooters and distant clanging could
be heard outside. Helen switched on a light.
"A maniac!" said Macfee. "The man's a maniac."
"Oh no," said Lanark. "I've known him a long time, and
he's not a maniac. As a private person I don't trust him, but
he seems to have thoroughly grasped the political situation.
And that speech sounded honest to me."
"He's a friend of yours?"
"No, a friend of my wife."
Macfee leaned over and grabbed Lanark's lapels and said,
"What's the score?"
"Jimmy!" cried Helen.
Lanark cried, "What's wrong?"
"That's what I'm asking you! You've a council passport, right?

And you work for social stability, right? You know Sludden, right? So just tell me what you folk are trying to do!"

Lanark had been half dragged across Helen's lap, his ear was pressed against her thigh and comforting warmth began flowing through it. He said dreamily, "We're trying to kill Unthank. Some of us."

"Christ, that isn't news. We've known that for ages in the shops! 'All right,' I said. 'Let the place die as long as my weans are spared.' But you bastards are really putting the boot in now, aren't you? *Aren't you*?"

Macfee shifted a hand to grip Lanark's nostrils and cover his mouth. Lanark found he was watching a bulging reflection of his face and Macfee's hand on the side of a shiny kettle on a shelf a few inches away. The reflection flickered and grew dim and he supposed that when it went black he would be unconscious. He felt no pain so he was not much worried. Then he heard slapping sounds and Helen panting, "Let *go*, let him *go*." he was released and heard much louder slapping sounds. Helen moaned, then yelled, "Clear out, mister! Leave us! Leave us alone!"

He found and pulled a handle and scrambled sideways out the door and slammed it shut. He hesitated beside the mohome, which was rocking slightly. Muffled noises came from the front seat and a frail childish wailing from the back. His eye was distracted by a lit poster on a gable showing an athletic couple in bathing costume playing beach ball with two laughing children. The message above said MONEY IS TIME. TIME IS LIFE. BUY MORE LIFE FOR YOUR FAMILY FROM THE QUANTUM INTERMINABLE. (THEY'LL LOVE YOU FOR IT.)

CHAPTER 39. Divorce

"Let the place die as long as my weans are spared." Jimmy's words had brought Sandy alarmingly to mind. Lanark ran from the park and along some empty streets, trying to retrace his steps. A warm heavy rain began falling and the gutters filled rapidly. The surrounding houses were unfamiliar. He turned a corner, came to a railing and looked down over several levels of motorway at the dark tower and bright spire of the cathedral. He sighed with relief, climbed the rail and scrambled down a slope of slippery wet grass. The water was nearly two feet deep at the edge of the road and flowing swiftly sideways like a stream. He waded through to the drier lanes. The only vehicle he saw was a military jeep which whizzed round a curve sending out sizzling arcs of spray, then slowed down and stopped beside him.

"Come here!" cried a gruff voice. "I've a gun, so no funny business."

Lanark went closer. A fat man in a colonel's uniform sat beside the driver. The fat man said, "How many of you are there?"

"One."

"Do you expect me to believe that? Where are you going?"

"The cathedral."

"Don't you know you're trespassing?"

"I'm just crossing a road."

"Oh, no! You are crossing a freeway. Freeways are for the exclusive use of wheeled carriages propelled by engines burning refined forms of fossilized fuel, and don't forget it. . . . Good heavens, it's Lanark, isn't it?"

"Yes. Are you McPake?"

"Of course. Get inside. Where did you say you were going?"

Lanark explained. McPake said, "Take us there, Cameron,"
then he leaned back, chuckling. "I thought we had a riot on
our hands when we saw you. We're on the watch for them,
you know, at times like these."
The jeep turned down toward the cathedral square. Lanark
said, "I suppose Rima told you about Alexander?"
McPake shook his head. "Sorry, I only know one Rima. She
used to hang about with Sludden in the old Elite days. Had
her myself once. What a woman! I thought she took off for
the institute when you did."
"Sorry, I'm getting confused," said Lanark.

He sat in a state of miserable excitement until the jeep
put him down at the cathedral gates. In the doorway he heard
organ strains, and the floor inside held a scattering of elderly
and middle-aged people (But *I'm* middle-aged, he thought),
standing between the rows of chairs and singing that time,
like an ever-rolling stream, bears all her sons away, they fly,
forgotten, as the dream dies at the opening day. He hurried
past them with his mouth shaping denunciations, opened the
small door, and rushed up the spiral stair, and along the window
ledge, through the organ loft and past the cubicles of the attic.
Rima and Alex were in none of them. He rushed to the kitchen
and stared at Frankie and Jack, who looked up, startled, from
a card game. He said, "Where are they?" There was an embarrassed silence; then Frankie said in a small voice, "She said
she left a note for you."
He hurried back and found the empty cubicle. A note lay on
the carefully made bed.

Dear Lanark,
I expect you won't be surprised to find us gone. Things haven't been
very good lately, have they. Alexander and I will be living with Sludden,
as we arranged, and on the whole it's better that you aren't coming
too. Please don't try to find us—Alex is naturally a bit upset by all
this and I don't want you to make him worse.
*   You probably think I've gone with Sludden because he has a*
big house, and is famous, and is a better lover than you in most
ways, but that isn't the real reason. It may surprise you to hear that
Sludden needs me more than you do. I don't think you need anybody.
No matter how bad things get, you will always plod on without caring
what other people think or feel. You're the most selfish man I know.
*   Dear Lanark, I don't hate you but whenever I try to write some-*
thing friendly it turns out nasty, perhaps because if you give the devil

*your little finger he bites off the whole arm. But you've often been
nice to me, you aren't really a devil.*

Love

Rima

*P.S. I'm coming back to collect some clothes and things. I may see
you then.*

He undressed slowly, got into bed, switched off the light and
fell asleep at once. He woke several times feeling that something
horrible had happened which he must tell Rima about, then
he remembered what it was. Lying drearily awake he sometimes
heard the cathedral bell tolling the hours. Once it struck five
o'clock and when he awoke later it was striking three, which
suggested that the regular marking of time had not slowed it
down much.

At last he opened his eyes to the electric light. She stood
by the bed quietly taking clothes from the chest of drawers.
He said, "Hullo."
"I didn't mean to wake you."
"How's Sandy?"
"Very quiet but quite happy, I think. He has plenty of room
to run about and Sludden lives outside the danger zone so
there's no stink, of course."
"There's no stink here."
"In another twenty-four hours I'm sure even you will begin
to notice it."
She snapped the suitcase shut and said, "I wanted to pack this
before I left but I was afraid you would suddenly come in
and get hysterical."
"When have you seen me hysterical?" he asked peevishly.
"I don't remember. Of course that's partly your trouble, isn't
it? Sludden and I often discuss you, and he thinks you would
be a very valuable man if you knew how to release your emo-
tions."
He lay rigid, clenching his fists and teeth in order not to scream.
She placed the suitcase by the bed foot and sat on it, twisting
a handkerchief. She said, "Oh, Lanark, I don't like hurting
you but I must explain why I'm leaving. You think I'm greedy
and ungrateful and prefer Sludden because he's a far better
lover, but that's not why. Women can live quite comfortably
with a clumsy lover if he makes them happy in other ways.
But you're too serious all the time. You make my ordinary
little feelings seem as fluffy and useless as bits of dust. You
make life a duty, something to be examined and corrected.

Do you remember when I was pregnant, and said I wanted a girl, and you said you wanted a boy so that someone would like the baby? You've always tried to *balance* me as if I were a badly floating boat. You've brought no joy to my happiness or sorrow to my misery, you've made me the loneliest woman in the world. I don't love Sludden *more* than you, but life with him seems open and free. I'm sure Alex will benefit too. Sludden plays with him. You would only explain things to him."
Lanark said nothing. She said, "But we enjoyed ourselves sometimes, didn't we? You've been a friend to me—I'm not sorry I met you."
"When can I visit Sandy?"
"I thought you were going away to Provan soon."
"Not if Sandy isn't going."
"If you phone us first you can come anytime. Frankie has the number and the address. We'll be needing a babysitter."
"Tell Sandy I'll see him soon and I'll visit him often. Goodbye."
She stood, lifted the case, hesitated and said, "I'm sure you would be happier if you complained more about things."
"Would complaining make you like me and want to stay? No, it would make it easier for you to leave. So don't think—"
He stopped with open mouth, for heavy grief came swelling up his throat till it broke out in loud, dry choking sobs like big hiccups or the slow ticking of a wooden clock. Wetness flooded his eyes and cheeks. He stretched a hand toward her and she said softly, "Poor Lanark! You really are suffering," and went softly out and softly closed the door behind her. Eventually the sobbing stopped. He lay flat with a leaden weight in his chest. He thought wistfully of getting drunk or smashing furniture, but all activity seemed too tiring. The leaden weight kept him flat on his back till he fell asleep.

Later someone laid a hand on his shoulder and he opened his eyes sharply saying, "Rima?"
Frankie stood by the bed with food on a tray. He sighed and thanked her and she watched him eat. She said, "I've taken your clothes away—they were terribly dirty. But there's a new suit and underthings laid out for you downstairs in the vestry."
"Oh."
"I think you need a shave and a haircut. Jack was a barber, once. Will I ask him to see to it?"
"No."
"Can Sludden speak to you?"
He stared at her.

She flushed and said, "I mean, if he comes to see you, you won't lose your temper or attack him, will you?"

"I certainly won't lose my dignity because I'm faced by someone with none of his own."

She giggled and said, "Good. I'll tell him that."

She removed the tray and later Sludden entered and sat by the bed, saying, "How do you feel?"

"I don't like you, Sludden, but the only people I do like depend on you. Tell me what you want."

"Yes, in a minute. I'm glad you agreed to see me, but of course I knew you would. What Rima and I admire in you is your instinctive self-control. That makes you a very, very valuable man."

"Tell me what you want, Sludden."

"We're sensible modern men, after all, not knights who've been jousting for the love of a fair lady. I dare say the fair lady picked you up somewhere, but you were too weighty for her so she dropped you and picked me up instead. I'm a lightweight. Women enjoy lifting me. But you're made of sterner stuff, which is why I'm here."

"Please tell me what you want."

"I want you to stop pitying yourself and get out of bed. I want you to do a difficult, important job. The committee sent me here. They ask you to go to Provan and speak for Unthank in the general assembly of council states."

"You're joking!" said Lanark, sitting up. Sludden said nothing. "Why should they ask me?"

"We want someone who's been through the institute and knows the council corridors. You've worked for Ozenfant. You've spoken to Monboddo."

"I've quarrelled with the first and I don't like the second."

"Good. Stand up in Provan and denounce them for us. We don't want to be represented by a diplomat now, we want someone tactless, someone who will tell delegates from other states exactly what is happening here. Use your nose and take back some of our stink to its source."

Lanark sniffed. The air had an unpleasant familiar smell. He said, "Send Grant. He understands politics."

"Nobody trusts Grant. He understands politics, yes, but he wants to change them."

"Ritchie-Smollet."

"He doesn't understand politics at all. He believes everyone he meets is honestly doing their best."

"Gow."

"Gow owns shares in Cortexin, the company that fouled us up. He makes belligerent noises but he would only pretend to fight the council."

"And you?"

"If I left the city for more than a week our administration would collapse. There would be nobody in control but a lot of civil servants who want to clear out as soon as they can. We're under very strong attack, inside and out."

"So I've been chosen because nobody else trusts one another," said Lanark. An intoxicating excitement began to fill him and he frowned to hide it. He saw himself on a platform, or maybe a pedestal, casting awe over a vast assembly with a few simple, forceful words about truth, justice and brotherhood. He said suddenly, "How would I get to Provan?"

"By air."

"But do I cross a zone, I mean an incaldrical zone, I mean—"

"An intercalendrical zone? Yes, you do."

"Won't that age me a lot?"

"Probably."

"I'm not going. I want to stay near Sandy. I want to help him grow up."

"I understand that," said Sludden gravely. "But if you love your son—if you love Rima—you'll work for them in Provan."

"My family isn't in the danger area now. It's living with you."

Sludden smiled painfully, stood up and walked the floor of the cubicle. He said, "I will tell you something only one other person knows. You'll have to be quiet about it till you reach Provan, but then you must tell the world. The whole of the Greater Unthank region is in danger, and not just from a typhoid epidemic, though that is probable too. Mrs. Schtzngrm has analyzed a sample of the poison—two firemen died getting it for her—and she says it has begun filtering down through the Permian layer. As you probably know, the continents, though not continuous with it, are floating on a superdense mass of molten—"

"Don't blind me with science, Sludden."

"If the pollution isn't cleared up we're going to have tremors and subsidences in the earth's crust."

"Something must be done!" cried Lanark, aghast.

"Yes. The knowledge of what to do belongs to the institute. The machinery to do it belongs to the creature. Only the council can force them to act together."

"I'll go," said Lanark quietly, and mainly to himself. "But first I must see the boy."

"Get dressed in the vestry and I'll take you to him," said Sludden briskly. "And by the way, if you've no objection we'll have you declared provost: Lord Provost of Greater Unthank. It doesn't mean anything—I'll still be senior executive officer—but you'll be going among people with titles, and a title of your own helps to impress that kind."

Lanark pulled on the old greatcoat like a dressing gown, thrust his bare feet into the mud-caked shoes and followed Sludden downstairs to the vestry. His feelings were pulled between a piercing sad love for Sandy and an excited love of his own importance as a provost and delegate. Nothing interrupted the colloquy between these two loves. A warm bath was ready for him, and afterward he sat in a bathrobe while Jack shaved and trimmed him and Frankie manicured his fingernails. He put on clean new underwear, socks, shirt, a dark blue necktie, and a three-piece suit of light grey tweed, and beautifully polished black shoes; then he withdrew to the lavatory, excreted into a plastic chamberpot fitted inside the lavatory pan and had the comfortable feeling that someone else was expected to empty it. There was a mirror above the blocked lavatory sink; a medicine cabinet with a mirror for a door hung on the wall facing it. By moving the door to an angle he managed to see himself in profile. Jack had removed the beard and trimmed the moustache. His greying hair, receding from the brow, swept into a bush behind the ears: the effect was impressive and statesmanlike. He placed his hands on his hips and said quietly, "When Lord Monboddo says that the council has done its best for Unthank he is lying to us—or has been lied to by others."

He returned to the vestry and Sludden escorted him out to a long black car by the cathedral door. They climbed into the back seat and Sludden said, "Home, Angus," to the chauffeur.

They sped swiftly through the city and Lanark was too occupied with himself to notice much, except when the pervading stink grew unusually strong as the car crossed the riverbed by a splendid new concrete bridge. Heaps of bloated black plastic bags were scattered across the cracked mud. Sludden said glumly, "Nowhere else to dump them."

"On television you said these bags were odour-proof."

"They are, but they burst easily."

They came to a private housing scheme of neat little identical bungalows, each with a small garden in front and a garage alongside. The car stopped at one with a couple of old-fashioned ornamental iron lampposts outside the gate. Sludden led the way to the front door and fumbled awhile for his key. Lanark's heart beat hard thinking he would meet Rima again. Through an uncurtained plate-glass window on one side he saw into a firelit sitting room where four people sat sipping coffee at a low table before the hearth. Lanark recognized one of them. He said, "Gilchrist is in there!"

"Good. I invited him."

"But Gilchrist is on the side of the council!"

"Not on the sanitary question. He's on our side on that, and it's important to present a broad front when dealing with journalists. Don't worry, he's a great fan of yours."

They entered a small lobby. Sludden took a note from a telephone stand, read it and frowned. He said, "Rima's gone out. Alex will be upstairs in the television room. I suppose you'd prefer to see him first."

"Yes."

"Go through the first door on your right at the top."

He climbed a narrow, thick-carpeted stair and quietly opened a door. The room he entered was small and had three armchairs facing a television set in the corner. Two dolls wearing different kinds of soldier uniform lay on the floor among a litter of plastic toy weapons. A table had a monopoly game spread on it and some drawings on sheets of paper. Alexander sat on the arm of the middle chair, stroking a cat curled on the seat and watching the television screen. Without turning he said, "Hullo, Rima," and then, glancing round, "Hullo."

"Hullo, Sandy."

Lanark went to the table and looked at the drawings. He said, "What are these?"

"A walking flower, a crane lifting a spider over a wall, and a space invasion by a lot of different aliens. Would you like to sit down and watch television with me?"

"Yes."

Alexander shoved the cat off the seat and Lanark sat down. Alexander leaned against him and they watched a film like the film Lanark had seen in Macfee's mohome, but the people killing each other in it were soldiers, not road users. Alexander said, "Don't you like films about killing?"

"No, I don't."

"Films about killing are my favourites. They're very real, aren't they?"

"Sandy. I'm going to leave this city for a long time."

"Oh."

"I wish I could stay."

"Mum said you would come and see me often. She doesn't mind us being friends."

"I know. When I told her I would visit you often I didn't know I would have to go away."

"Oh."

Lanark felt tears behind his eyes and realized his mouth was straining to girn aloud. He felt it would be horrible for a boy to remember a pitiable father and turned his face away and hardened the muscles of it to keep the grief inside. Alexander had turned his face to the television set. Lanark got up and moved clumsily to the door. He said, "Goodbye."

"Goodbye."

"I've always liked you. I always will like you."

"Good," said Alexander, staring at the screen. Lanark went outside, sat on the stairs and rubbed his face hard with both hands. Sludden appeared at the foot and said, "I'm sorry but the press are in a hurry."

"Sludden, will you look after him properly?"

Sludden climbed some steps toward him and said, "Don't worry! I know I played around a lot when I was younger but I've always liked Rima and I'm past wanting a change. Alex will be safe with me. I *need* a home life nowadays."

Lanark looked hard into Sludden's face. The shape seemed the same but the substance had changed. This was the eager, slightly desperate face of a burdened and caring man. With a pang of pity Lanark knew Sludden would have very little domestic peace with Rima. Lanark said, "I don't want to talk to journalists."

"Don't worry. Just appearing to them is the main thing."

A shaded lamp on the mantelpiece cast an oval of soft light on the small group before the hearth. Sludden, Gilchrist, a quiet-looking man and a reckless-looking man sat on a long leather sofa facing the fire. A grey-haired lady Lanark had seen in the chapterhouse sat on an armchair with a briefcase on her lap. Lanark pushed his own chair as far back into the shadow

as possible. Sludden said, "These two gentlemen fully understand the situation. They're on our side, so there's no need
to worry."

The quiet man said quietly, "We aren't interested in the detailed
character stuff. We just want to convey that the right man has
been found for the right job."

"A new figure strides into the political arena," said the reckless
man. "Where does he come from?"

"From Unthank," said Sludden. "He and I were close friends
in our early days. We hung about sowing our wild oats with
the same bohemian crowd, measuring out our life with coffee
spoons and trying to find a meaning. I did nothing at all in
those days but Lanark, to his credit, produced one of the finest
fragments of autobiographical prose *and* social commentary it
has been my privilege to criticize."

"No use to our readers," said the reckless man. The quiet
man said, "We can use it. What happened then?"

"He entered the institute and worked with Ozenfant. Although
a mainstay of the energy division, his qualities were *not*
appreciated and eventually, sickened by bureaucratic ineptitude,
he returned to Unthank: but not before registering a strong
personal protest to the lord president director."

"Room for a bit of dramatic detail here," said the reckless
man. "Exactly why did you quarrel with Ozenfant?"

Lanark tried to remember. At last he said, "I didn't quarrel
with him. He quarrelled with me, about a woman."

"Better leave that out," said Sludden.

"All right," said the quiet man. "He returned to Unthank.
And then?"

"I can tell you what happened then," said Gilchrist amiably.
"He devoted himself to public service by working in the Central
Centre for Employment, Stability and Surroundings. I was his
boss and I soon realized he was something of a saint. When
confronted by human suffering he had absolutely no patience
with red tape. To be frank, he often went too fast for me,
and that is why he is exactly the lord provost the region needs.
I can imagine no better politician to represent Greater Unthank
at the forthcoming general assembly."

"Good!" said the reckless man. "I wonder if Provost Lanark
would care to say something quotable about what he is going
to *do* at the Provan assembly?"

After thinking for a while Lanark said boldly, "I will try to
tell the truth."

"Couldn't you make it more emphatic?" said the reckless man.

"Couldn't you say, 'Come hell or high water, I will tell the world the TRUTH'?"

"Certainly not!" said Lanark crossly. "Water has nothing to do with my visit to Provan."

"Come what may, the world will hear the truth," murmured the quiet man. "We'll quote you as saying that."

"Very good, gentlemen!" said Sludden, standing up. "Our provost is leaving now. It's a very ordinary departure so you needn't watch. If you want a photograph Mr. Gilchrist's secretary can provide one. I'm sorry my wife was not here to offer you stronger refreshment, but you will find a bottle of sherry and a half bottle of whisky on the telephone-stand outside. Consume them at your leisure. Mr. Gilchrist will drive you back into town."

Everybody stood up.

Sludden showed Gilchrist and the journalists out. The grey-haired lady sighed and said, "Communicating with the press is a science I will nefer understand. This briefcase, Mr. Lanark, holts passcart, identification paper and three reports relating to the Unthank region. Before you speak in Provan I advise you to master them. There is a seismological report on the effect of pollution upon the Merovicnic discontinuity. There is a sanitary report on the probability of typhoid and related epidemics. There is a social report cuffering all the olt ground— no region our size has so much unemployment, uses so much corporal punishment in schools, has so many children cared for by the state, so much alcoholism, so many adults in prison or such a shortage of housing. It is all very olt stuff but people should be reminded. The seismological report is the only von whose language is at all technical because it contains an analysis of certain deep Permian samples vich *may* haf a commercial value. I haf put in a dictionary of scientific terms to help you out."

"Thank you," said Lanark, taking the case. "Are you Mrs. Schtzngrm?"

"Eva Schtzngrm, yes. There is von other matter personal to your*self,*" she said, lowering her voice. "In crossing the intercalendrical zone by air I think you vill pass very rapidly through the menopause barrier."

"What?" said Lanark, alarmed.

"No neet to worry. You are not a voman and so vill not be greatly changed. But you may haf very odd experiences of contraction and expansion which neet not be referred to aftervards. Don't vorry about them. Don't vorry."

Sludden looked round the door and said, "Angus has set up the lights. Let's go to the airfield."

They went through a kitchen to a back door and followed an electric cable which snaked up a path between seedy cabbage stumps.

"Remember," said Sludden, "your best tactic is open denunciation. It's pointless complaining to the council chiefs when the other delegates aren't present, and vice versa. The leaders must be shamèd into making concrete promises in the hearing of the rest."

"I wish you were going instead," said Lanark. They reached an overgrown privet hedge whose top leaves were black against a low glowing light. Sludden, then Lanark, then Mrs. Schtzngrm pushed through a gap onto the airfield. This was almost too narrow to be called a field, being a grassy triangular space on the summit of a hill completely surrounded by back gardens. A square tarpaulin was spread on the grass with three electric lights placed round it, and in the centre of the tarpaulin, upon very broad feet and short bowed legs, stood something like a bird. Though too large for an eagle it had the same shape and brownish gold feathers. The figures U-1 were stencilled on the breast. In the back between the folded wings was an opening about eighteen inches wide, though overlapping feathers made it seem narrower. As far as Lanark could see the interior was quilted with blue satin. He said, "Is this a bird or a machine?"

"A bit of both," said Sludden, taking the briefcase from Lanark's hand and tossing it into the cavity.

"But how can it fly when it's hollow inside?"

"It draws vital energy from the passenger," said Mrs. Schtzngrm.

"I haven't enough energy to fly that to another city."

"A credit cart vill allow the vehicle to draw energy from your future. You haf a cart?"

"Here," said Sludden. "I took it from his other suit. Angus, the chair, please."

The chauffeur brought a kitchen chair from the darkness and placed it beside the bird; Lanark, feebly protesting, was helped onto it by Sludden.

"I don't like doing this."

"Just step inside, Mr. Delegate."

Lanark put one foot in the cavity, then the other. The bird rocked and settled as he slid down inside; then the head came up and turned completely round so that he was faced by the down-curving dagger point of the great beak. "Give it this," said Sludden, handing him the credit card. Lanark held it by an extreme corner and thrust it shyly toward the beak, which snapped it up. A yellow light went on in the glassy eyes. The head turned away and lowered out of sight. Mrs. Schtzngrm said, "He cannot fly till you haf put yourself mostly inside. Remember, the less you think the faster he vill go. Do not fear for your goot clothing, the interior is sanitizing and vill launder and trim you while you sleep."

The smooth strong satin inside the bird supported Lanark as though he sat in a chair, but when he pulled his arms in it stretched him out and the rear end sank until his feet inside the neck felt higher than his face. This looked out of the cleft between two brown wings, which started rising higher and higher on each side. Squinting forward he could see a bungalow roof with a yellow square of window. The black shape of someone's head and shoulders looked out of this, and if the window belonged to Sludden's house the watcher was surely Sandy and at once the grotesque flimsy aircraft and being a delegate and a provost seemed stupid evasions of the realest thing in the world and he shouted "No!" and began struggling to get out but at that moment the arching wings on each side thrashed down and with a thunderous *wump-wump-wump* he was flung upward feet first like a javelin and a sore blast of cold air on the brow knocked him out of his senses.

CHAPTER 40. Provan

He wakened cradled in stillness and looking at a bright full moon. The surrounding sky held a few big stars. His eyes were so dazzled that he rested them on the deep spaces between, but other stars started glittering there, and then whole constellations; he could not watch a space, however tiny, without the silver dust of a galaxy coming to glimmer in it. With outspread wings his aircraft seemed hanging, slightly tilted, between the ceiling of stars and a floor of smooth clouds which spread, like them, from horizon to horizon, and was that most mysteriously splendid of all colours, whiteness seen by a dim light. This thinned and opened under him and for a moment the craft seemed to overturn, for the bright moon shone through the opening. He was looking down into the sky reflected in a circular lake, reflected and magnified, for a black speck in the centre of the lower moon was clearly a reflection of his bird-machine. The lake, though sombre, had colour of its own. A jet black halo surrounded the reflected moon, and a ring of deep blue water flecked with stars surrounded that. To left and right was a beach of pure sand as pearly-pale as the clouds, and the round lake and its beaches were enclosed by two curving shores which made the shape of an eye. And Lanark saw that it was an eye, and the feeling which came to him then was too new to have a name. His mouth and mind opened wide and the only thought left was a wonder if he—a speck of a speck floating before that large pupil—was seen by it. In an effort to think something else he looked up at the stars but looked down again almost at once, and the eye was nearer now, he could only see the stars reflected in the depth. There was a sound like remote thunder or the breathings of wind in the ear. "Is . . . is . . . is . . ." it said. "Is . . . if . . . is. . . ." He knew that half the stars were seeing the other

half and smiled slightly, not knowing up from down or caring
which was which. Then, dazed by infinity, he did not fall asleep
but seemed to float out into it.

He wakened next in pale cold azure. He was above a
plain of snowy clouds with a blue bird-like shadow skimming
over them on one side and on the other, not far above the
horizon, a small piercing sun which seemed to shoot golden
wires at his eyes when he glimpsed it. Sometimes he passed
through fountains of birdsong squirting up through rifts in the
clouds and looked down for a moment on grass or rocks a
mile or so beneath, but the only steady sound was the quietly
thudding wings of the eagle-machine muted by the thin air.
His body lay relaxed and warm on the firm satin. His face
lay in a pool of cold air as refreshing as a rinse of cold water.
On the horizon ahead he saw a mountain of white cloud as
single as a milk jug on the edge of a bare table. A bird-shaped
black dot, casting a fleck of shadow, seemed to cross the side
of it. Later, when the peak and precipices of the mountain
floated above him, creamy and dazzling toward the sun and
toning into blue shadow away from it, he saw that the cloudy
plain ended here and a real mountain stood under the cloud
one. It had a sharp summit and granite precipices and was
highest of a jagged range rising from heathery purple moors.
It combined the massiveness of great sculptures with the most
delicately imagined detail. A drifting movement on the shadowy
side of a glen resolved into a herd of deer. A small loch on
the moor had a waterfall spilling out of it and an angler, knee
deep, near the edge. He saw differently coloured fields with
white farmhouses along a shore, and a bay where the sand
under shallow water was lemon-yellow with reddish gardens
of weed. Farther out the water was ribbed by sea swells and
ruffled all over by little waves that sparkled where the sunlight
caught them. He passed over a pale green, slow-foaming triangle of wake with a long tanker moving onward at the tip. Then
conversational sounds came from inside his eagle-machine, and
he pulled his head in out of the sunlight.

A small voice near his toes was saying ". . . identify self.
This is Provan Air Authority addressing the U-1 flight from
Unthank. Repeat: will passenger please identify self. Over."
"I am the Lord Provost of the Greater Unthank region," said
Lanark firmly, yet with elation, "and delegate to the general
assembly of council states."
"Please rep—please rep—please repeat. Over."

Lanark said it again.

"The U-1 flight from Unthank may proceed to Hampden as planned on beam co—beam co—beam coordinate zero flux zero parahelion 43 minutes 19 point nought 7 seconds epihelion ditto neg—ditto neg—ditto negating impetus reversal flow 22 point nought 2—nought 2—nought 2—nought 2—nought 2 beyond the equinoctial of Quebus on the international nerve—national nerve—national nerve-circuit-decimal-calendar-cortexin-quantum-clock. Message understood? Over."

"It sounds like gibberish to me," said Lanark.

"Proceed as planned. Repeat: as planned. Repeat: as planned. Out."

There was a click and silence. He lay thinking of how he kept being pushed into certain actions, and how people kept talking to him as though he had planned them. But perhaps the message had not been for him but for his aircraft. It had sounded very like a machine talking to a machine. He pushed his head out into sunlight again.

He was flying up a wide and winding firth with very different coasts. To the right lay green farmland with clumps of trees and reservoirs in hollows linked by quick streams. On the left were mountain ridges and high bens silvered with snow, the sun striking gold sparkles off bits of sea loch between them. On both shores he saw summer resorts with shops, church spires and crowded esplanades, and clanging ports with harbours full of shipping. Tankers moved on the water, and freighters and white-sailed yachts. A long curving feather of smoke pointed up at him from a paddle steamer churning with audible chunking sounds toward an island big enough to hold a grouse moor, two woods, three farms, a golf course and a town fringing a bay. This island looked like a bright toy he could lift up off the smoothly ribbed, rippling sea, and he seemed to recognize it. He thought, 'Did I have a sister once? And did we play together on the grassy top of that cliff among the yellow gorsebushes? Yes, on that cliff behind the marine observatory, on a day like this in the summer holidays. Did we bury a tin box under a gorse root in a rabbit hole? There was a halfcrown piece in it and a silver sixpence dated from that year, and a piece of our mother's jewellery, and a cheap little notebook with a message to ourselves when we grew up. Did we promise to dig it up in twenty-five years? And dug it up two days later to make sure it hadn't been stolen? And were we not children then? And was I not happy?'

The shores grew steeper, more wooded and close together; the firth was pinched between them to a water-lane marked by buoys and light-towers. In places docks embanked it and vessels were being built or unloaded beneath the arms of cranes. Then the high land sloped away left and right and he came to a valley, a broad basin of land filled by a city with the river gleaming toward a centre of spires, towers and high white blocks. The eagle-machine left the river and soared in a long curve over sloping hills to the south, then to the east, then to the north. It crossed tenements of clean stone enclosing gardens where children played and lines of washing flapped in a slow breeze. There was a holiday in this city for the air was transparent and the bowling greens and tennis courts busy with players. The width and beauty of the view, its clearness under the sun seemed not only splendid but familiar. He thought, 'All my life, yes, all my life I've wanted this, yet I seem to know it well. Not the names, no, the names have gone, but I recognize the places. And if I really lived here once, and was happy, how did I lose it? Why am I only returning now?'

Sometimes he heard a sound like a slow explosion, a huge soft roaring from the city centre, and looking over there he saw tiny bird shapes moving to and fro. A shadow touched him and looking upward he saw, overhead toward the east, a great eagle crossing his course with the sign Z-1 on the underside of the breast. He realized his own craft was following a spiral path aimed at the city centre and getting lower all the time. It soared down the tree-filled gorge of another river, a small one linking parks full of strollers and sunbathers. Children on a grassy slope waved handkerchiefs at him and he thought, 'Soon I'll see the university.' A moment later he looked down on twin quadrangles framed by pinnacled rooftops. He thought, 'Soon we'll reach the river with the big dock basin and cranes and warehouses', but this time he was wrong. The small river entered a mainstream which spread out into arms of quiet water, but these lay among paths and trees surrounding a gigantic sports stadium. Figures were racing and vaulting round the tracks, on the rich green grass of the centre rested athletes in variously coloured suits, from the crowded terraces a dull hub-bub of applause welled into a roar. Lanark's aircraft joined five or six others circling overhead. At intervals one would drop toward a white canvas square spread before the main grandstand with red, blue and black target rings painted on

it. A voice over a loudspeaker was saying ". . . and now Posky,
Podgorny, Paleologue and Norn are entering the last lap; and
just descending, bang on target, is Premier Kostoglotov of the
Scythian People's Republic; and Norn and Paleologue are passing, yes, passing Podgorny into second place, almost neck and
neck, and the gap between them and Posky is closing fast"—
here a great roar went up—
"and the Toltec of Tiahuanaco dips toward the target just as
Posky falls into third place and now Norn leads, then Paleologue, then Posky with Podgorny a very poor fourth; and here
comes the Provost of Unthank—I'm sorry the *Lord* Provost
of *Greater* Unthank—dropping toward the target just as Norn,
yes, Norn, yes, Norn of Thule breaks the tape, closely followed
by Paleologue of Trebizond and Posky of Crim Tartary."

Lanark's eagle-machine thumped down on the canvas and
stood rocking slightly. Six men in dust coats seized it and carried
it a few yards to a row of similar machines standing against a
long narrow platform. Lanark gripped his briefcase and was
helped onto the platform by a girl in a scarlet skirt and blouse
who said hurriedly, "The Unthank delegate, yes?"
"Yes."
"This way, please, you're half a minute behind schedule."
She led him down some steps, through groups of relaxing athletes, across a momentarily bare cinder track and into a doorway
under the terracing of the main grandstand. After the wide
spaces of the sky it was perplexing to trot up a narrow passage
in artificial light. He decided that whatever happened he would
remain dour, sceptical and unimpressed. They came to a hall
with open lifts along the walls. The girl ushered him into one,
saying, "Go up to the executive gallery, they're expecting you.
Leave your luggage with me; I'll make sure it reaches your
room in the delegates' repose village."
"No, I'm sorry, these documents are vital," said Lanark. He
saw a row of buttons in a polished metal panel and touched
one beside the words EXECUTIVE GALLERY. The lift ascended
and he watched his reflection in the polished panel with satisfac-
tion. Though older he was even more dignified than in the
vestry lavatory. He had grown a pointed, compact, captainish
little white beard, his cheeks were smooth and rosy, the effect
was of well-groomed efficiency. The lift door opened and Wilkins, looking exactly as Lanark remembered him, shook his
hand, saying, "Provost Sludden! Am I right?"
"No, Wilkins. My name is Lanark. We've met before."

Wilkins peered closely and said, "Lanark! My God, so you are. What's happened to Sludden?"

"He is coping at present with a very dangerous sanitary problem. The Greater Unthank regional committee have judged it wiser for me to represent the city."

Wilkins smiled crookedly and said, "That man is a fox: a ninth-generation ecological fox. Never mind. Join the queue, join the queue."

"Wilkins, our sanitary problem is assuming catastrophic dimensions. I have more than one report in this briefcase which shows that people will start dying soon and—"

"This is a social reception, Lanark, public health will be debated on Monday. Just join the queue and say hello to your hosts."

"Hosts?"

"The Provan executive officer and Lord and Lady Monboddo. Join the queue, join the queue."

They were in a broad curving corridor with glass double-doors on one side and a queue moving steadily through. Lanark noticed a woman in a silver sari and a brown man in a white toga but most people wore sober uniforms or business suits and had the wary look of important people who, without showing friendship, are prepared to respond judiciously to it in others. They were an easy crowd to join. At the glass door a loud voice announced the arrivals to a company beyond: "Senator Sennacherib of New Alabama. Brian de Bois Guilbert, Grand Templar of Languedoc and Apulia. Governor Vonnegut of West Atlantis. . . ."

He reached the door and heard the satisfying cry, "Lord Provost Lanark of Greater Unthank," and shook hands with a hollow-cheeked man who said, "Trevor Weems of Provan. Glad you could come."

A stately woman in a blue tweed gown shook his hand and said, "Had you a nice trip?"

Lanark stared at her and said, "Catalyst."

"Call her Lady Monboddo," said Ozenfant, who was standing beside her. He shook Lanark's hand briskly. "Time changes all the labels, as you yourself are proving also."

A girl in a scarlet skirt and blouse took Lanark's arm and led him down some steps saying, "Hello, I'm called Libby. I expect you need some refreshment. Shall I get you a snack from the buffet? Pâté de something? Breast of something? Locusts and honey?"

"Was Ozenfant . . . ? Is Ozenfant . . . ?"

"The new lord president director, yes hadn't you heard?
Doesn't he look tremendously fit? I wonder why his wife is
wearing that hairy frock? Perhaps you aren't hungry. Neither
am I. Let's tuck into the booze instead, there's heaps of it.
Just sit there a minute."
He sat down at the end of a long leather sofa and looked
perplexedly around.

He was on the highest and largest of four floors which
descended like steps to a wall of window overlooking the stadium. Half the people standing around seemed to be delegates
and stood talking in quiet little groups. Girls in scarlet lent
some liveliness to the company by carrying trays between the
groups with flirtatious quickness, but they were balanced by
silent, robust men who stood watchfully by the walls wearing
black suits and holding glasses of whisky which they did not
sip. On a glass-topped table near the sofa lay a sheaf of pamphlets
entitled **ASSEMBLY PROGRAMME.** Lanark lifted and
opened one. He read a printed letter from Trevor Weems
welcoming the delegates on behalf of the people of Provan
and trusting their stay would be a happy one. There was no
possibility of danger to life or limb, as the newest sort of security
staff had been rented from the Quantum-Cortexin group; the
Red Girls, however, were human and anxious to help with
any difficulty the delegates could bring to them. Then came
six pages of region names listed alphabetically from Armorica
to Zimbabwe. Lanark saw that the Greater Unthank delegate
was given as Provost Sludden. Then came a page headed:

FIRST DAY

**HOUR 11. Arrival and reception of delegates by Lord
and Lady Monboddo**

After this a press conference was listed, a lunch, an "opportunity
for social and informal lobbying," a sheepdog trial, a pipe band
contest, a dinner with speeches, a performance by the Erse
Opera Company of Purser's *Misfortunes of Elphin,* a firework
display and a party. Lanark turned a page impatiently and found
something less frivolous.

SECOND DAY

HOUR 8.50.   Breakfast. Lobbying.

HOUR 10.   World Education Debate.

Chairman, Lord Monboddo.

Opening speech: "Logos into Chaos." The Erse
delegate and sociosophist Odin MacTok analyzes
the disastrous impact of literacy on the undereducated.

Speeches.   Motions.   Voting.

HOUR 15.   Lunch. Lobbying.

HOUR 17.   World Food Debate.

Chairman, Lord Monboddo.

Opening speech: "Excrement into Aliment." The
Bohemian delegate and Volstat research scholar
Dick Otoman explains how organic pollutions can
be pre-processed to revitalize each other within
the human body.

Speeches.   Motions.   Voting.

HOUR 22.   Dinner. Lobbying.

THIRD DAY

HOUR 8.50.   Breakfast. Lobbying.

HOUR 10.   Public Order Debate.

Chairman, Lord Monboddo.

Opening speech: "Revolutionary Stasis." Kado
Motnic, sociometrist and delegate of the People's
Republic of Paphlogonia describes the application
of short-nerve-circuitry to libido-canalization in the
infra-supra-25-40 spectrum.

Speeches.   Motions.   Voting.

HOUR 15.   Lunch. Lobbying.

HOUR 17.   World Energy Debate.

Chairman, Lord Monboddo.

Opening speech: "Biowarp." South Atlantis delegate and Algolagnics director Timon Kodac presents gene-warping as the solution to the fossil-
fuel failure.

Speeches.   Motions.   Voting.

HOUR 22.   Dinner. Lobbying.

FOURTH DAY

HOUR 8.50.   Breakfast. Lobbying.

HOUR 10.   **World Health Debate.**
                                        Chairman, Lord Monboddo.
Opening speech: "Kindness, Kin and Capacity."
Hanseatic delegate and sociopathist Moo Dackin
explains why healthy norms must be preserved
by destroying other healthy norms.
Speeches.   Motions.   Voting.

HOUR 15.   **Lunch, social and informal.**
HOUR 17.   **The Subcommittees report. Voting.**
HOUR 21.   **Press conference.**
HOUR 22.   **Dinner. Speeches.**
                                        Master of Ceremonies, Trevor Weems.
Opening speech: "Then, Now and Tomorrow." Six
millennia of achievement will be outlined by the
Chairman of the Assembly, Moderator of the Ex-
pansion Project, Director of the Institute and Presi-
dent of the Council, the Lord Monboddo. Trevor
Weems, Chief Executive Officer of the Provan Ba-
sin, will propose a vote of thanks. Toadi Monk,
Satrap of Troy and Trebizond, will move the vote
of thanks to the hosts.

HOUR 25.   **The delegates depart.**

Before reading all this Lanark had been gripped by a large
undirected excitement. Since wakening to sunlight in his aircraft
that morning he had felt himself nearing the centre of a great
event, approaching a place where he would utter, publicly, a
word that would change the world. The sight of Wilkins, the
catalyst and Ozenfant-Monboddo had not damaged this feeling.
He had been startled, but so had they, which was satisfying.
But the assembly programme disconcerted him. It was like seeing the plans of a vast engine he meant to drive and finding
he knew nothing about engineering. What did "Speeches. Motions. Voting" mean? What was "Lobbying" and why did it
happen at mealtimes? Did the other delegates understand these
things?

The gallery was very crowded now and two men sat at
the other end of the sofa sipping pint glasses of black beer
and gazing at the active little figures on the sunlit sports field
below. One of them said cheerfully, "It's great to see all this
happening in Provan."

"Is it?"

"Oh, come now, Odin, you've worked as hard as anyone to bring the assembly here."

The other said morosely, "Bread and circuses. Bread and circuses. A short spell of reasonable wages and long holidays while they plunder us and then *wham!* The chopper. Provan will be turned into another Greater Unmentionable Region."

Lanark said eagerly, "Excuse me, are you complaining about the condition of this city?"

The morose man had thick white hair, a body like a wrestler's and a pinkish battered face like a boxer's. He looked at Lanark balefully for a moment, then said, "I think I've a right to do that. I live here."

"Then you don't know how lucky you are! I'm from a region with an unusually dangerous sanitary problem, and Provan strikes me as the most splendidly situated—"

"Are you a delegate?"

"Yes."

"So you've just arrived by air."

"Yes."

"Then don't talk to me about Provan. You're in the early stages of a Gulliver complex."

Lanark said coldly, "I don't understand you."

"The first recorded aerial survey happened when Lemuel Gulliver, a plain, reasonable man, was allowed to stand on his feet beside the capital of Lilliput. He saw well-cultivated farms surrounding the homes, streets, and public buildings of a very busy little people. He was struck by the obvious ingenuity and enterprise of the rulers, the officials and the workmen. It took him two or three months to discover their stupidity, greed, corruption, envy, cruelty."

"You pessimists always fall into the disillusion trap," said the cheerful man cheerfully. "From one distance a thing looks bright. From another it looks dark. You think you've found the truth when you've replaced the cheerful view by the opposite, but true profundity blends all possible views, bright as well as dark."

The morose man grinned and said, "Since nearly everyone clings to the cloud-cuckoo view it's lucky one or two of us aren't afraid to look at the state of the sewers."

"Sorry I took so long," said the Red Girl, placing a tray on the table. "I thought it might be fun to try a gaelic coffee."

"I'm glad you mentioned sewers," said Lanark eagerly, "I come from Unthank, which is having trouble with its sewers. In fact the future of the whole region is being menaced—I mean, decided—by this assembly, and I've been sent here as advocate for the defence. But the programme"—he waved it—"tells me nothing about where and when to speak. Can you advise me?"

"There's no need to be so serious on the first day," said the Red Girl.

"The future of a crippled region," said the morose man slowly, "is usually hammered out by one of the subcommittees."

"Which subcommittee? When and where does it meet?"

"This is a friendly social reception!" said the Red Girl, looking distressed. "Can't we keep all this heavy stuff till later? There's going to be *such* a lot of it."

"Shut up, dear," said the morose man. "Wilkins knows all the ropes. You'd better ask him."

"Listen," said the Red Girl. "I'll take you to Nastler. He knows everything about everything, and he's expecting to see you soon in the Epilogue room. He told me so."

"Who is Nastler?"

"Our king. In a way. But he's not at all grand," said the Red Girl evasively. "It's hard to explain."

The morose man guffawed and said, "He's a joker. You'll get nothing out of him."

Lanark opened his briefcase, locked the assembly programme inside and stood up.

"I understand that you are employed to help me with my difficulties," he told the Red Girl. "I will speak to both Wilkins and this Nastler person. Which can I see first?"

"Oh Nastler, definitely," said the red girl, looking relieved. "He's an invalid, anyone can see him anytime. But won't you drink your coffee first?"

"No," said Lanark, and thanked the morose man, and followed the Red Girl into the crowd.

Weems and the Monboddos were still shaking hands with the queue by the door, which was a short one now. As Lanark passed them the announcer was saying, "Chairman Fu of Xanadu. Proto-Presbyter Griffith-Powys of Ynyswitrin. Premier Multan of Zimbabwe."

The Red Girl led him along the outer corridor till they came to a white panel without hinges or handle. She said, "It's a door. Go through it."

"Aren't you coming?"

"If you're going to talk politics, I'm going to wait outside."

As Lanark pressed the surface he noticed a big word on it:

EPILOGUE

He entered a room with no architectural similarity to the building he had left. The door on this side had deeply moulded panels and a knob, the ceiling was bordered by an elaborate cornice of acanthus sprays, there was a tall bay window with the upper foliage of a chestnut tree outside and an old stone tenement beyond. The rest of the room was hidden by easels holding large paintings of the room. The pictures seemed brighter and cleaner than the reality and a tall beautiful girl with long blond hair reclined in them, sometimes nude and sometimes clothed. The girl herself, more worried and untidy than her portraits, stood near the door wearing a paint-stained butcher's apron. With a very small brush she was adding leaves to a view of the tree outside the window, but she paused, pointed round the edge of the picture and told Lanark, "He's there."

A voice said, "Yes, come round, come round."

Lanark went behind the picture and found a stout man leaning against a pile of pillows on a low bed. His face, framed by wings and horns of uncombed hair, looked statuesque and noble apart from an apprehensive, rather cowardly expression. He wore a woollen jersey over a pyjama jacket, neither of them clean, the coverlet over his knees was littered with books and papers, and there was a pen in his hand. Glancing at Lanark in a sly sideways fashion he indicated a chair with the pen and said, "Please sit down."

"Are you the king of this place?"

"The king of Provan, yes. And Unthank too. And that suite of rooms you call the institute and the council."

"Then perhaps you could help me. I am here—"

"Yes, I know roughly what you want and I would like to help. I would even offer you a drink, but there's too much intoxication in this book."

"Book?"

"This world, I meant to say. You see I'm the king, not the government. I have laid out landscapes, and stocked them with people, and I still work an occasional miracle, but governing is left to folk like Monboddo and Sludden."

"Why?"

The king closed his eyes, smiled and said, "I brought you here to ask that question."

"Will you answer it?"

"Not yet."

Lanark felt very angry. He stood up and said, "Then talking to you is a waste of time."

"Waste of time!" said the king, opening his eyes. "You clearly don't realize who I am. I have called myself a king—that's a purely symbolic name, I'm far more important. Read this and you'll understand. The critics will accuse me of self-indulgence but I don't care."[1]

With a reckless gesture he handed Lanark a paper from the bed. It was covered with childish handwriting and many words were scored out or inserted with little arrows. Much of it seemed to be dialogue but Lanark's eye was caught by a sentence in italics which said: *Much of it seemed to be dialogue but Lanark's eye was caught by a sentence in italics which said:*

Lanark gave the paper back asking, "What's that supposed to prove?"

"I am your author."

Lanark stared at him. The author said, "Please don't feel embarrassed. This isn't an unprecedented situation. Vonnegut has it in *Breakfast of Champions* and Jehovah in the books of Job and Jonah."

"Are you pretending to be God?"

"Not nowadays. I used to be part of him, though. Yes, I am part of a part which was once the whole. But I went bad and was excreted. If I can get well I may be allowed home before I die, so I continually plunge my beak into my rotten liver and swallow and excrete it. But it grows again. Creation festers in me. I am excreting you and your world at the present moment. This arse-wipe"—he stirred the papers on the bed—"is part of the process."

"I am not religious," said Lanark, "but I don't like you mixing religion with excrement. Last night I saw part of the person you are referring to and it was not at all nasty."

"You saw part of God?" cried the author. "How did that happen?"

Lanark explained. The author was greatly excited. He said, "Say those words again."

"*Is . . . is . . . is . . .* , then a pause, then *Is . . . if . . . is. . . .*"

"If?" shouted the author sitting upright. "He actually said if? He wasn't simply snarling 'Is, is, is, is, is,' all the time?"

Lanark said, "I don't like you saying 'he' like that. What I saw may not have been masculine. It may not have been human. But it certainly wasn't snarling. What's wrong with you?"

The author had covered his mouth with his hands, apparently

---

1. To have an objection anticipated is no reason for failing to raise it.

to stifle laughter, but his eyes were wet. He gulped and said, "One *if* to five *is*es! That's an incredible amount of freedom. But can I believe you? I've created you honest, but can I trust your senses? At a great altitude *is* and *if* must sound very much alike."

"You seem to take words very seriously," said Lanark with a touch of contempt.

"Yes. You don't like me, but that can't be helped. I'm primarily a literary man," said the author with a faintly nasal accent, and started chuckling to himself.

The tall blond girl came round the edge of the painting wiping her brush on her apron. She said defiantly, "I've finished the tree. Can I leave now?"

The author leaned back on his pillows and said sweetly, "Of course, Marion. Leave when you like."

"I need money. I'm hungry."

"Why don't you go to the kitchen? I believe there's some cold chicken in the fridge, and I'm sure Pat won't mind you making yourself a snack."

"I don't want a snack, I want a meal with a friend in a restaurant. And I want to go to a film afterward, or to a pub, or to a hairdresser if I feel like it. I'm sorry, but I want money."

"Of course you do, and you've earned it. How much do I owe?"

"Five hours today at fifty pence an hour is two pounds fifty. With yesterday and the day before and the day before is ten pounds, isn't it?"

"I've a poor head for arithmetic but you're probably right," said the author, taking coins from under a pillow and giving them to her. "This is all I have just now, nearly two pounds. Come back tomorrow and I'll see if I can manage a little extra."

The girl scowled at the coins in her hand and then at the author. He was puffing medicinal spray into his mouth from a tiny hand-pump. She went abruptly behind the painting again and they heard the door slam.

"A strange girl," murmured the author, sighing. "I do my best to help her but it isn't easy."

Lanark had been sitting with his head propped on his hands. He said, "You say you are creating me."

"I am."

"Then how can I have experiences you don't know about?

You were surprised when I told you what I saw from the aircraft."

"The answer to that is unusually interesting; please attend closely. When *Lanark* is finished (I am calling the work after you) it will be roughly two hundred thousand words and forty chapters long, and divided into books three, one, two and four."

"Why not one, two, three and four?"

"I want *Lanark* to be read in one order but eventually thought of in another. It's an old device. Homer, Vergil, Milton and Scott Fitzgerald used it.[2] There will also be a prologue before book one, an interlude in the centre, and an epilogue two or three chapters before the end."

"I thought epilogues came after the end."

"Usually, but mine is too important to go there. Though not essential to the plot it provides some comic distraction at a moment when the narrative sorely needs it. And it lets me utter some fine sentiments which I could hardly trust to a mere character. And it contains critical notes which will save research scholars years of toil. In fact my epilogue is so essential that I am working on it with nearly a quarter of the book still unwritten. I am working on it here, just now, in this conversation. But you have had to reach this room by passing through several chapters I haven't clearly imagined yet, so you know details of the story which I don't. Of course I know the broad general outline. That was planned years ago and mustn't be changed. You have come here from my city of destruction, which is rather like Glasgow, to plead before some sort of world parliament in an ideal city based on Edinburgh, or London, or perhaps Paris if I can wangle a grant from the Scottish Arts Council[3] to go there. Tell me, when you were landing this morning, did you see the Eiffel Tower? Or Big Ben? Or a rock with a castle on it?"

"No. Provan is very like—"

"Stop! Don't tell me. My fictions often anticipate the experiences they're based upon, but no author should rely on that sort of thing."

Lanark was so agitated that he stood and walked to the window

2. Each of the four authors mentioned above began a large work *in medias res,* but none of them numbered their divisions out of logical sequence.
3. In 1973, as a result of sponsorship by the poet Edwin Morgan, the author received a grant of £300 from the Scottish Arts Council for the purpose of helping him write his book, but it was never assumed that he would use the money to seek out exotic local colour.

to sort out his thoughts. The author struck him as a slippery person but too vain and garrulous to be impressive. He went back to the bed and said, "How will my story end?"

"Catastrophically. The Thaw narrative shows a man dying because he is bad at loving. It is enclosed by your narrative which shows civilization collapsing for the same reason."

"Listen," said Lanark. "I never tried to be a delegate. I never wanted anything but some sunlight, some love, some very ordinary happiness. And every moment I have been thwarted by organizations and things pushing in a different direction, and now I'm nearly an old man and my reasons for living have shrunk to standing up in public and saying a good word for the only people I know. And you tell me that word will be useless! That you have *planned* it to be useless."

"Yes," said the author, nodding eagerly. "Yes, that's right." Lanark gaped down at the foolishly nodding face and suddenly felt it belonged to a horrible ventriloquist's doll. He raised a clenched fist but could not bring himself to strike. He swung round and punched a painting on an easel and both clattered to the floor. He pushed down the other painting beside the door, went to a tall bookcase in a corner and heaved it over. Books cascaded from the upper shelves and it hit the floor with a crash which shook the room. There were long low shelves around the walls holding books, folders, bottles and tubes of paint. With sweeps of his arm he shoved these to the floor, then turned, breathing deeply, and stared at the bed. The author sat there looking distressed, but the paintings and easels were back in their old places, and glancing around Lanark saw the bookcases had returned quietly to the corner and books, folders, bottles and paint were on the shelves again.

"A conjuror!" said Lanark with loathing. "A damned conjuror!"

"Yes," said the conjuror humbly, "I'm sorry. Please sit down and let me explain why the story has to go like this. You can eat while I talk (I'm sure you're hungry) and afterward you can tell me how you think I could be better. Please sit down." The bedside chair was small but comfortably upholstered. A table had appeared beside it with covered dishes on a tray. Lanark felt more exhausted than hungry, but after sitting for a while he removed a cover out of curiosity. There was a bowl beneath of dark red oxtail soup, so taking a spoon he began to eat.

"I will start," said the conjuror, "by explaining the physics of the world you live in. Everything you have experienced and are experiencing, from your first glimpse of the Elite café to the metal of that spoon in your fingers, the taste of the soup in your mouth, is made of one thing."

"Atoms," said Lanark.

"No. Print. Some worlds are made of atoms but yours is made of tiny marks[4] marching in neat lines, like armies of insects, across pages and pages and pages of white paper. I say these lines are marching, but that is a metaphor. They are perfectly still. They are lifeless. How can *they* reproduce the movement and noises of the battle of Borodino, the white whale ramming the ship, the fallen angels on the flaming lake?"

"By being read," said Lanark impatiently.

"Exactly. Your survival as a character and mine as an author depend on us seducing a living soul into our printed world and trapping it here long enough for us to steal the imaginative energy which gives us life. To cast a spell over this stranger I am doing abominable things. I am prostituting my most sacred memories into the commonest possible words and sentences. When I need more striking sentences or ideas I steal them from other writers, usually twisting them to blend with my own. Worst of all I am using the great world given at birth— the world of atoms—as a ragbag of shapes and colours to make this second-hand entertainment look more amusing."

"You seem to be complaining," said Lanark. "I don't know why. Nobody is forcing you to work with print, and all work involves some degradation. I want to know why your readers in their world should be entertained by the sight of me failing to do any good in mine."

"Because failures are popular. Frankly, Lanark, you are too stolid and commonplace to be entertaining as a successful man. But don't be offended; most heroes end up like you. Consider the Greek book about Troy. To repair a marriage broken by adultery, a civilization spends ten years smashing another one. The heroes on both sides know the quarrel is futile, but they continue

---

4. This is a false antithesis. Printed paper has an atomic structure like anything else. "Words" would have been a better term than "print," being less definably concrete.

INDEX OF PLAGIARISMS

There are three kinds of literary theft in this book:
BLOCK PLAGIARISM, where someone else's work is printed as a distinct typographical unit, IMBEDDED PLAGIARISM, where stolen words are concealed within the body of the narrative, and DIFFUSE PLAGIARISM, where scenery, characters, actions or novel ideas have been stolen without the original words describing them. To save space these will be referred to hereafter as Blockplag, Implag, and Difplag.
ANON.
Chap. 29, para. 2. The couplet ends a verse on a monument now standing beside a pedestrian lane under a flyover of an intersection of the Monkland Motorway and Cathedral Street, Glasgow.
ANON.
Chap. 30, para. 12. Blockplag of inscription on cairn on moor

beside the String Road near Black-waterfoot on Isle of Arran, Firth of Clyde.
ANON.
Chap. 43. Ozenfant's speech. Blockplag of first stanza of Middle English epic poem *Gawain and the Green Knight*, omitting 3rd and 4th lines, "The tyke that the trammels of treason there wrought/Was tried for his treachery, the truest on earth" (the translation is also anonymous).
BLACK ANGUS
See Macneacail, Aonghas.
BLAKE, WILLIAM
Chap. 19, para. 1. Implag of poem "The Clod and the Pebble" from *Songs of Experience.*
Chap. 35, last paragraph. Implag. Ritchie-Smollet quotes "The Little Vagabond" from *Songs of Experience.*
BORGES, JORGE LUIS
Chap. 43, Ozenfant's speech. Blockplag from short essay "The Barbarian and the City."
BOYCE, CHRISTOPHER
Chap. 38, para. 16. The encounter between the "sharp red convertible" and the motorcyclists is an Implag from the short story "Shooting Script."
BROWN,
GEORGE DOUGLAS
Books 1 and 2 owe much to the novel *The House with the Green Shutters* in which heavy paternalism forces a weakminded youth into dread of existence, hallucination, and crime.
BUNYAN, JOHN
Chap. 9, para. 10. Blockplag of first paragraph of the *Relation of the Holy War Made by Shaddai Upon Diabolus for the Regaining of the Metropolis of the World; or the losing and taking again of the town of Mansoul.*
BURNS, ROBERT
Robert Burns' humane and lyrical rationalism has had no impact upon the formation of this book, a fact more sinister than any exposed by mere attribution of sources. See also Emerson.
CARLYLE, THOMAS
Chap. 27, para. 5. "I can't believe," etc., is an Implag of the youthful sage of Ecclefechan's query of his mother, "Did God

it because they think willingness to die in a fight is proof of human greatness. There is no suggestion that the war does anything but damage the people who survive it.

"Then there is the Roman book about Aeneas. He leads a group of refugees in search of a peaceful home and spreads agony and warfare along both coasts of the Mediterranean. He also visits Hell but gets out again. The writer of this story is tender toward peaceful homes, he wants Roman success in warfare and government to make the world a peaceful home for everyone, but his last words describe Aeneas, in the heat of battle, killing a helpless enemy for revenge.

"There is the Jewish book about Moses. It's very like the Roman one about Aeneas, so I'll go on to the Jewish book about Jesus. He is a poor man without home or wife. He says he is God's son and calls all men his brothers. He teaches that love is the one great good, and is spoiled by fighting for things. He is crucified, goes to Hell, then to Heaven which (like Aeneas's peaceful world) is outside the scope of the book. Jesus taught that love is the greatest good, and that love is damaged by fighting for things; but if (as the song says) "he died to make us good" he too was a failure. The nations who worshipped him became the greediest conquerors in the world.

"Only the Italian book shows a living man in Heaven. He gets there by following Aeneas and Jesus through Hell, but first loses the woman and the home he loves and sees the ruin of all his political hopes.

"There is the French book about the giant babies. Pleasing themselves is their only law so they drink and excrete in a jolly male family which laughs at everything adults call civilization. Women exist for them, but only as rubbers and ticklers.

"There is the Spanish book about the Knight of the Dolorous Countenance. A poor old bachelor is driven mad by reading the sort of books *you* want to be in, with heroes who triumph here and now. He leaves home and fights peasants and innkeepers for the beauty which is *never* here and now, and is mocked and wounded. On his deathbed he grows sane and warns his friends against intoxicating literature.

"There is the English book about Adam and Eve. This describes a heroic empire-building Satan, an amoral, ironical, boundlessly creative God, a lot of warfare (but no killing) and all centered on a married couple and the state of their house and garden. They disobey the landlord and are evicted, but he promises them accommodation in his own house if they live and die penitently. Once again success is left outside the scope of the book. We are last shown them setting out into a world to raise children they know will murder each other.

"There is the German book about Faust, an old doctor who grows young by witchcraft. He loves, then neglects, a girl who goes mad and kills his baby

Almighty come down and make wheelbarrows in a shop?'' The device of giving a ponderous index to a work of ponderous fiction is taken from *Sartor Resartus.*

CARROLL, LEWIS
Chap. 41, para. 3. The taste of the white rainbow is a Difplag of the taste in the bottle marked "drink me" in *Alice in Wonderland.*

CARY, JOYCE
Chaps. 28 and 29. Difplags of the novel *The Horse's Mouth.* Here and elsewhere Duncan Thaw is a hybrid formed by uniting Gulley Jimson (the Blake-quoting penniless painter of a mural illustrating the biblical Genesis in a derelict church) with his untalented working-class disciple, Nosey Barbon.

CHASE, JAMES HADLEY
Chap. 9, para. 1. Blockplag of first two paragraphs of *No Orchids for Miss Blandish.*

COLERIDGE, SAMUEL TAYLOR
Chap. 41, para. 12. This reference to God, orphans and Hell is a debased Implag of "An orphan's curse would drag to hell/A spirit from on high," from *The Rime of the Ancient Mariner.*
Chap. 26, para. 10. The warmth which gushes in Thaw's chest at the kind sister's words, freeing him from the constriction which came when he prayed God that Marjory be killed, is a difplag of that "spring of love" the Ancient Mariner felt for the watersnakes, and which freed him from the Nightmare Life-in-Death caused by killing the albatross.

CONRAD, JOSEPH
Chap. 41, para. 6. Kodac's speech contains a dispersed Implag of names and nouns from the novel *Nostromo.*

DISNEY, WALT
In Book 3, the transforming of Lanark's arm and the turning of people into dragons is a Difplag of the transformed hero's nose and turning of bad boys into donkeys from the film *Pinocchio.* So is the process of purification by swallowing in the last paragraphs of Chap. 6. (*See also* GOD and JUNG.)

ELIOT, T. S.
Chap. 10, para. 4. "I'm something commonplace that keeps getting hurt" is a drab Difplag of the "notion of some infinitely gentle,/Infinitely suffering thing" in *Preludes.*

EMERSON, RALPH WALDO
Ralph Waldo Emerson has not been plagiarized.

EVARISTI, MARCELLA
Chap. 45, para. 3. "Dont knife the leaf" is from the song *Lettuce Bleeds.*

FITZGERALD, F. SCOTT
Epilogue, para. 1. The sentence "You don't like me" etc. is from McKisco's bedroom dialogue with Rosemary Hoyte in Book 1 of *Tender Is the Night.* Chap. 10, para. 6. "We think a lot of new friends" etc. echoes Dick Diver's remark to Rosemary on the beach.

FREUD, SIGMUND
Difplags in every chapter. Only a writer unhealthily obsessed by all of Dr. Freud's psycho-sexual treatises would stuff a novel with more oral, anal and respiratory symbols, more Oedipal encounters with pleasure-reality/Eros-thanatos substitutes, more recapitulations of the birth-trauma than I have space to summarize. (*See also* DISNEY, GOD and JUNG.)

GLASHAN, JOHN
Chap. 38, para. 13. The snapping noise in Miss Maheen's head is an Implag from the "Snapping Song" from "Earwigs Over the Mountains" sung by the Social Security choir in *The Great Meths Festival.*

GOD
Chap. 6, paras. 11, 12, 13, 14. The purification by swallowing is a Difplag from the verse drama *Jonah.* (*See also* DISNEY and JUNG.)

GOETHE, JOHANN WOLFGANG VON
Chap. 35, para. 1. *"Wer immer strebend"* etc. is from the verse drama *Faust,* angel chorus Act V, Scene VII. Bayard Taylor translates this as "Whoe'er aspires unweariedly is not beyond redeeming"; John Anster as "Him who, unwearied, still strives on/We have the power to save" and Hopton Upcraft as "It's a great life/If you don't weaken."

son. He becomes banker to the emperor, abducts Helen of Troy and has another, symbolic son who explodes. He steals land from peasants to create an empire of his own and finances it by piracy. He abandons everything he tires of, grabs everything he wants and dies believing himself a public benefactor. He is received into a Heaven like the Italian one because 'man must strive and striving he must err' and because 'he who continually strives can be saved.' Yah! The only person in the book who strives is the poor devil, who does all the work and is tricked out of his wages by the angelic choir showing him their bums.[5] The writer of this book was depraved by too much luck. He shows the sort of successful man who captains the modern world, but doesn't show how vilely incompetent these people are. *You* don't need that sort of success.

"It is a relief to turn to the honest American book about the whale. A captain wants to kill it because the last time he tried to do that it bit off his leg while escaping. He embarks with a cosmopolitan crew who don't like home life and prefer this way of earning money. They are brave, skilful and obedient, they chase the whale round the world and get themselves all drowned together: all but the storyteller. He describes the world flowing on as if they had never

5. *"Von hinten anzusehen—Die Racker sind doch gar zu appetitlich"* is little more than a line. Louis MacNeice omits it from his translation as inessential because it reduces the devil's dignity. The author's amazing virulence against Goethe is perhaps a smokescreen to distract attention from what he owes him. *See* GOETHE and WELLS in the Index of Plagiarisms.

existed. There are no women or children in this book, apart from a little black boy whom they accidentally drive mad.

"Then there is the Russian book about war and peace. That has fighting in it, but fighting which fills us with astonishment that men can so recklessly, so resolutely, pester themselves to death. The writer, you see, has fought in real battles and believed some things Jesus taught. This book also contains"—the conjuror's face took on an amazed expression—"several believable happy marriages with children who are well cared for. But I have said enough to show that, while men and women would die out if they didn't usually love each other and keep their homes, most of the world's great stories[6] show them failing spectacularly to do either."

6. The index proves that *Lanark* is erected upon an infantile foundation of Victorian nursery tales, though the final shape derives from English language fiction printed between the 40's and 60's of the present century. The hero's biography after death occurs in Wyndham-Lewis's trilogy *The Human Age,* Flann O'Brien's *The Third Policeman* and Golding's *Pincher Martin.* Modern afterworlds are always infernos, never paradisos, presumably because the modern secular imagination is more capable of debasement than exaltation. In almost every chapter of the book there is a dialogue between the hero (Thaw or Lanark) and a social superior (parent, more experienced friend or prospective employer) about morality, society or art. This is mainly a device to let a self-educated Scot (to whom "the dominie" is the highest form of social life) tell the world what he thinks of it: but the glum flavour of these episodes recalls three books by disappointed socialists which appeared after the second world war and centred upon what I will call dialogue under threat: *Darkness at Noon* by Arthur Koestler, *1984* by George Orwell, and *Barbary Shore* by Norman Mailer. Having said this, one is compelled to

Epilogue, para. 1. "I am part of that part which was once the whole" is an Implag from Mephistopheles' speech in *Faust* Act I, Scene III: *"Ich bin ein Theu des Theus, der Angango alles war."*

GOLDING, WILLIAM
See footnote 6.

GOODMAN, LORD
Chap. 38, para. 9. "Greed isn't a pretty thing but envy is far, far worse" is a slightly diffuse Implag from the speech in which the great company lawyer compared those who fight for dividends with those who fight for wages and declared his moral preference for the former.

GUARDIAN
Chap. 36, para. 8. The newspaper extract is a distorted Blockplag of the financial report from Washington, July 9, 1973.

HEINE, HEINRICH
Chap. 34, para. 5. "screeching, shrieking, yowling, growling, grinding, whining, yammering, skammering, trilling, chirping" etc. contains Implag from the Hellnoise described in Chap. 1 of *Reisebilder* in Leland's translation.

HIND, ARCHIE
Epilogue, para. 14. The disciplines of cattle slaughter and accountancy are dramatized in the novel *The Dear Green Place.*

HOBBES, THOMAS
Books 3 and 4 are Difplags of Hobbes's daemonic metaphor *Leviathan,* which starts with the words "By art is created that great Leviathan called a Commonwealth or State (in Latin, *Civitas*), which is but an artificial man." Describing a state or tribe as a single man is as old as society—Plutarch does it in his life of Coriolanus—but Hobbes deliberately makes the metaphor a monstrous one. His state is the sort of creature Frankenstein made: mechanical yet lively; lacking ideas, yet directed by cunning brains; morally and physically clumsy, but full of strength got from people forced to supply its belly, the market. In a famous title page this state is shown threatening a whole earth with the symbols of warfare and religion. Hobbes named it from the verse drama Job, in which God

describes it as a huge water beast he is specially proud to have made because it is "king of all the children of pride." The author of *The Whale* thought it a relation of his hero. (*See* MELVILLE.)

HOBSBAUM, DR. PHILIP
Chap. 45, paras. 6, 7, 8. The battle between the cloth and wire monkeys is a Difplag of *Monkey Puzzle:*

Wire monkeys are all
    elbows, knees and teeth.
Cloth monkeys can be leant
                        upon.
Wire monkeys endure,
        repel invaders.
Cloth monkeys welcome all
                comers.
They set up wire monkeys to
    test the youngsters' hunger,
Cloth monkeys their loneliness.

Wire monkeys suckle, give food.
Cloth monkeys are barren.

You will see the youngster
    turn to the wire monkey
For sustenance merely
Then go back and embrace
        the cloth monkey
Who affords nothing.

When frightened the youngster
    will bury its head in
            the soft
Warm protruding bosom of the
                    cloth.
The wire monkey stands
    against the blast.
Everyone prefers cloth monkeys.

HUME, DAVID
Chap. 16, para. 9. Blockplag from treatise: *An Enquiry Concerning Human Understanding.*

IBSEN, HENRIK
Books 3 and 4. These owe much to the verse drama *Peer Gynt*, which presents an interplay between a petit-bourgeois universe and supernatural regions which parody and criticise it. (*See also* KAFKA.)

IMPERIAL GAZETTEER OF SCOTLAND, 1871
Chap. 25, para. 1. This is not the simple Blockplag it seems. It unites extracts from the *Monkland Canal* entry and the *Monkland and Kirkintilloch Railway* entry which preceeds that.

JOYCE, JAMES
Chap. 22, para. 5. This monologue by a would-be artist to a

"Which proves," said Lanark, who was eating a salad, "that the world's great stories are mostly a pack of lies." The conjuror sighed and rubbed the side of his face. He said, "Shall I tell you the ending you want? Imagine that when you leave this room and return to the grand salon, you find that the sun has set and outside the great windows a firework display is in progress above the Tuileries garden."

"It's a sports stadium," said Lanark.

"Don't interrupt. A party is in progress, and a lot of informal lobbying is going on among the delegates."

"What is lobbying?"

"Please don't interrupt. You move about discussing the woes of Unthank with whoever will listen. Your untutored eloquence has an effect beyond your expectations, first on women, then on men. Many delegates see that their own lands are threatened by the multinational companies and realize that if something isn't quickly done the council won't be able to help them either. So

ask why the "conjuror" introduces an apology for his work with a tedious and brief history of world literature, as though summarizing a great tradition which culminates in himself! Of the eleven great epics mentioned, only one has influenced *Lanark.* Monboddo's speech in the last part of *Lanark* is a dreary parody of the Archangel Michael's history lecture in the last book of *Paradise Lost* and fails for the same reason. A property is not always valuable because it is stolen from a rich man. And for this single device thieved (without acknowledgement) from Milton we find a confrontation of fictional character by fictional author from Flann O'Brien; a hero, ignorant of his past, in a subfuse modern Hell, also from Flann O'Brien; and, from T. S. Eliot, Nabokov and Flann O'Brien, a parade of irrelevant erudition through grotesquely inflated footnotes.

tomorrow when you stand up in the great assembly hall to speak for your land or city (I haven't worked out which yet), you are speaking for a majority of lands and cities everywhere. The great corporations, you say, are wasting the earth. They have turned the wealth of nations into weapons and poison, while ignoring mankind's most essential needs. The time has come etcetera etcetera. You sit down amid a silence more significant than the wildest applause and the lord president director himself arises to answer you. He expresses the most full-hearted agreement. He explains that the heads of the council have already prepared plans to curb and harness the power of the creature but dared not announce them before they were sure they had the support of a majority. He announces them now. All work which merely transfers wealth will be abolished, all work which damages or kills people will be stopped. All profits will belong to the state, no state will be bigger than a Swiss canton, no politician will draw a larger wage than an agricultural labourer. In fact, all wages will be lowered or raised to the national average, and later to the international average, thus letting people transfer to the jobs they do best without artificial feelings of prestige or humiliation. Stockbrokers, bankers, accountants, property developers, advertisers, company lawyers and detectives will become schoolteachers if they can find no other useful work, and no teacher will have more than six pupils per class. The navy and air forces will be set to providing children everywhere with free meals. The armies will dig irrigation ditches and plant trees. All human excrement will be returned to the land.

tolerant student friend is a crude Difplag of similar monologues in *A Portrait of the Artist as a Young Man.*

JUNG, CARL
Nearly every chapter of the book is a Difplag of the mythic "Night Journey of the Hero" described in that charming but practically useless treatise *Psychology and Alchemy.* This is most obvious in the purification by swallowing at the end of chapter 6. (*See also* DISNEY, GOD and FREUD.) But the hero, Lanark, gains an unJungian political dimension by being swallowed by Hobbes's Leviathan. (*See* HOBBES.)

KAFKA, FRANZ
Chap. 39, last paragraph. The silhouette in the window is from the last paragraph of *The Trial.*

KELMAN, JIM
Chap 47. God's conduct and apology for it is an extended Difplag of the short story *Acid:*

In this factory in the north of England acid was essential. It was contained in large vats.

Gangways were laid above them. Before these gangways were made completely safe a young man fell into a vat feet first. His screams of agony were heard all over the department. Except for one old fellow the large body of men was so horrified that for a time not one of them could move. In an instant this old fellow who was also the young man's father had clambered up and along the gangway carrying a big pole. Sorry Hughie, he said. And then ducked the young man below the surface. Obviously the old fellow had had to do this because only the head and shoulders . . . in fact, that which had been seen above the acid was all that remained of the young man.

KINGSLEY, REVEREND CHARLES
Most of *Lanark* is an extended Difplag of *The Water Babies,* a Victorian children's novel thought unreadable nowadays except in abridged versions. *The Water Babies* is a dual book. The first half is a semi-realistic, highly sentimental account of an encounter between a young chimney sweep from an indus-

trial slum and an upper-class girl who makes him aware of his inadequacies. Emotionally shattered, in a semi-delirious condition, he climbs a moorland, descends a cliff and drowns himself, in a chapter which recalls the conclusion of Book 2. He is then reborn with no memory of the past in a vaguely Darwinian purgatory with Buddhist undertones. At one point the hero, having stolen sweets, grows suspicious, sulky and prickly all over like a seaurchin! The connection with dragonhide is obvious. He is morally redeemed by another encounter with the upper-class girl, who has died of a bad cold, and then sets out on a pilgrimage through a grotesque region filled with the social villainies of Victorian Britain. (*See also* MacDONALD.)

KOESTLER, ARTHUR
See footnote 6.
LAWRENCE, D. H.
See footnote 12.
LEONARD, TOM
Chap. 50, para. 3. "In a wee while, dearie" is an Implag of the poem "The Voyeur."
Chap. 49. General Alexander's requiem for Rima is a Blockplag of the poem "Placenta."
LOCHHEAD, LIZ
Chap. 48, para. 25. The android's discovery by the Goddess is a Difplag of *The Hickie.*

I mouth
sorry in the mirror when I see
the mark I must have
                made just now
loving you.
Easy to say it's alright
adultery
like blasphemy is for
            believers but
even in our
situation simple etiquette
                    says
love should leave us
            both unmarked.
You are on loan to me
            like a library book
and we both know it.
Fine if you love both of us
but neither of us
            must too much show it.

In my misted mirror
you trace two toothprints
on the skin of your
            shoulder and sure
you're almost quick enough

I don't know how Monboddo would propose to start this new system, but I could drown the practical details in storms of cheering. At any rate, bliss it is in this dawn to be alive, and massive sums of wealth and technical aid are voted to restore Unthank to healthy working order. You board your aircraft to return home, for you now think of Unthank as home. The sun also rises. It precedes you across the sky; you appear with it at noon above the city centre. You descend and are reunited with Rima, who has tired of Sludden. Happy ending. Well?"

Lanark had laid down his knife and fork. He said in a low voice, "If you give me an ending like that I will think you a very great man."

"If I give you an ending like that I will be like ten thousand other cheap illusionists! I would be as bad as the late H. G. Wells! I would be worse than Goethe.[7] Nobody who knows a thing about life or politics will believe me for a minute."

Lanark said nothing. The conjuror scratched his hair furiously with both hands and said querulously, "I understand your resentment. When I was sixteen or seventeen *I* wanted an ending like that. You see, I found Tillyard's study of the epic in Dennistoun public library, and he said an epic was only written when a new society was giving men a greater chance of liberty. I decided that what the *Aeneid* had been to the Roman Empire my epic would be to the Scottish Cooperative Wholesale Republic, one of the many hundreds of

7. This remark is too ludicrous to require comment here.

small peaceful socialist republics which would emerge (I thought) when all the big empires and corporations crumbled. That was about 1950. Well, I soon abandoned the idea. A conjuror's best trick is to show his audience a moving model of the world as it is with themselves inside it, and the world is not moving toward greater liberty, equality and fraternity. So I faced the fact that my world model would be a hopeless one. I also knew it would be an industrial-west-of-Scotland-petitbourgeois one, but I didn't think that a disadvantage. If the maker's mind is prepared, the immediate materials are always suitable.

"During my first art school summer holiday I wrote chapter 12 and the mad-vision-and-murder part of chapter 29. My first hero was based on myself. I'd have preferred someone less specialized but mine were the only entrails I could lay hands upon. I worked poor Thaw to death, quite cold-bloodedly, because though based on me he was tougher and more honest, so I hated him. Also, his death gave me a chance to shift him into a wider social context. You are Thaw with the neurotic imagination trimmed off and built into the furniture of the world you occupy.[8] This makes you much more capable of action and slightly more capable of love.

"The time is now"—the conjuror glanced at his wristwatch, yawned and lay back on the pillows—"the time is

8. But the fact remains that the plots of the Thaw and Lanark sections are independent of each other and cemented by typographical contrivances rather than formal necessity. A possible explanation is that the author thinks a heavy book will make a bigger splash than two light ones.

to smile out bright and
                clear for me
as if it was O.K.

Friends again, together in
            this bathroom
we finish washing love away.

McCABE, BRIAN
Chap. 48, para. 2. The Martian headmaster is from the short story *Feathered Choristers*.
MacCAIG, NORMAN
Chap. 48, para. 22. The cursive adder is from the poem *Movements*.
MacDIARMID, HUGH
Chap. 47, para. 22. Major Alexander's remark that "Inadequate maps are better than no maps; at least they show that the land exists" is stolen from *The Kind of Poetry I Want*.
MacDONALD, REVEREND GEORGE
Chap. 17, *The Key*, is a Difplag of the Victorian children's story *The Golden Key*. The journey of Lanark and Rima across the misty plain of Chap. 33 also comes from this story, as does the death and rebirth of the hero halfway through (*see also* KINGSLEY) and the device of casually ageing people with spectacular rapidity in a short space of print.
MacDOUGALL, CARL
Chap. 41, para. 1. *Poxy nungs* is the favourite expletive of the oakumteaser in the colloquial verse drama *A View from the Rooftops*.
McGRATH, TOM
Chap. 48, para. 22. The android's circuitous seduction of God is from the play, *The Android Circuit*.
MacNEACAIL, AONGHAS
See Nicolson, Angus.
MANN, THOMAS
Chap. 34, para. 5. "Screeching, shrieking, yowling, growling, grinding, whining, yammering, stammering, trilling, chirping" etc. contains Implag of the devil's account of Hellnoise in the novel. *Doktor Faustus*, translated by H. T. Lowe-Porter.
MAILER, NORMAN
See footnote 6.
MARX, KARL
Chap. 36, paras. 3 and 4. Grant's long harangue is a Difplag of the pernicious theory of history as class warfare embodied in *Das Kapital*.

MELVILLE, HERMAN
See footnote 12.
MILTON, JOHN
See footnote 6.
MONBODDO, LORD
Chap. 32, para. 3. The reference to James Burnett, Lord Monboddo, demonstrates the weakness of the fabulous and allegorical part of *Lanark.* The "institute" seems to represent that official body of learning which began with the ancient priesthoods and Athenian academies, was monopolized by the Catholic Church and later dispersed among universities and research foundations. But if the "council" represents government, then the most striking union of "council" and "institute" occurred in 1662 when Charles II chartered the Royal Society for the Advancement of the Arts and Sciences. James Burnett of Monboddo belonged to an Edinburgh Corresponding Society which advanced the cause of science quite unofficially until granted a royal charter in 1782. He was a court of session judge, a friend of King George and an erudite metaphysician with a faith in satyrs and mermaids, but has only been saved from oblivion by the animadversions against his theory of human descent from the ape in Boswell's *Life of Johnson.* By plagiarizing and annexing his name to a dynasty of scientific Caesars the author can only be motivated by Scottish chauvinism or a penchant for resounding nomenclature. A more fitting embodiment of government, science, trade and religion would have been Robert Boyle, son of the Earl of Cork and father of modern chemistry. He was founder of the Royal Society, and his strong religious principles also led him to procure a charter for the East India Company, which he expected to propagate Christianity in the Orient.
NicGUMARAID, CATRIONA
Like all lowland Scottish literateurs, the "conjuror" lacks all understanding of his native Gaelic culture. The character and surroundings of the Rev. McPhedron in Chap. 13, the least convincing chapter in the

1970, and although the work is far from finished I see it will be disappointing in several ways. It has too many conversations and clergymen, too much asthma, frustration, shadow; not enough countryside, kind women, honest toil. Of course not many writers describe honest toil, apart from Tolstoy and Lawrence on haymaking, Tressel on housebuilding and Archie Hind on clerking and slaughtering. I fear that the men of a healthier age will think my story a gafuffle of grotesquely frivolous parasites, like the creatures of Mrs. Radcliffe, Tolkien and Mervyn Peake. Perhaps my model world is too compressed and lacks the quiet moments of unconsidered ease which are the sustaining part of the most troubled world. Perhaps I began the work when I was too young. In those days I thought light existed to show things, that space was simply a gap between me and the bodies I feared or desired; now it seems that bodies are the stations from which we travel into space and light itself. Perhaps an illusionist's main job is to exhaust his restless audience by a show of marvellously convincing squabbles until they see the simple things we really depend upon: the movement of shadow round a globe turning in space, the corruption of life on its way to death and the spurt of love by which it throws a new life clear. Perhaps the best thing I could do is write a story in which adjectives like *commonplace* and *ordinary* have the significance which *glorious* and *divine* carried in earlier comedies. What do you think?"

"I think you're trying to make the readers admire your fine way of talking."

"I'm sorry. But yes. Of course," said the conjuror huffily. "You should know by now that I have to butter them up[9] a bit. I'm like God the Father, you see, and you are my sacrificial Son, and a reader is a Holy Ghost who keeps everything joined together and moving along. It doesn't matter how much you detest this book I am writing, you can't escape it before I let you go. But if the readers detest it they can shut it and forget it; you'll simply vanish and I'll turn into an ordinary man. We mustn't let that happen. So I'm taking this opportunity to get all of us agreeing about the end so that we stay together right up to it."

"You know the end I want and you're not allowing it," said Lanark grimly. "Since you and the readers are the absolute powers in this world you need only persuade them. My wishes don't count."

"That *ought* to be the case," said the conjuror, "but unluckily the readers identify with your feelings, not with mine, and if you resent my end too much I am likely to be blamed instead of revered, as I should be. Hence this interview.

"And first I want us all to admit that a long life story cannot end happily. Yes, I know that William Blake sang on his deathbed, and that a president of the French Republic died of heartfailure while fornicating on the office sofa,[10] and that in 1909 a dental patient in Wumbijee, New South Wales, was struck by lightning after receiving a

---

9. In this context to butter up means to flatter. The expression is based upon the pathetic fallacy that because bread tastes sweeter when it is buttered, bread enjoys being buttered.

10. The president in question was Felix Fauré, who died in 1909 upon the conservatory sofa, not office sofa, of the Elysée Palace.

---

book, seem to be an effort to supply that lack. As a touchstone of his failure I print these verses by a real Gael. See also MacNeacail, Aonghas.

Nan robh agam sgian
ghearrainn ás an ubhal
an grodadh donn a th'ann
a leòn's a shàraich mise.

Ach mo chreach-s' mar thà
chan eil mo sgian-sa biorach
's cha dheoghail mi ás nas mò
an loibht' a sgapas annad.

NICOLSON, ANGUS
See Black Angus.

O'BRIEN, FLANN
See footnote 6.

ORWELL, GEORGE
Chap. 38. The poster slogans and the social stability centre are Difplags of the Ingsoc posters and Ministry of Love in *1984.*

PENG, LI
Books 3 and 4. These owe much to *Monkey,* the Chinese comic classic eclectic novel, first Englished by Arthur Waley, which shows the interplay between an earthly pilgrimage and heavenly and hellish supernatural worlds which parody it. (*See also* KAFKA.)

PLATH, SYLVIA
Chap. 10, para. 10. "I will rise with my flaming hair and eat men like air" is an Implag of the last couplet of "Lady Lazarus," with "flaming" substituted for "red."

POE, EDGAR ALLAN
Chap. 8, para. 7. The "large and lofty apartment" is an Implag from the story *The Fall of the House of Usher.* Chap. 38, para. 16. The three long first sentences are Implag from *The Domain of Arnheim.* The substitution of "pearly" pebbles for "alabaster" pebbles comes from Poe's other description of water with *c.* pebbly bottom in *Eleonora.*

POPE, ALEXANDER
Chap. 41, para. 6. Timon Kodac's statement "Order is heaven's first law" is from the poetic *Essay on Man.*

PRINCE, REV. HENRY JAMES
Chap. 43, Monboddo's speech. "Stand with me on the sun" is from *Letters addressed by H. J. Prince to his Christian Brethren at St. David's College, Lampeter.*

PROPPER, DAN

Chap. 28, para. 7. McAlpin's statement of Propper's law is a distorted Implag from *The Fable of the Final Hour:* "In the 34th minute of the final hour the Law of Inverse Enclosure was redis-covered and a matchbox was de-clared the prison of the uni-verse, with two fleas placed inside as warders."

QUINTILIANUS
MARCUS FABRICIUS
Chap. 45, para. 5. Grant's "form of self-expression second only to the sneeze" is an Implag from Book 11 of the *Institutio Oratoria* translated by John Bul-wer in his *Chironomia.*

REICH, WILHELM
Book 3. The dragonhide which infects the first six chapters is a Difplag of the muscular con-striction Reich calls "armour-ing."

REID, TINA
Chap. 48, para. 15. The an-droid's method of cleaning the bed is a Difplag of *Jill the Grip-per* from *Licking the Bed Clean.*

SARTRE, JEAN-PAUL
Chap. 18, para. 6. Chap. 21, para. 12. These are Difplags of the negative epiphanies experi-enced by the hero of *Nausea.*

SAUNDERS,
DONALD GOODBRAND
Chap. 46. The peace-force led by Sergeant Alexander is blocked by God in a land whose shapes and colours come from *Ascent:*

The white shape is Loch Fionn,
Intimate with corners.
From here, the foothills
　　　　　　of Suilven,
The white shape is Loch Fionn.

The green shape is Glencanisp,
Detailed with rocks,
From here, the shoulder
　　　　　　of Suilven,
The green shape is Glencanisp.

The blue shape is the seas.
The blue shape is the skies.
From here, the summit
　　　　　　of Suilven,
My net returns glittering.

SHAKESPEARE, WILLIAM
Books 1 and 2 owe much to the play *Hamlet* in which heavy pa-ternalism forces a weak-minded youth into dread of existence, hallucinations and crime.

SITWELL, EDITH
Chap. 41, para. 12. "Speaking

dose of laughing gas.[11] The God of the real world can be believed when such things happen, but no serious enter-tainer dare conjure them up in print. We can fool people in all kinds of elabo-rate ways, but our most important things must seem likely and the likeliest death is still to depart this earth in a 'fiery-pain-chariot' (as Carlyle put it), or to drift out in a stupefied daze if there's a good doctor handy. But since the dis-maying thing about death is loneliness, let us thrill the readers with a descrip-tion of you ending *in company.* Let the ending be worldwide, for such a calam-ity is likely nowadays. Indeed, my main fear is that humanity will perish before it has a chance to enjoy my forecast of the event. It will be a metaphorical ac-count, like Saint John's, but nobody will doubt what's happening. Attend!

"When you leave this room you will utterly fail to contact any helpful officials or committees. Tomorrow, when you speak to the assembly, you will be applauded but ignored. You will learn that most other regions are as bad or even worse than your own, but that does not make the leaders want to coop-erate: moreover, the council itself is maintaining its existence with great dif-ficulty. Monboddo can offer you noth-ing but a personal invitation to stay in

11. The township of Wumbijee is in southern Queensland, not new South Wales, and even at the present moment in time (1976) is too small to support a local dentist. In 1909 it did not exist. The laughing gas incident is therefore probably apocryphal but, even if true, gives a facetious slant to a serious statement of principle. It will leave the readers (whom the author pre-tends to cherish) uncertain of what to think about his work as a whole.

Provan. You refuse and return to Unthank, where the landscape is tilted at a peculiar angle, rioters are attacking the clock towers and much of the city is in flame. Members of the committee are being lynched, Sludden has fled, you stand with Rima on the height of the Necropolis watching flocks of mouths sweep the streets like the shadows of huge birds, devouring the population as they go. Suddenly there is an earthquake. Suddenly the sea floods the city, pouring down through the mouths into the corridors of council and institute and short-circuiting everything. (That sounds confusing; I haven't worked out the details yet.) Anyway, your eyes finally close upon the sight of John Knox's statue—symbol of the tyranny of the mind, symbol of that protracted male erection which can yield to death but not to tenderness—toppling with its column into the waves, which then roll on as they have rolled for . . . a very great period. How's that for an ending?"

"Bloody rotten," said Lanark. "I haven't read as much as you have, I never had the time, but when I visited public libraries in my twenties *half* the science-fiction stories had scenes like that in them,[12] usually at the end. These banal world destructions prove nothing but the impoverished minds of those who can think of nothing better."

The conjuror's mouth and eyes opened wide and his face grew red. He began speaking in a shrill whisper which swelled to a bellow: *"I am not writing*

12. Had Lanark's cultural equipment been wider, he would have seen that this conclusion owed more to *Moby Dick* than to science fiction, and more to Lawrence's essay on *Moby Dick* than to either.

purely as a private person," and much of the religious sentiment, are Im- and Difplag from the section of *Facade* which starts "Don't go bathing in the Jordan, Gordon."

SMITH, W. C.
Chap. 28. Blockplag from hymn "Immortal, Invisible, God Only Wise" with distorted final line.

SPENCE, ALAN
Chap. 45, para. 9. The fine colours are taken from the anthology *Its Colours They Are Fine.*

THACKERAY, WILLIAM MAKEPEACE
Chap. 11, para. 5. The bag and listed contents are a Plag, Block- and Dif-, from the Fairy Blackstick's bag in *The Rose and the Ring.*

THOMAS, DYLAN
Chap. 29, para. 5. Contains small Implag and Difplag from the prose poem "The Map of Love." Chap. 42, para. 5. Lanark's words when urinating are a distorted Implag of the poem "Said the Old Ramrod."

TOTUOLA, AMOS
Books 3 and 4. These owe much to *The Palm Wine Drinkard,* another story whose hero's quest brings him among dead or supernatural beings living in the same plane as the earthly. (*See also* KAFKA.)

TURNER, BILL PRICE
Chap. 46, para. 1. "The sliding architecture of the waves" is from *Rudiment of an Eye.*

URE, JOAN
Chap. 48, para. 8. The batman's wife is singing her own version of the song in the review *Something may come of it:* "Nothing to sing about/getting along/very pedestrianly./People in aeroplanes/singing their song/continue to fly over me./Something they've got that I've not?/Something I've got that they've not?/Nothing to sing about./Nothing to sing about."

VONNEGUT, KURT
Chap. 43, Monboddo's speech. The description of the earth as a "moist blue-green ball" is from the novel *Breakfast of Champions.*

WADDEL, REVEREND P. HATELY
Chap. 37, para. 4. The overheard prayer is from Rev. Waddel's lowland Scottish translation of Psalm 23.

science fiction! Science-fiction stories have no real people in them, and all my characters are real, real, real people! I may astound my public by a dazzling deployment of dramatic metaphors designed to compress and accelerate the action, but that is not science, it is magic! Magic! As for my ending's being banal, wait till you're inside it. I warn you, my whole imagination has a carefully reined-back catastrophist tendency; you have no conception of the damage my descriptive powers will wreak when I loose them on a theme like THE END."

"What happens to Sandy?" said Lanark coldly.

"Who's Sandy?"

"My son."

The conjuror stared and said, "You have no son."

"I have a son called Alexander who was born in the cathedral."

The conjuror, looking confused, grubbed among the papers on his bed and at last held one up, saying, "Impossible, look here. This is a summary of the nine or ten chapters I haven't written yet. If you read it you'll see there's no time for Rima to have a baby in the cathedral. She goes away too quickly with Sludden."

"When you reach the cathedral," said Lanark coldly, "you'll describe her having a son more quickly still."

The conjuror looked unhappy. He said, "I'm sorry. Yes, I see the ending becomes unusually bitter for you. A child. How old is he?"

"I don't know. Your time goes too fast for me to estimate."

After a silence the conjuror said querulously, "I can't change my overall plan

now. Why should I be kinder than my
century? The millions of children
who've been vilely murdered this century is—*don't hit me!"*

Lanark had only tensed his muscles but
the conjuror slid down the bed and
pulled the covers over his head; they
subsided until they lay perfectly flat on
the mattress. Lanark sighed and dropped his face into his hand. A little voice
in the air said, "Promise not to be violent."

Katrina Veronica Margaret Inge
Inge Inge Inge Inge Inge Inge
Inge Inge Inge Inge Inge Inge
Inge Inge Inge Inge Inge Marian
Beth Liz Betty Daniele Angel
TinaJanetKate; the final descent
to healthy commonplace and
finding a silk smooth you inside
that husk are Blockplags, Im-
plags, Difplags of *The Marriage
of Heaven and Hell* translated
into clear images and sublime
distances by William Blake and
William Turner for the benefit
of all makers of useful and
lovely things.

Lanark snorted contemptuously. The bedclothes swelled up in
a man-shaped lump but the conjuror did not emerge. A muffled
voice under the clothes said, "I didn't need to play that trick.
In a single sentence I could have made you my most obsequious
admirer, but the reader would have turned against both of
us. . . . I wish I could make you like death a little more. It's
a great preserver. Without it the loveliest things change slowly
into farce, as you will discover if you insist on having much
more life. But I refuse to discuss family matters with you. Take
them to Monboddo. Please go away."

"Soon after I came here," said Lanark, lifting the briefcase
and standing up, "I said talking to you was a waste of time.
Was I wrong?"

He walked to the door and heard mumbling under the bedclothes. He said, "What?"

". . . know a black man called Multan . . ."

"I've heard his name. Why?"

". . . might be useful. Sudden idea. Probably not."

Lanark walked round the painting of the chestnut tree, opened
the door and went out.[13]

13. As this "Epilogue" has performed the office of an introduction to the
work as a whole (the so-called "Prologue" being no prologue at all, but
a separate short story), it is saddening to find the "conjuror" omitting
the courtesies appropriate to such an addendum. Mrs. Florence Allan typed
and retyped his manuscripts, and often waited many months without payment
and without complaining. Professor Andrew Sykes gave him free access
to copying equipment and secretarial help. He received from James Kelman
critical advice which enabled him to make smoother prose of the crucial
first chapter. Charles Wild, Peter Chiene, Jim Hutcheson, Stephanie Wolf
Murray engaged in extensive lexical activity to ensure that the resulting
volume had a surface consistency. And what of the compositors employed
by Kingsport Press of Kingsport, Tennessee, to typeset this bloody book?
Yet these are only a few out of thousands whose help has not been acknowl-
edged and whose names have not been mentioned.

CHAPTER 41. Climax

He looked down, startled, at Libby, who lay curled with her
legs under her in the angle between wall and carpet looking
unconscious. She was a gracefully plump, dark-haired girl. Her
skirt was shorter and blouse silkier than he remembered, and
her sulky slumbering face looked far more childish than the
clothes. She opened her eyes saying "What?" and sat up and
glanced at her wristwatch. Without blame she said, "You've
been hours in there. Hours and hours. We've missed the opera."

She held out a hand and he helped her up. She said, "Did
he feed you?"

"He did. Now I would like to speak to Wilkins."

"Wilkins?"

"Or Monboddo. On second thought, I would prefer to see
Monboddo. Is that possible?"

She stared at him and said, "Do you never relax? Don't you
ever enjoy yourself?"

"I did not come here to relax."

"Sorry I asked."

She walked down the corridor. He followed, saying, "Listen, if I'm being rude I apologize, but I'm very worried just
now. And anyway, I've always been bad at enjoying myself."

"Poor old you."

"I'm not complaining," said Lanark defensively. "Some very
nice things have happened to me, even so."

"When, for instance?"

Lanark remembered when Sandy was born. He knew he must
have been happy then or he wouldn't have rung the cathedral
bell, but he couldn't remember what happiness felt like. His

past suddenly seemed a very large, very dreary place. He said tiredly, "Not long ago."

In the hall beside the lift doors she halted, faced him and said firmly, "I don't know where Monboddo and Wilkins are just now. I expect they'll drop in later when the party starts, so I'll give you some advice. Play it gelid. I see you've got it bad, Dad, but the hard sell is no go on day one when everybody's casing each other. The real hot lobbyists start cashing their therms halfway through countdown on day two. And there's something else I'd like to tell you. The Provan executive pays my salary whether I stay with you or not. If you want me to vanish say 'vanish' and I'll vanish. Or else come for a quiet drink with me and talk about *anything* but this general bloody awful assembly. Even their language gives me the poxy nungs."

Lanark stared at her, seeing how attractive she was. The sight was a great pain. He knew that if she let him kiss her petulant mouth he would feel no warmth or excitement. He looked inside himself and found only a hungry ungenerous cold, a pained emptiness which could neither give nor take. He thought, 'I am mostly a dead man. How did this happen?' He muttered, "Please don't vanish."

She took his arm and led him toward the gallery saying slyly, "I bet I know one thing you enjoy."

"What?"

"Bet you enjoy being famous."

"I'm not."

"Modest, eh?"

"No, but I'm not famous either."

"Think I'd have waited all these hours outside Nastler's door if you'd been an ordinary delegate?"

Lanark was too confused to answer. He pointed to a silent crowd of black-suited security men on each side of the glass door and said, "What are they doing here?"

"They're staying outside to make the party less spooky."

Though nearly empty the gallery throbbed with light rhythmical music. In the night sky outside the window the pink-tipped petals of several great chrysanthemums were spreading out from golden centres among the stars and dipping down toward the floodlit stadium where tiny figures thronged the terraces and crowded upon dance floors, one at each end of the central field. The chrysanthemums faded and a scarlet spark shot through them, drawing a long tail of white and green dazzling feathers. The floor along the window was furnished with piles of huge coloured cushions. The floor above that had a twelve-man orchestra at one end, though at present the only player was a clarinettist blowing a humorous little tune and a drummer softly stroking the cymbals with wire brushes. The floor above that had four well-laden buffets along it, and the top floor had many empty little chairs and tables, and a bar at each end, and four girls sitting on stools by one of the bars. Libby led Lanark over to them and said, "Martha, Solveig, Joy and the other Joy, this is you-know-who from Unthank." Martha said, "It can't be."

Solveig said, "You look far too respectable."

Joy said, "Shall I put your briefcase behind the bar? It'll be safe there."

The other Joy said, "My mother is a friend of yours, or says she used to be."

"Is she called Nancy?" said Lanark glumly, handing over the briefcase and sitting down. "Because if she is I met you when you were a baby."

"No, she's called Gay."

"Don't remind him of his age," said Libby. "Be a mother yourself and mix us two white rainbows. (She's good at white rainbows.)"

Solveig was the largest of the girls and the other Joy was the smallest. They were all about the same age and had the same casually friendly manners. Lanark was not very conscious of them as distinct people but he was soothed by being the only man among them. Libby said, "We've got to persuade Lanark that he's famous."

They all laughed and the other Joy, who was measuring drops of liquor into a silver canister, said, "But he knows. He must know."

"What am I famous for?" said Lanark.

"You're the man who does these weird, weird things for no reason at all," said Martha. "You smashed Monboddo's telescreen when he was conducting a string quartet."

"You fought with him over a dragon-bitch and blocked the whole current of the institute," said Solveig.

"You told him exactly what you thought of him and walked straight out of the council corridors into an intercalendrical zone. On foot!" said Joy.

"We're mad keen to see what you do tonight," said the other Joy. "Monboddo's terrified of you."

Lanark started explaining how things had really happened, but the corners of his mouth had risen and were squeezing out his cheeks and narrowing his eyes; he could not help his face being contorted, his tongue gagged by a huge silly grin, and at last he shook his head and laughed. Libby laughed too. She was leaning on the bar, her hip brushing his thigh. Martha told him, "Libby's using you to make her boyfriend jealous."

"No I'm not. Well, just a bit, I am."

"Who's your boyfriend?" asked Lanark, smiling.

"The man with the glasses down there. The drummer. He's horrible. When his music isn't going right for him nothing goes right for him."

"Make him as jealous of me as you like," said Lanark, patting her hand. The other Joy gave him a tall glass of clear drink and they all watched him closely as he sipped. The first sip tasted soft and furry, then cool and milky, then thin and piercing like peppermint, then bitter like gin, then thick and warm like chocolate, then sharp like lemon but sweetening like lemonade. He sipped again and the flow of tastes over his tongue was wholly different, for the tip tasted black currant, blending into a pleasant kind of children's cough mixture in the centre and becoming like clear beef gravy as it entered the throat, with a faint aftertaste of smoked oysters. He said, "The taste of this makes no sense."

"Don't you like it?"

"Yes, it's delicious."

They laughed as if he'd said something clever. Solveig said, "Will you dance with me when the music starts?"

"Of course."

"What about me?" said Martha.

"I intend to dance once with everybody—except the other Joy. I'm going to dance twice with the other Joy."

"Why?"

"Because being unusually kind to someone will give me a feeling of power."

Everyone laughed again and he sipped the drink feeling worldly and witty. A small man with a large nose arrived and said, "You all seem to be having a good time, do you mind if I join in? I'm Griffith-Powys, Arthur Griffith-Powys of Ynyswitrin. Lanark of Unthank, aren't you? I only just missed you this morning, but I heard you'd been hard at it. It was good to know somebody was knocking the gelid lark. We've had too much of that. You'll be sounding off loud and clear tomorrow, I hope?"

The gallery was filling with older people who were clearly
delegates or delegates' wives, and others in their thirties who
seemed to be secretaries and journalists. There were more red
girls too, though few of them now wore the whole red uniform.
Groups were forming but the group round Lanark was the
largest. Odin, the pink-faced morose man, came over and asked,
"Any luck with His Royal Highness?"
"None. In fact he said he wasn't a king at all but a conjuror."
"Young people must find the modern world very confusing,"
said Powys, patting Martha's arm paternally. "So many single
people have different names and so many different people have
the same name. Look at Monboddo. We've all known at least
two Monboddos and the next one will likely be a woman.
Look at me! Last year I was Arch Druid of Camelot and Cad-
bury. This year, what with ecumenical pressure and regionaliza-
tion, I'm Proto-Presbyter of Ynyswitrin, yet I'm the same man
doing the same job."
Odin said in a low voice, "Here comes the enemy."
Five black men of different heights entered, two in business
suits, two in military uniform and the tallest in caftan and fez.
Martha shivered and said, "I hate the black bloc—they drink
nothing stronger than lemonade."
"Well, I *love* them," said Libby stoutly. "I think they're charming. And Senator Sennacherib drinks whisky by the quart."
"What I can't take is bloody Multan's air of superiority," said
Odin. "I know we sold and flogged his ancestors, which proves
we're vicious; but it doesn't prove he's much good."
"Is that Multan?" said Lanark. The blacks had descended to
the next floor and were standing at one of the buffets. "Excuse
me a minute," said Lanark. He passed quickly through the
other groups, descended three or four steps and approached
the black bloc. "Please," he said to the tall man in the fez,
"are you Multan of Zimbabwe?"
"Here is General Multan," said the tall man, indicating a small
man in military uniform. Lanark said, "May I speak to you,
General Multan? I've been told you . . . we might be able
to help each other."
Multan regarded Lanark with an expression of polite amuse-
ment. He said, "Who told you that, man?"
"Nastler."
"Don't know this Nastler. How does he say we be useful?"
"He didn't, but my own region—Greater Unthank—is having
trouble with—well, many things. Almost everything. Is yours?"
"Oh, sure. Our plains are overgrazed, our bush is underculti-

vated, our minerals are owned by foreigners, the council sends us airplanes, tanks and bulldozers and our revenues go to Algolagnics and Volstat to buy fuel and spare parts to work them. Oh, yes, we got problems."

"Oh."

"I don't expect help from your sort, man, but I listen hard to anything you say."

Multan held a plate of sweet corn and chopped meat in one hand and ate delicately with the other for a minute or two, closely watching Lanark, who could now hear the dance orchestra playing very loudly, for the nearest groups had fallen silent and an attentive and furtive murmuring came from the rest of the gallery. Lanark felt his face blush hotter and hotter.

Multan said, "Why you go on standing there if you got nothing to say?"

"Embarrassment," said Lanark in a low voice. "I started this conversation and I don't know how to end it."

"Let me help you off the hook, man. Come here, Omphale." A tall elegant black woman approached. Multan said, "Omphale, this delegate needs to talk to a white woman."

"But I'm black. As black as you are," said the woman in a clear, hooting voice.

"Sure, but you got a white voice," said Multan, moving away. Lanark and the woman stared at each other then Lanark said, "Would you care to dance?"

"No," said the woman and followed Multan.

Suddenly, on a note of laughter, all the conversations started loudly again. Lanark turned, blushing, and saw the two Joys laughing at him openly. They said "Poor Lanark!" and "Why did he leave the friends who love him?" Each linked an arm with him and led him down steps to a side of the dance floor where Odin, Powys, the other girls and some new arrivals had gathered. They received him so genially that it was easy to smile again.

"I could have told you it was useless talking to that bastard," said Odin. "Have a cigar."

"But wasn't it exciting?" said Libby. "Everybody expected something gigantic to happen. I don't know what."

"The opening of a new intercontinental viaduct, perhaps," said Powys jocularly. "The unrolling across the ocean of a fraternal carpet on which all the human races could meet and sink into one human race and get Utopia delivered by parachute with their morning milk, no?"

"Congratulations! You've done something rather fine," said

Wilkins, shaking his hand. "The rebuff doesn't matter. What counts is that you put the ball fair and square into their arena *and* they know it. One of you girls should get this man a drink."

"Wilkins, I want to talk to you," said Lanark.

"Yes, the sooner the better. There are one or two unexpected developments we must discuss. Shall we breakfast together first thing tomorrow at the delegates' repose village?"

"Certainly."

"You don't mind rising early?"

"Not at all."

"Good. I'll buzz your room before seven, then."

"Please, sir," said Solveig very meekly, "please can I have the dance you promised me earlier, please, please?"

"In a wee while, dearie. Let me finish my drink first," said Lanark kindly.

As he sipped a second white rainbow he looked out at the starry field of the sky where rockets bloomed, tinting thousands of upturned faces in the stadium beneath with purple, white, orange and greenish-gold. He was leaning on a rail guarding the drop to the lowest and narrowest floor and he also saw in the window a dark distinct reflection of himself, the captainish centre of a company standing easily in midair under the flashing fireworks and above the crowd. He nodded down at the people below and thought, 'Tomorrow I will defend you all.' He brought the cigar to his lips, turned round and carefully surveyed the gallery. His group was still the largest, though Wilkins had left it and was moving among the others. Lanark even saw him pause for a word with Multan. He thought tolerantly, 'I must keep my eye on that fellow; he's a fox, an ecological fox of the first water. . . . Fox? Ecological? First water? I don't usually think in words like these but they seem appropriate here. Yes, tomorrow I will talk to Wilkins. There will be some shrewd bargaining but no compromise. No compromise. I'll play it by ear. I'll play it hot, gelid, dirty, depending on how he deals the deck. I'll cash every therm in my suit, and then some, but no compromise! If a region's to be thrown to the crocodiles it won't be Unthank; upon that I am resolved. Monboddo is afraid of me: understandably. The hell with the standings, the top rung is up for grabs! All bets are off, the odds are cancelled, it's anybody's ballgame! The horses are all drugged, the track is glass . . . what is happening to my vocabulary? This cigar is intoxicating. Good thing I noticed: stub it out, stay calm, sip your drink. . . . I know why this is called a white rainbow. It's clear like water, yet on the tongue it spreads out into all the tastes on an artist's peacock palette (badly put). It contains as many tastes as there are colours in the mother of pearly stuff lining an abalone seashell. Poetry. Shall I tell the other Joy? She mixed this drink, she's standing over there, what a clever attractive little . . . I used to prefer big women but . . . oh, if my hand were between her small . . .'

"I am pleased to encounter you, sir," said a quiet, bald man with rimless spectacles, shaking Lanark's hand. "Kodac, Timon Kodac of South Atlantis. God knows why they chose me as a delegate. My true field is research, for Algolagnics. But it's nice to visit other continents. My mother's people hailed from Unthank."

Lanark nodded and thought, 'She is smiling at me just as Libby smiled. I thought Libby meant to seduce me but she had a boyfriend. All young attractive healthy girls have young attractive healthy boyfriends. I've heard that young girls prefer older men, but I've never seen it.'

"That's a very good woman you've got," said Kodac.

Lanark stared at him. Kodac said, "That little old professor. What's her name? Schtzngrm. That was quite a report she sent to the council. You know, the preliminary report with the Permian deep pollution samples. It made us sit up, in Algolagnics, when we got word of it. Oh, yes, we have our sources."

Lanark smiled, nodded and sipped. He thought, 'Surely her face is making me smile at her? It's so merry and intelligent, so quick to be surprised and amused. I will smile, but not much. A leader should be an audience, not a performer. His crowd should feel he is noticing, assessing, appreciating them, but from a position of strength.'

Kodac said, "Of course what interests us is her *final* report, giving the locations. I believe you are seeing Wilkins tomorrow. He's a very, very shrewd man, best man the council owns. We have a lot of respect for Wilkins at Algolagnics. So far we've always been one or two paces ahead of him, but it's been a hassle. By the way, a lot of us in Algolagnics feel Unthank has had a pretty raw deal from the council. It doesn't surprise us that you and Sludden are taking an independent line. More power to you! And speaking unofficially, I know these are also the sentiments of the Tunc-Quidative and Quantum-Cortexin clusters. But I suppose they've told you that?"

Lanark nodded gravely and thought, 'If she knew what her odd, thoroughly alive young face makes me feel, and how I

envy the seam in her jeans which goes down over her stomach
and over the little mound between the thighs and through
and up between behind . . . if she knew how much less than
a leader I am, I would bore her. I must give her the same
smile I am giving this bald man who is hinting something:
the knowing smile which tells them I know more than they
know I know.'

"Hey!" said Kodac chuckling. "See that little tulip watching
you over there? Bet you she would go like a bomb. Yes, I'm
sure Wilkins is just wild to get his hands on that final report
of yours. If he knows it exists. Does he?"

Lanark stared at him. Kodac laughed, patted Lanark's shoulder
and said, "A straight question at last, eh? I'm sorry, but though
government and industry are interlocking we ain't *fully* interlocking. Not yet. We support each other because order is Heav-
en's first law, but remember Costaguana? Remember when the
Occidental Republic split off from it? That could never have
happened without our support. Of course we weren't called
Algolagnics then; that was in the time of the old Material Interests Corporation. Boy, what a gang of pirates *they* were! And
the mineral was silver, which doesn't thrust as hard as a certain
other mineral, you follow?"

Lanark smiled bitterly and thought, 'The only feeling she gives
me is stony pain, the pain of being slightly alive in a pot-bellied
old body with thinning hair. But leaders need to be mostly
dead. People want solid monuments to cling to, not confused
men like themselves. Sludden was wise to send me. *I* can never
melt.'

"Your glass is empty," said Kodac, taking it. "I'll find a girl
to fill it; I need a drink myself."

"Don't be nasty to me, Lanark," said the other Joy, smiling
in front of him. "You promised me two dances, remember?
Surely you can give me one?"

Without waiting for a reply she drew him out among the dancers.

        Bitterness fell from him. The firm bracelet of her fingers
round his wrist gave lightness and freedom. He laughed and
held her waist, saying, "And Gay is your mother? Has the
wound in her hand healed?"

"Was she ever wounded? She never tells me anything."

"What does she do nowadays?"

"She's a journalist. Let's not talk about her; surely I'm enough
for you?"

Holding her was hard, at first, for the music was so quick and jerky that the other men and women danced without touching each other. Lanark danced to the slower sound of the whole room, whose main noise was conversation. Heard all together the conversations sounded like a waterfall blattering into a pool and made the orchestra seem the chirping of excited insects. At first the other dancers collided with him but later they moved to the side of the floor and stood cheering and clapping. The orchestra lapsed raggedly into silence and the other Joy broke away and ran into the crowd. He followed her through laughter to his group and found her talking vigorously to the other girls. She faced him and asked, "Was that not nearly incest?"

He stared at her. She said, "You are my father, aren't you?"

"Oh, no! Sludden is. Probably."

"Sludden? My mother never tells me anything. Who is Sludden? Is he successful? Is he good-looking?"

Lanark said gently, "Sludden is a very successful man, and women find him very attractive. Or used to. But I don't want to talk about him tonight."

He turned sadly away and looked at the crowded gallery where the dancing had resumed. On the faces of all these strangers he saw such familiar expressions of worry, courage, happiness, resignation, hope and failure that he felt he had known them all his life, yet they had surprising variety. Each seemed a world with its own age, climate and landscape. One was fresh and springlike, another rich, hot and summery. Some were mildly or stormily autumnal, some tragically bleak and frozen. Someone was standing by his side and her company let him admire these worlds peacefully, without wanting to conquer or enter them. He heard her sigh and say, "I wish you were more careful," and he turned and saw Lady Monboddo. Her face looked younger, more solemn and lonely than he remembered. Her breasts were bigger and a floor-length gown of stiff tapestry patterned with lions and unicorns gave her a pillar-like look. Lanark said gladly, "Catalyst!"

"That was my job, not my name. I think you should leave this place and go to bed, Lanark."

"I would, if I could go with you," said Lanark, placing an arm round her waist. She frowned at him as though his face was a page she was trying to read. He withdrew his arm awkwardly and said, "I'm sorry if I'm greedy, but I don't think these little girls like me much. And you and I were nearly very good friends once."

"Yes. We could have done anything we liked together. But you ran away to a dragon-bitch."

"But good came of it!" said Lanark eagerly. "She didn't stay a dragon long and we have a son now. He's very tall and healthy for his age, and seems intelligent too, and may be quite a kind person when he grows up."

She still stared at his face as if trying to read it. He looked away, saying uncomfortably, "Don't worry about me. I'm not drunk, if that's what you're thinking."

When he looked back she had gone and Martha stood there offering a glass and saying, "I mixed this one. It doesn't taste very nice but it's strong. Please, sir, will it soon be time for me to dance with you?"

"Why do you girls keep replacing each other?" said Lanark moodily, "I've had no time to know any of you yet."

"We think a lot of new friends can have more fun together than a pair of old friends."

"So when will you leave me?"

"Maybe I'll stay with you. Tonight," said Martha, looking at him unsmilingly.

"Maybe!" said Lanark sceptically, and drank.

At first the taste was sickly sweet and then so appallingly bitter that he gulped it hastily. Somewhere he could hear Powys saying ". . . wants the council to ban the manufacture of footwear, because the earth, you see, is like the body of a mother, and direct contact with her keeps us healthy and sane. He says the recent increase in warfare and crime is caused by composition rubber shoe soles which insulate us from the cthonic current and leave us a prey to the lunar current. Once I would have laughed, of course, but modern science is reinstating so much that we regarded as superstition. It seems that hedgehogs really *do* suck the teats of cows. . . ."

Lanark was lying outspread on cushions upon the lowest floor of all. Someone had removed his shoes and his feet gently explored the softer parts of a silk-clad body. His cheek lay on another one, each hand was snug between a pair of canvas-covered thighs and someone caressed his neck. The sounds of the gallery and orchestra were subdued and distant but he could hear two people talking high above his head.

"It's nice to see women combining to make a man feel famous."

"Drivel. They're making him a sot."

"I believe he comes from a region where coitus is often reached through stupefaction."

"And just as often missed."

"I hate these voices," said Lanark. There was whispering and he was gently raised and helped forward. A door closed somewhere and all noises stopped.

He said loudly, "I am walking . . . along a corridor."

Someone whispered, "Open your eyes."

"No. Touch tells me you are near me but eyes talk about the space between."

Another door closed and he lay down among whispers like falling leaves and felt his clothes removed. Someone whispered "Look!" and he opened his eyes long enough to meet a thin-lipped small smiling mouth in a glade of dark hair. Softly, sadly, he revisited the hills and hollows of a familiar landscape, the sides of his limbs brushing sweet abundances with surprisingly hard tips, his endings paddling in the pleats of a wet wound which opened into a boggy cave where little moans bloomed like violets in the blackness. There were dank odours and even a whiff of dung. Losing his way he lay on his back feeling that he too was a landscape, a dull flat one surrounding a tower sticking up into a dark and heavy sky. In the darkness above he felt people climbing off and onto his tower and swinging there with rhythmical gasps or shrieks. He hoped they were enjoying themselves and was glad of the company, and he kissed and caressed to show this; then everything turned over and he was the heavy sky pressing the tower into the land below, yet he felt increasingly lost, knowing the tower could stand for hours and never fire a gun. Someone whispered, "Won't you give yourself?"

"I can't. Half my strength is locked in fear and hatred."

"Why?"

"I don't remember."

"How would you like to show it?"

"I would like to . . . I can't say. You'd be disgusted."

"Tell us."

"I would like . . . I can't tell you. You would laugh."

"Risk it."

"I want you to hate and fear me too, but be unable to escape. I want you captured and bound, and waiting helplessly in perfect dread for the slash of my whip, the touch of my branding iron. And then, at the climax of your terror, what enters you is simply naked me—ah! You would have . . . to . . . be . . . de . . . lighted. Then."

The land and foundation melted and he was thrusting, biting, grunting and clutching among squealing jelly meats like a carnivorous pig with fingers. Later on, feeling expended, he lay again in kindness gently rooting in soft clefts, rocking and drifting on smoothness, afloat and basking in softness. He clasped a waist, his penis nestled between two gentle mounds and he was filled with kind nowhere.

He was knee-deep in a cold quick little burn gurgling over big rounded stones, some black, some grey, some speckled like oatmeal. He was tugging some of the stones out and carefully flinging them onto the bank a yard or two upstream where Alexander, about ten years old, very brown, and wearing red underpants, was building a dam with them. The hot sun on Lanark's neck, the chill water round his legs, the ache in his back and shoulders suggested he had been doing this for a long time. He hauled out an extra large black and dripping boulder, heaved it into the heather, then climbed up and lay flat on his back beside it, breathing hard. He closed his eyes against the profound blue and the dazzle came hot dark red through his lids. He could hear the water and the click of stones. Alexander said, "This water keeps getting through."
"Plug the holes with moss and gravelly stuff."
"I don't believe in God, you know," said Alexander.
Lanark blinked sideways and watched him wrenching clods from the bank. He said, "Oh?"
"He doesn't exist. Grampa told me."
"Which Grampa? Everyone has two."
"The one who fought in France in the first war. Give me a lot of that moss."
Without sitting up Lanark plucked handfuls from a dank mossy cushion nearby and chucked them lazily over. Alexander said, "The first war was the most interesting, I think, even though it had no Hitler or atomic bombs. You see, it mostly happened in one place, and it killed more soldiers than the second war."
"Wars are only interesting because they show how stupid we can be."
"Say that sort of thing as much as you like," said Alexander amiably, "but it won't change me. Anyway, Grampa says there isn't a God. People invented him."
"They invented motorcars too, and there are motorcars."
"That's nothing but words. . . . Shall we go for a walk? I can show you Rima, if you like."
Lanark sighed and said, "All right, Sandy."
He stood up while Alexander climbed out of the burn. Their clothes lay on a flat rock and they had to shake small red ants

off them before dressing. Alexander said, "Of course my real name is Alexander."

"What does Rima call you?"

"Alex, but my *real* name is Alexander."

"I'll try to remember that."

"Good."

They walked down the burn to a place where it vanished into a dip in the moor. Lanark saw it fall from his feet down a reddish rock into a pool at the head of a deep glen full of bushes and trees, mostly birch, rowan and small oaks. A couple, partly screened by the roots of a fallen mountain ash, lay on some grass beside the pool. The woman seemed asleep and Lanark saw more of the man, who was reading a newspaper. He said, "That isn't Sludden."

"No, that's Kirkwood. We don't see Sludden nowadays."

"Why not?"

"Sludden became too dependent."

"Kirkwood isn't?"

"Not yet."

"Sandy, do you think Rima would like to see me?"

Alexander looked uncertainly into the glen, then pointed the other way saying, "Wouldn't you like to walk with me to the top of that hill?"

"Yes. I would."

They turned and walked uphill toward a distant green summit. Alexander flung himself down for a rest at the top of the first slope and did the same thing halfway up the next. Soon he was resting for two minutes every minute or two. Lanark said irritably, "You don't need as much rest as this."

"I know how much rest I need."

"The sun won't hang around the sky forever, Sandy. And it bores me, sitting still so often."

"It bores me walking all the time."

"Well, I'll go on at a slow steady pace and you catch up with me when you like," said Lanark, standing up.

"Yah!" cried Alexander on a strong whining note. "You must be right all the time, mustn't you? You won't leave anyone in peace, will you? You have to spoil everything, haven't you?"

Lanark lost his temper, thrust his face toward Alexander's and hissed, "You hate visiting the country, don't you?"

"Have I been howling and whining like this all the time? If I hated the country I would have been, wouldn't I?"

"Stand up."

"No. You'll hit me."

"I certainly will *not.* Stand up!"

Alexander stood up, looking worried. Lanark went behind him, gripped his body under the armpits and with a strong heave managed to sit him on his shoulders. Staggering slightly he set off through a plantation of tiny fir trees. A minute later Alexander said, "You can put me down now."

Lanark plodded on up the slope.

"I said you can put me down. I can walk now."

"Not till . . . we leave . . . these trees."

The weight at first had been so heavy that Lanark told himself he would only walk ten paces, but after that he went another ten, and then another, and now he thought happily, 'I could carry him forever by taking ten steps at a time.' But he put him down at the far side of the plantation and rested on the heather while Alexander hurried ahead. Eventually Lanark followed and overtook him on a ridge where heather and coarse brown grass gave place to a carpet of turf. The land here dipped into a hollow then rose to the steep cone of the summit. Alexander said, "You see that white thing on top?"

"Yes."

"It's a triangle point."

"A triangulation point."

"That's right, a triangule point. Come on."

Alexander started straight toward the summit. Lanark said, "Stop Sandy, that's the difficult way. We'll take this path to the right."

"The straight way in the shortest, I can *see* it is."

"But it's the steepest too. This path keeps to the high ground, it will save a lot of effort."

"You go that way then."

"I will, and I'll reach the top before you do. This path was made by sensible people who knew which way was the quickest."

"You go that way then," said Alexander and rushed straight down into the hollow.

Lanark walked up the path at an easy pace. The air was fresh and the sun warm. He thought how good it was to have a holiday. The only sound was the *Wheep! Wheep!* of a distant moorbird, the only cloud a faint white smudge in the blueness over the hilltop. In the hollow on his left he sometimes saw Alexander scrambling over a ridge and thought tolerantly, 'Silly of him, but he'll learn from experience.' He was wondering sadly about Alexander's life with Rima when the path became a ladder of sandy toeholes kicked in the steepening turf. From here the summit seemed a great green dome, and staring up at it Lanark saw an amazing sight. Up the left-hand curve, silhouetted against the sky, a small human figure was quickly climbing. Lanark sighed with pleasure, halted and looked away into the blue. He said, "Thank you!" and for a moment glimpsed the ghost of a man scribbling in a bed littered with papers. Lanark smiled and said, "No, old Nastler, it isn't you I thank, but the cause of the ground which grew us all. I have never given you much thought, Mr. cause, for you don't repay that kind of effort, and on the whole I have found your world bearable rather than good. But in spite of me and the sensible path, Sandy is reaching the summit all by himself in the sunlight; he is up there enjoying the whole great globe that you gave him, so I love you now. I am so content that I don't care when contentment ends. I don't care what absurdity, failure, death I am moving toward. Even when your world has lapsed into black nothing, it will have made sense because Sandy once enjoyed it in the sunlight. I am not speaking for mankind. If the poorest orphan in creation has reason to curse you, then everything high and decent in you should go to Hell. Yes! Go to Hell, go to Hell, go to Hell as often as there are vicitms in your universe. But I am not a victim. This is my best moment. Speaking purely as a private person, I admit you to the kingdom of Heaven, and this admission is final, and I will not revoke it."

Near the top of the slope he began to grow breathless. The turf of the summit was broken by low gnarls of rock. The concrete triangulation pillar stood on one and Alexander was using it as a backrest. He had the air of man sprawling on a comfortable sofa in his own house and seemed not to see Lanark at first, then patted invitingly the rock beside him, and when Lanark sat down he leaned against him and they looked a long time at the view. In spite of their height the sea was only a soft dark line on the horizon. The land up to it was wide low hills given over to pasture, and there were strips of windbreak wood with half-reaped fields of grain in the valleys between. Lanark and Alexander faced a steep side of the hill which sloped straight down to a red-roofed town with crooked streets and a small ancient palace. This had round towers with conical roofs and a walled garden open to the public. Many figures were moving between the bright bushes and flowerbeds, and there was a full car-park outside. Alexander said, "It would be nice to go down there."

"Yes."

"But Mum might worry."

"Yes, we must go back."

They sat a little longer and when the sun was three-quarters across the sky they arose and descended to the moor by a path which led round a small loch. Two men with thick moustaches, one carrying a rifle, came up the path and nodded to Lanark as they passed. The rifle man said, "Will I shoot the delegate?" and the other laughed and said, "No, no, we mustn't kill our delegate."

Shortly after, Alexander said, "Some jokes make me tremble with fear."

"I'm sorry."

"It can't be helped. Are you really a delegate?"

Lanark had been pleased by the recognition but said firmly, "Not now. I'm on holiday just now."

The loch was embanked as a reservoir on one side and on the grass of the embankment a dead seagull lay with outspread wings. Alexander was fascinated and Lanark picked it up. They looked at the yellow beak with the raspberry spot under the tip, the pure grey back and snowy breast which seemed unmarked. Alexander said, "Should we bury it?"

"That would be difficult without tools. We could build a cairn over it."

They collected stones from the shingle of the lochside and heaped them over the glossy feathers of the unmarked body. Alexander said, "What happens to it now?"

"It rots and insects eat it. There are a lot of red ants around here; they'll pick it to a skeleton quite fast. Skeletons are interesting things."

"Could we come back for it tomorrow?"

"No, it probably needs several weeks to reach the skeleton stage."

"Then say a prayer."

"You told me you didn't believe in God."

"I don't, but a prayer must be said. Put your hands like this and shut your eyes."

They stood on each side of the knee-high cairn and Lanark shut his eyes.

"You begin by saying *Dear God.*"

"Dear God," said Lanark, "we are sorry this gull died, especially as it looks young and healthy (apart from being dead). Let there be many young, living gulls to enjoy the speed and freshness this one missed; and give us all enough happiness and courage to die without feeling cheated; moreover . . ." He hesitated. A voice whispered, "Say amen."
"Amen."

Something cold stung his cheeks. He opened his eyes and saw the sky dark with torn, onrushing clouds. He was alone with nothing at his feet but a scatter of stones with old bones and feathers between them. He said "Sandy?" and looked around. There was nothing human on the moor. The light was fading from two or three sunset streaks in the clouds to the west. The heather was crested with sleet; the wind whipped more of it into his face.
"Sandy!" he screamed, starting to run. "Sandy! Sandy! *Alexander!*"
He plunged across the heather, tripped and fell into darkness. He wrestled awhile with something entangling, then realized it was blankets and sat up.

He was in a square room with cement floor and tiled walls like a public lavatory. It seemed large, perhaps because the only furniture was a lavatory pan in one corner without seat or handle to flush it. He lay in the diagonally opposite corner on part of the floor raised a foot above the rest and covered with red linoleum. The door of the place had a metal surface, and he knew it was locked. He had a headache and felt filthy and was sure something dreadful had happened. He pulled the blankets around him and huddled up, biting the thumb knuckle and trying to think. His main feeling was of filth, disorder and loss. He had lost someone or something, a secret document, a parent, or his self-respect. The past seemed a muddle of memories without sequence, like a confused pile of old photographs. To sort them out he tried recalling his life from the start.

First he had been a child, then a schoolboy, then his mother died. He became a student, tried to work as a painter and became very ill. He hung uselessly round cafés for a time, then took a job in an institute. He got mixed up with a woman there, lost the job, then went to live in a badly governed place where his son was born. The woman and child left him, and for no very clear reason he had been sent on a mission to some sort of assembly. This had been hard at first, then easy, because he was suddenly a famous man with important papers in his briefcase. Women loved him. He had been granted an unexpected holiday with Sandy, then something cold had stung his cheek—

His thoughts recoiled from that point like fingers from a scalding plate, but he forced them back to it and gradually more recent, more depressing memories came to him.

CHAPTER 42. Catastrophe

There had been a sky dark with onrushing clouds. He had been alone with some scattered rocks, old bones and feathers at his feet and had looked round saying "Sandy?" but there was nobody else on the moor and the light was fading from two or three sunset streaks in the clouds to the west. He had run across the heather screaming Alexander's name and tripped and fallen into darkness. He had wrestled a while with something entangling, then realized it was a downy quilt, flung it aside and sat up.

He was in bed in a darkened room with a headache and a feeling of terrible loss. He was sure he had come here with people who had been kind to him, but who were they? Where had they gone? His hand found and flicked the switch of a bedlight. The room was a dormitory with a pair of beds to each wall and dressing tables between them loaded with female cosmetics. The walls had coloured posters of male singers on them and notices saying things like JUST BECAUSE YOU'RE PARANOID DON'T THINK THEY AREN'T PLOTTING AGAINST YOU. His clothes were scattered about the floor. He groaned, rubbed his head, got up and quickly dressed. He felt that something very good had happened recently. It may not have been love, but it had left him ready for love. Delight had opened him, prepared him for someone who wasn't there. He was anguished by the absence of someone to hold and whisper to affectionately, someone to hold him and speak lovingly back. He left the room and hurried along a dark corridor toward a sound of music and voices behind a door. He pushed the door open and stood blinking in the light. The voices stopped then someone shouted, "Look out! Here he comes again!" and a huge explosion of laughter went up.

The gallery was emptier than he remembered. Most people lay on cushions on the lowest floor and he hurried through them looking left and right. He remembered meeting a thin-lipped smiling little mouth in a glade of dark hair and cried to a laughing mouth among dark hair, "Is it you? Were you with me?"

"When?"

"In the bedroom?"

"Oh, no, not me! Wasn't it Helga? The woman dancing up there?"

He rushed onto the dance floor, crying, "Are you Helga? Were you with me in the bedroom?"

"Sir," said Timon Kodac, who was dancing with her, "this lady is my wife."

Laughter came from every side though nobody else was dancing and the only player was a saxophonist. The rest of the orchestra sat with girls on cushions round the floor and he suddenly saw Libby very clearly. She leaned against the drummer, a middle-aged man with horn-rimmed glasses. Her gracefully plump young body yearned toward him, little ripples flowed up it, thrusting her shoulder into his armpit, a breast against his side. Lanark hurried over and said, "Libby, please, was it—was it you, please?"

"Nyuck!" she said with a disgusted grimace. "Certainly not!"

"It's all sliding away from me," wept Lanark, covering his eyes. "Sliding into the past, further and further. It was lovely, and now it has turned to jeering."

A hand seized his arm and a voice said, "Take a grip of your-self."

"Don't let go," said Lanark opening his eyes. He saw a small, lean, young-looking man with crew-cut hair, black sweater, slacks and sandshoes.

The man said, "You're being bloody embarrassing. I know what you need. Come with me."

Lanark let himself be led up to the top floor, which was completely empty. He said, "Who are you?"

"Think a bit."

The voice sounded familiar. Lanark peered closely and saw deep little creases at the corners of the eyes and mouth which showed that this smooth, pale, ironical face belonged to quite an old man.

He said, "You can't be Gloopy."

"Why not?"

"Gloopy, you've changed. You've improved."

"Can't say the same for you."

"Gloopy, I'm lonely. Lost and lonely."

"I'll help you out. Sit there."

Lanark sat at a table. Gloopy went to the nearest bar and returned with a tall glass. He said, "There you are. A rainbow." Lanark gulped it and said, "I thought you were operating as a lift, Gloopy."

"Doesn't do to stay too long at the same thing. What is it you want? Sex, is it?"

"No, no, not just sex, something more gentle and ordinary." Gloopy frowned and drummed his fingers on the tabletop. He said, "You'll have to spell it out more definite than that. Think carefully. Male or female? How old? What posture?"

"I want a woman who knew and liked me a long time ago and still likes me. I want her to take me in her arms easily, casually, as if it was a simple thing to do. She'll find me cold and unresponsive at first, I've lived too long alone, you see, but she mustn't be put off by that. We'll sleep together calmly all night, and then I'll lose my fear of her and toward morning I'll wake with an erection and she'll caress me and we'll make love without worry or fuss. And spend all day in bed, eating, reading and cuddling happily, making love if we feel like it and not *bothered* by each other."

"I see. You want a mother figure."

"No!" yelled Lanark. "I don't want a mother figure, or a sister figure, or a wife figure, I want a woman, an attractive woman who likes me more than any other man in the world yet doesn't pester me!"

"I can probably fix you up with something like that," said Gloopy. "So stop shouting. I'll give you one more drink, and then we visit your rooms in Olympia. All types of attractive bints in Olympia."

"My rooms? Olympia?"

"Olympia is the delegates' repose village. Didn't they tell you?"

"Are you a pimp, Gloopy?" said Lanark, gulping another white rainbow.

"Yeah. One of the best in the business. There's a great need for us in times like these."

"Times like what, Gloopy?"

"Don't you read the glossies? Don't you watch the talk shows?

Ours is an era of crumbling social values. This is the age of
alienation and non-communication. The old morals and manners are passing away and the new lot haven't come in yet.
Result is, men and women can't talk about what they want
from each other. In an old-fashioned flower culture like Tahiti
a girl would wear a pink hibiscus blossom behind her left ear,
which meant, I got a good boyfriend but I'd like to have two.
So the boys understood her, see? The European aristocracy
used to have a very sophisticated sex language using fans, snuff-
boxes and monocles. But nowdays people are so desperate for
lack of a language that they've taken to advertising in newspapers. You know the kind of thing! *Forty-three-year-old wealthy
but balding accountant whose hobby is astronomy would like to meet
one-legged attractive not necessarily intelligent girl who wouldn't mind
spanking him with a view to forming a lifelong attachment.* That's
just not good enough. Too much room for accident. What
society needs is me, a sensitive trustworthy middleman with
wide connections and access to a good Tunc-Quidative-Cor-
texin-Cluster-Computer."

"Smattera fact, Gloop," said Lanark shyly, "sometimes I am
a . . . a . . . a . . ."

"Yeah?"

"a . . . a . . . an imaginary sadist."

"Yeah?"

"Not a damaging sadist. Namaginary one. So from standpoint
of occasional perverse frolic it would help matters if lady nques-
tion, along with the other points numerated, which *are* the
'sential points, make no mistake about that, these other points
I numerated are the 'sential ones . . . where was?"

"Perverse frolic."

"Good. I'd like her *not* to be namaginary masochist, because
I want to give her imaginary pain, not imaginary pleasure."

"Yeah. Defeat whole purpose."

"So I require namaginary *weaker* sadist than myself."

"Yeah, difficult, but I might just manage to swing it. Come
on, then."

Gloopy steered him through the dozen Quantum-Cortexin
security men who remained outside the gallery and opened a
door beside the doors of the lifts. They walked down a paved
path between lawns and trees with Chinese lanterns in them.
Lanark said, "I thought we were very high up, Gloop."

"Only on the inside. The stadium is built in an old dock basin,
you see. The river's down here, Narky boy."

They passed a wharf where small pleasure boats were gently rocking and came to a smooth sheet of water with lamps along the far shore. Lanark stopped and pointed dramatically to the long reflections of the lights in the dark water.

"Gloop!" he cried. "Poem. Listen. 'Magine these lights stars, right? Here goes. Twilit lake, sleek as clean steel—"

"This is a river and it's nearly dawn, Narky boy."

"Doninerrupt. You're not a cricit, Gloop, you're a chamberlain, like Munro. Know Munro, no? Nindividual who delivers folk from one chamber to nother. Listen. Twilit lake, sleek as clean steel, each star a shining spear in your deep. Pottery. I have been twitted, in my time, with solidity, Gloop. Dull solid man of few words, me. But *pottery* is lukring in these dethps, Gloop!" said Lanark, thumping his chest. He thumped too hard and started coughing.

"Lean on me, Nark," said Gloopy.

Lanark leaned on him and they came to a footbridge which crossed the water in one slender white span to a shining arrangement of glass cubes and lantern-hung trees on the other shore.

"Olympia," said Gloopy.

"Nice," said Lanark. In the middle of the bridge he stopped again saying, "No fireworks now, so we have waterworks, yes? It's urgent that I piss."

He did so between two railings and was disappointed to see his urine jet two feet forward and then fall straight down. "When I was a small-bellied boy!" he cried, "tumbling ninepin over the dolly mixture daisies, my piss had an arc of thirteen feet. A greybeard now, belly flabby from abuse of drink, I cannot squirt past my reflection. Piss. A word which sounds like what it means. A rare word."

"Police," muttered Gloopy.

"No, Gloop, you are wrong. Police does not sound like what it means. It is too like polite, please and nice."

Gloopy was running down the slope of the bridge toward the village. When he reached the shore he turned his head for a moment and yelled, "All right, officers! Just a perverse frolic!"

Lanark saw two policemen advancing toward him. He zipped up his trousers and hurried after Gloopy. As he reached the shore two men stepped onto the bridge and stood blocking the way. They wore black suits. One held out a hand and said in a dull voice, "Pass please."

"I can't, you're blocking the way."

"Show your pass, please."

"I don't have one. Or if I do it's in my briefcase—I've left that somewhere. Do I need a pass? I'm a delegate, I have rooms here, please let me through."

"Identify self."

"Provost Lanark of Greater Unthank."

"There is no Provost Lanark of Greater Unthank."

Lanark noticed that the man's eyes and mouth were shut and the voice came from a neatly folded white handkerchief in his breast pocket. His companion was staring at Lanark with eyes and mouth wide open. A metal ring with a black centre poked out between his teeth. With great relief Lanark heard the voice of an ordinary human policeman behind him: "Just what's happening here?"

"There is no Provost Lanark of Greater Unthank," said the security man again.

"There is!" said Lanark querulously, "I know the programme says the Unthank delegate is Sludden but it's wrong, there was an unexpected last-minute change. *I* am the delegate!"

"Identify self."

"How *can* I without my briefcase? Where's Gloopy? He'll vouch for me, he's a very important pimp, you've just let him through. Or Wilkins, send for Wilkins. Or Monboddo! Yes, contact the bloody Lord Monboddo, he knows me better than anyone."

In his own ears the words seemed shrill and unconvincing. The voice from the security man's pocket sounded like a record slowing to a stop: "Proof-burden property of putative prover."

"What the hell does that mean?"

"It means, Jimmy, that you'd better come quietly with us," said a policeman, and Lanark felt a hand grip each shoulder. He said feebly, "My name is Lanark."

"Don't let it worry you, Jimmy."

The security men stepped back. The policemen pushed Lanark forward, then sideways and down to a landing stage. Lanark said, "Aren't you taking me to the repose village?"

They pushed him onto the deck of a motor launch, then down into a cabin. He said, "What about Nastler? He's your king, isn't he? *He* knows me."

They pushed him down on a bench and sat on a bench opposite. He felt the launch move out into the river and was suddenly so tired that he had to concentrate to keep from falling down.

Later he saw the planks of another landing stage, and a pavement which continued for a long time, then a few stone steps, a doormat and some square rubber tiles fitted edge to edge. He was allowed to lean on a flat surface. A voice said, "Name?"

"Lanark."

"Christian or surname?"

"Both."

"Are you telling me your name is Lanark Lanark?"

"If you like. I mean yes yes yes yes yes."

"Age?"

"Ndtermate. I mean indeterminate. Past halfway."

Someone sighed and said "Address?"

"Nthank cathedral. No, 'Lympia. Olympia."

There was some muttering. He noticed the words "bridge" and "security" and "six fifty." That jerked him awake. He stared across a counter at a police sergeant with a grey moustache who was writing in a ledger. He saw a room full of desks where two policewomen were typing and the number 6.94 very big and black was framed upon the wall. With a click it charged to 6.95. He realized that a decimal clock had a hundred minutes an hour and licked his lips and tried to talk quickly and clearly.

"Sergeant, this is urgent! An important phone call is probably going through just now to my rooms in the delegates' repose village; can it be diverted here? It's from Wilkins, Monboddo's secretary. I've been drunk and foolish, I'm sorry, but there may be a public disaster if I can't speak to Wilkins!"

The sergeant stared at him hard. Lanark had flung out his hands appealingly and now saw they were filthy. His waistcoat was unbuttoned, his suit crumpled. There was a bad smell in the room and he noticed, with a shudder, that it came from a brown crusted stain on his trouser leg. He said, "I know I look detestable but politicians can't always be wise! Please! I'm not asking for myself but for the people I represent. Put me on to Wilkins!"

The sergeant sighed. He took an assembly programme from under the counter and studied a back page printed in small type. He said, "Is Wilkins a surname or a Christian name?"

"Surname, I think. Does it matter?"

The sergeant pushed the programme over the counter saying, "Which?"

A list of names headed COUNCIL STAFF filled ten pages. In the first four Lanark found Wilkins Staple-Stewart, the Acting Secretary for Internal-External Liaison, Peleus Wilkins, Procurator Designate for Surroundings and Places, and Wendel Q.

Wilkins, Senior Adviser on Population Energy Transfer.

"Listen!" said Lanark. "I'll phone every Wilkins in the list till
I get the—no! No, I'll phone Monboddo and get the full name
from him; he knows me even if his damned robots don't. I'm
sorry the hour is so early, but . . ."

He hesitated, for his voice sounded unconvincing again and
the sergeant was slowly shaking his head. "Let me prove who
I am!" said Lanark wildly. "My briefcase is in Nastler's room
in the stadium—no, I gave it to Joy, a Red Girl, a hostess in
the executive gallery; she put it behind the bar for me I must
get it back it contains a vitally important document please this
is vital—"

The sergeant, who was writing in the ledger, said "All right,
lads."

Lanark felt a hand clapped on each shoulder and cried, "But
what am I charged with? I've hurt nobody, molested nobody,
insulted nobody. What am I charged with?"

"With being a pisser," said a policeman holding him.

"All men are pissers!"

"I am charging you," said the sergeant, writing, "under the
General Powers (Consolidation) Order, and what you need
is a nice long rest."

And as he was led away Lanark found himself yawning hugely.
The hands on his shoulder grew strangly comforting. Surely
he had often been pushed forward by strong people who
thought he was wicked? The feeling was less dreamlike than
childlike.

He was led into a small narrow room with what looked
like bunks piled with folded blankets along one wall. He climbed at once to the top bunk and lay down, but they laughed
and said, "No, no, Jimmy!"

He climbed down and they gave him two blankets to carry
and led him to another door. He went through and it was
slammed and locked behind him. He wrapped the blankets
round him, lay on a platform in a corner and slept.

And now he was awake and wildly miserable. He sprang
up and walked in a circle round the floor, crying, "Oh! I have
been wicked, *stupid,* evil, *stupid,* daft daft daft *daft* and stupid,
stupid! And it happened exactly when I thought myself a fine
great special splendid man! How did it happen? I meant to
find Wilkins and talk to him sensibly, but the women made
me feel famous. Did they want to destroy me? No, no, they

treated me like something special because it made *them* feel special but all the time nothing good was being made, nothing useful was done. I was drunk, yes, with white rainbows, yes, but mostly with vanity; nobody is as crazy as a man who thinks he is important. People tried to tell me things and I ignored them. What was Kodac hinting at? Valuable minerals, special reports, government ignorance, it sounded like dirty trickery but I should have listened carefully. And . . . Catalyst . . . why didn't I ask her name? She tried to warn me and I thought she wanted to sleep with me. Yah! Greed and idiocy. *I forgot the reports!* I lost the reports without even reading them, I was seduced by people I can't even remember (but it was lovely). And how did I come to be paddling in that burn with Sandy? What was that but a useless bit of happiness put in to make my fall more dreadful? (But it was wonderful.) Oh, Sandy, what kind of father have you been cursed with? I left you to defend you and have turned into a ludicrous lecherous discredited stinking goat!''

He stopped and stared at some things he had not noticed beside the platform: three plastic mugs of cold tea and three paper plates of rolls with cold fried sausages in them. He grabbed the rolls and with tears trickling down his cheeks gulped and swallowed between sentences, saying, "Three mugs, three plates, three meals: I've been a whole day in here, the first day of the assembly is over. . . . When will I be let out? . . . I was fooled by false love because I never knew the true kind, not even with Rima. Why? I was faithful to her not because I loved her but because I *wanted* love, it is *right* that she left me it is *right* that I'm locked up here, I deserve much worse. . . . But who will speak for Unthank? . . . Who will cry out against that second-hand second-rate creator who thinks a cheap stupid *disaster* is the best ending for mankind? O, heavens, heavens fall and crush me! . . . .''

He noticed that self-denunciation was becoming a pleasure and sprang up and beat his head hard against the door; then stopped because it hurt too much. Then he noticed someone else was shouting and banging too. The door had a slit like a small letterbox at eye level. He looked through and saw another door with a slit immediately opposite. A voice from there said, "Have you a cigarette Jimmy?''

"I don't smoke. Do you know the time?''

"It was two in the morning when they brought me in and that was a while ago. What did they get you for?''

"I pissed off a bridge.''

"The police," said the voice bitterly, "are a shower of bastards. Are you sure you don't have a cigarette?"

"No, I don't smoke. What did they get you for?"

"I hammered a man up a close and called the police a shower of bastards. Listen, they can't treat us like this. Let's batter our doors and yell till they give us some fags."

"But I don't smoke," said Lanark, turning away.

His main feeling now was of physical filth. The lavatory pan suddenly flushed and he examined it. The water looked and smelled pure. He undressed, wet a corner of a blanket and scrubbed himself hard all over. He draped a dry blanket round him like a toga, rinsed his underclothes several times in the pan and hung them on the rim to dry. He scraped with his nails the crust of vomit from the trouser leg and rubbed the place with the wettened blanket. The creased cloth offended him. Though thirsty he had only been able to empty one mug of cold tea. He spread the trousers on the platform and rubbed them steadily in small circles with the mug base, pressing down hard. He did this a long time without seeing an improvement, but whenever he stopped there was nothing else to do. The door opened and a policeman entered with a mug and a plate of rolls. He said, "What are you doing?"

"Pressing my trousers."

The man collected the other mugs and plates. Lanark said, "When will I get out, please?"

"That's up to the magistrate."

"When will I see the magistrate?"

The policeman went outside, slamming the door. Lanark ate, drank the hot tea and thought, 'The assembly has begun the work of the second day.' He began pressing again. Whenever he stopped he felt so evil and useless, evil and trivial that he bit his hands till the pain was an excuse for screaming, though he did it quietly and undramatically. Another policeman brought lunch and Lanark said, "When will I see the magistrate?"

"The court sits tomorrow morning."

"Could you take my underclothes please and hang them somewhere to dry?"

The policeman went out, laughing heartily. Lanark ate, drank, then walked in a circle, flapping the underpants in one hand, the vest in the other. He thought, 'I suppose the assembly is discussing world order just now.' A feeling of hatred grew in him, hatred of the assembly, the police and everyone who wasn't in the cell with him. He decided that when he was released he would immediately piss on the police station steps, or smash a window, or set fire to a car. He bit his hands some more, then worked at pressing trousers and drying underclothes till long after the evening tea and rolls. He felt too restless to lie down, and when the underwear was only slightly damp he dressed, polished his shoes with the blanket and sat waiting for breakfast and the magistrates' court. He thought drearily, 'Perhaps I'll be in time for the pollution debate.'

And then he wakened with a headache, feeling filthy again. Three mugs of cold tea, three plates of rolls lay beside the platform. He thought, 'My life is moving in circles. Will I always come back to this point?' He didn't feel wicked any more, only trivial and useless. Another policeman opened the door and said, "Outside. Come on. Outside."
Lanark said feebly, "I would like to stay here a little longer."
"Outside, come on. This isn't a hotel we're running."

He was led to the office. A different sergeant stood behind the counter and an old lady wearing jeans and a fur coat stood in front. Her face was sharp and unpleasant; her thin hair, dyed blond, was pulled into an untidy bun on top of her head and the scalp showed between the strands. She said, "Hullo, Lanark."
The sergeant said, "You have this lady to thank for bailing you out."
She said, "Why didn't he appear in the magistrates court this morning?"
"Pressure of business."
"The court didn't look busy to me. Come on Lanark."
Her voice was harsh and grating. He followed her to the station steps and was slightly blinded by the honey-coloured light of an evening sun sparkling on the river beyond a busy roadway. He stopped and said, "I'm sorry. I don't know who you are."
She pulled off a fur gauntlet and with a queer, vulnerable gesture held out her hand, palm upward. One of the lines across it was deep, like a scar.
He said "Gay!" with immense regret, for though she had been ill when he last saw her she had also been attractive and young. He gazed into her lean old face, shaking his head, and her expression showed she had the same feeling about himself.

She pulled on the glove and slipped her arm round his, saying quietly, "Come on, old man. We can do something better than stand round regretting our age. My car is over there."

As they went toward it she said with sudden violence, "The whole business stinks! Everyone knew you disappeared two days ago; there were plenty of rumours but nothing was done. Twice daily I phoned every police station in the Provan region and they pretended they hadn't heard of you till an hour ago; then the marine police station admitted they had a prisoner who *might* be you. An hour ago! After the subcommittee reports had been read and voted on and all the smiling statements made to the press. Did you know I was a journalist? I write for one of those venomous little newspapers that decent people think should be banned: the sort that print nasty stories about rich, famous, highly respected citizens."

She opened the car door. He sat beside her and she drove off. He said, "Where are we going?"

"To the banquet. We'll be in time for the speeches at the end."

"I don't want to go to a banquet. I don't want the other delegates or anybody to see me or be reminded of me ever again."

"You're demoralized. It'll wear off. My daughter is a stupid, gelid little nung. If she'd looked after you none of this would have happened. Have you guessed who caused all this?"

"I blame nobody but myself."

She laughed almost merrily and said, "That's a splendid excuse for letting bastards walk all over you. . . . Do you really not know who pushed you into that trap?"

"Gloopy?"

"Sludden."

He looked at her. She frowned and said, "Perhaps Monboddo is in it too, but no, I don't think so. The big chief prefers not to know certain details. Wilkins and Weems are more likely, but if so Sludden has been too smart for them. Instead of neatly carving up Greater Unthank for the council my bloody ex-husband has handed it over to Cortexin lock, stock and ballocks."

"Sludden?"

"Sludden, Gow and all the other merry men. Except Grant. Grant objected. Grant may manage to start something."

"I don't understand you," said Lanark drearily. "Sludden sent me here to argue against Unthank's being destroyed. Will it be destroyed?"

"Yes, but not in the way they first planned. The council and creature-clusters meant to use it as a cheap supply of *human* energy, but they won't do that now till they've sucked out these lovely rich juices discovered by your friend Mrs. Schtzngrm."

"What of the pollution?"

"Cortexin will handle that. For the moment, at any rate."

"So Unthank is safe?"

"Of course not. Bits of it have become valuable property again, but only to a few people and for a short time. Sludden has sold your resources to an organization with worldwide power run by a clique for the benefit of a clique. That isn't safety. Why do you think were you sent here as a delegate?"

"Sludden said I was the best man available."

"Ha! Politically speaking you don't know your arse from your elbow. You don't even know what the word 'lobbying' means. You were fucking well *certain* to pox up everything, that's why Sludden made *you* delegate. And while people here got excited about you, and plotted against you, and passed big resolutions about world order and energy and pollution, Sludden and Cortexin were doing with Unthank exactly what they wanted. You aren't very intelligent, Lanark."

"I have begun to notice that recently," said Lanark, after a pause.

"I'm sorry old man, it isn't your fault. Anyway, I'm trying to make you angry."

"Why?"

"I want you to raise hell at this banquet."

"Why? I won't do it, but why?"

"Because this has been the smoothest, politest, most docile assembly in history. The delegates have handled each other as gently as unexploded bombs. All the dirty deals and greedy devices have been worked out in secret committees with nobody watching, nobody complaining, nobody reporting. We need somebody, just once, to embarrass these bastards with a bit of the truth."

"Sludden told me to do that."

"His reasons are not my reasons."

"Yes. He was a politician, you are a journalist, and I like neither of you. I like nobody except my son, and I'm afraid I'll never see him again. So I care for nothing."

The car was passing down a quiet street. Gay parked it suddenly by a vast brick wall and folded her arms on the wheel.

She said quietly, "This is terrible. In the days of the old Elite you were a definite, independent sort of man in your limited way. I was slightly afraid of you. I envied you. I was a silly weakling then, the mouthpiece of someone who despised me. And now that I've lost my looks and gained some sense and self-confidence you've gone as feeble as putty. Did Rima chew your balls off?"

"Please don't talk like that."

Gay sighed and said, "Where will we go?"

"I don't know."

"You're my passenger. Where do you want me to drive you?"

"Nowhere."

"All right," she said, reaching into the back seat. "Here's your briefcase. My daughter found it somewhere. It was empty, apart from a scientific dictionary and this pass with your name on it." She stuck a long strip of plastic into his breast pocket. "Get out."

He got out and stood on the kerb, trying to find comfort in the familiar smoothness of the briefcase handle. He expected the car to drive away but Gay got out too. She took his arm and led him to a double door, the only feature in a wilderness of wall. He said, "What place is this?" but she hummed softly to herself and touched a bell button. Each wing of the door suddenly swung inward and Lanark was appalled by the sight of two tight-mouthed security men. They spoke sharply and simultaneously, the voices springing from their shirtfronts: "Pass, please."

"You can see it in his pocket," said Gay.

"Identify self."

"He's the Unthank delegate, slightly late, and I'm from the press."

"Delegate may enter. No press may enter without the red card. No press may enter without the red card. Delegate may enter."

They moved apart, leaving a narrow space between them. Gay said, "Well, goodbye, Lanark. I'm sorry I won't be able to twist your arm when the right moment comes. But if you manage to improvise some guts, old man, I'll certainly hear about it."

She turned and walked away.

"Delegate may enter. Or Not," said the security men. "Delegate may enter. Or not. Invite expression of intention by progression or retrogression. Request expression of intention. Demand expression of intention. Command expression of intention!"

Lanark stood and pondered.

"Think hard!" said the security men. "In default of expression of intention, delegate demoted to condition of obstruction. Think hard! In def of exp of int del dem to con of ob think, conofobthink, conofobthink."

And although it made him shudder, he stepped through the narrow space between them because he could think of nowhere else to go.

CHAPTER 43. Explanation

A concrete floor, dusty and stained by pigeon droppings, lay under a high roof upheld by iron girders. From the doorway a long blue carpet ran into the shadowy distance. He walked down this till it touched a similar carpet at right angles. He turned the corner round a little gurgling fountain in a glass bowl and heard a hubbub of voices. A dozen security guards stood before the door of a circus tent. He went forward, holding out his pass and saying loudly, "Unthank delegate!"

A displeased looking girl in red shirt and jeans appeared between the black-clad men and said, "I'm surprised to see *you* here, Lanark. I mean, everything's finished. Even the food." It was Libby. He muttered that he had come for the speeches. "Why? They'll be horribly boring, and you look as if you hadn't washed for a week. Why do you want to hear speeches?"

He stared at her. She sighed and said, "Come inside, but you'll have to hurry."

He followed her through the door. The hubbub grew deafening as she led him along between the inner wall of the tent and a line of waiters carrying out trays laden with used dishes. He glimpsed the backs of people sitting at a table which curved away to the left and right. Libby pointed to an empty chair saying, "That was yours."

He slunk into it as quietly as possible. A neighbor stared at him, said "Good God, a ghost!" and started chuckling. It was Odin. "It's very, very, very good to see you," said Powys, the other neighbour. "What happened? We've been terribly alarmed about you."

The table formed a white-clothed circle filling most of the tent. There was a wineglass to each chair and a sign with

the guest's name and title facing outward. Red girls carried
bottles about inside the circle, filling glasses. Lanark explained
what had happened to him.

"I'm glad it was only that," said Powys. "Some people whispered you'd been shot or abducted by the security guards.
Of course we didn't really believe it. If we had we'd have
complained."

"That rumour did the assembly a power of good," said Odin
cheerfully. "A lot of cowardly loudmouths were afraid to say
a word during the big energy debate. Bloody idiots!"

"Well, you know," said Powys, "I don't mind admitting I was
worried too. These guards are ugly customers, and nobody
seems to know what their precise instructions are. Yes, the
business of the last few days has been settled with unusual
promptness, so you did not piss in vain. But it was reckless
of you to pollute their river. They're very fond of it."

Solveig came along the table filling wineglasses. He stared down
at the tablecloth, hoping not to be noticed. There was a sound
like a colossal soft cough then a perfectly amplified voice said,
"Ladies and gentlemen, you will be glad to hear that after an
absence of three days one of our most popular delegates has
returned. The witty, the venerable, the *not always perfectly sober*
Lord Provost Lanark of Greater Unthank is in his place at last."

Lanark's mouth opened. Though total silence had fallen he
seemed to hear a great roar go up. The multitude of glances
on him—mocking, he was sure, condescending, contemptuous,
amused—seemed to pierce and press him down. Someone
yelled, "Give the man a drink!"

He sobbed and laid his head on the tablecloth. The hubbub
of voices began again, but with more speculation than laughter
in it. He heard Odin murmur, "That wasn't necessary," and
Powys said, "No, they didn't need to rub it in like that."

There was another soft cough and the voice said, "My lords,
ladies and gentlemen, pray silence for Sir Trevor Weems,
Knight of the Golden Snail, Privy Councillor of Dalriada, Chief
Executive Officer of the Greater Provan Basin and Outer Erse
Confederacy."

There was some applause then Lanark heard the voice of
Weems.

"This is a strange occasion for me. The man sitting on
my left is the twenty-ninth Lord Monboddo. He has been many
things in his time: musician, healer, dragon-master, scourge
of the decimal clock, *enfant terrible* of the old expansion project,

stupor mundi of the institute and council debates. I have known him as all these things and opposed him as every one of them. A rash, rampant, raving intellectual, that's what I called him in the old days. Everyone remembers the unhappy circumstances in which his predecessor retired. I won't tell you what I thought when I heard the name of the new Monboddo. If I spoke too plainly our excellent Quantum-Cortexin security guards might be obliged to lead me away under the Special Powers (Consolidation) Order and lock me in a very small room for a very long time. The fact is, I was appalled. Our whole Provan executive was flung into profound gloom when we realized we would be hosts to a general assembly chaired by the dreadful *Ozenfant*. But what has been the outcome?" There was a pause. Weems said fervently, "Ladies and gentlemen, this has been the most smoothly run, clear-sighted, coherent assembly the council has ever convened! There are many reasons for this, but I believe future historians will mainly ascribe it to the tact, tolerance and intelligence of the man sitting on my left. He need not shake his head! If he is a rebel we need more of them. Indeed, I might even be persuaded to vote for a revolution—if the twenty-ninth Lord Monboddo undertook to lead it!"

There was some loud laughter.

By slow degrees Lanark had come to sit upright again. The centre of the circle was empty. Far to the right Weems stood beside Lord and Lady Monboddo. Microphones protruded from a low bank of roses on the tablecloth before him. All the guests on that side of the circle were pink. On the other side they were sallow or brown, with the five members of the black bloc directly facing Monboddo. Several dark delegates talked quietly among themselves, not attending to the speech. Weems was saying, ". . . will be far too deep for me, I'm afraid, and what I do understand I'll almost certainly disagree with. But he has heard so much from us in the past three days that it is only fair to allow him his revenge. And so, Lord Monboddo, I call on you to summarize the work of the council, Then, Now and Tomorrow."

Weems sat down amid applause. Monboddo had been smiling down at the table with half-shut eyes. He arose and stood with one hand resting on the table, the other in his pocket, the smiling head tilted a little to one side. He waited until applause, faint conversation, coughs and stirrings sank into silence. As the silence continued his figure, casual yet unmoving, gained power and authority until the whole great ring of guests was like an audience of carved statues. Lanark was amazed that so many could make so complete a silence. It weighed on him like a crystal bubble filling the top of the tent and pressing down on his skull: he could shatter it any time by yelling a single obscenity, but bit his lips hard to stop that happening. Monboddo began to speak.

> "Some men are born modest. Some achieve modesty. Some have modesty thrust upon them. I fear that Sir Trevor has firmly placed me in the last of these categories."

Laughter went up, especially from Weems.

> "Once I was an ambitious young department chief. I launched policies and had flashes of creative brilliance which, believe me, my friends, verged, I thought, upon genius! Well, ambition has met its nemesis. I now stand on the top tip of our vast pyramid and create nothing. I can only receive the brilliant proposals of younger, more actively placed colleagues and find ways to reconcile and promote them. I examine the options and discard, without emotions, those which do not fit our system. Such work uses a very *small* part of human intelligence."

"Oh, nonsense!" shouted Weems cheerfully.

> "Not nonsense, no, my friend. I promise you that in three years all the limited skills of a council supremo will be embodied in the circuits of a Quantum-Cortexin humanoid, just as the skills of secretaries and special policemen are embodied. It may be my privilege to be the last of the fully human Lords Monboddo. The idea would flatter my very considerable vanity, were it not for the great improvement people will see in government business when the change takes place. Everything will suddenly go much faster.

Yes, today human government stands at a very delicate point of balance. But before opening the path ahead I must describe the steps which brought us here.

"So stand with me on the sun some six thousand years ago and consider, with sharper eyes than the eagle, the moist blue-green ball of the third planet. The deserts are smaller than now, the forest jungles much bigger, for where soil is thick, shrubberies clog the rivers and spread them out into swampland. There are no broad tracts of fenced field, no roads or towns. The only sign of men is where the globe's western edge is rolling into the shadow of night. Some far-apart gleams are beginning on that dim curve, the fires of hunters in forest clearings, of fishers at river mouths, of wandering herdsmen and planters on the thin soil between desert and jungle, for we are too few to take good land from the trees. Our tiny tribal democracies have spread all over this world, yet we influence it less than our near relation the squirrel, who is important to the survival of certain hardwoods. We have been living here for half a million years, yet history, with its noisy collisions and divisions of code and property, has not yet started. No wonder the first historians thought men had been created a few centuries before themselves. No wonder later theorists called prehistoric men *childlike, savage, rude,* and thought they had wasted time in fighting and couplings even more ferocious than those of today.

"But big killings, like big buildings, need large populations to support them, and fewer people were born in 500,000 years of the stick-and-stone age than in the first 50 years of the twentieth century. Prehistoric men were too busy cooperating against famine, flood and frost to hate each other very much; yet they tamed fire and

animals, mastered joinery, cooking, tailor-
ing, painting, pottery and planting. These
skills still keep most of us alive. Compared
with the sowing and reaping of the first
grain crop, our own biggest achievement
(sending three men to and from a dead
world in a self-firing bullet) is a marvellously extravagant baroque curlicue on the
recentest page of human history."

"That's crap, Monboddo! And you know it!" yelled someone
across the circle from Lanark. There was laughter from the
darker-skinned delegates. Monboddo smirked at them before
continuing:

"I still represent modern government, Mr. Kodac, do not worry. But the
tools for harpooning other planets are still
in the primitive phase, and it does no harm
to admit that clever fellows like ourselves
need not be ashamed of our ancestors. All
the same, this petit-bourgeois world of
gamekeepers and peasant craftmen bores
me. Yes, it bores me. I thirst for the over-
weening exuberance of the Ziggurats and
Zimbabwes, the Great Walls and Cathe-
drals. What is lacking from this prehistoric
nature-park where sapient men have lived
so long with such little effect? Surplus is
lacking: that surplus of food, time and energy, that surplus of *men* we call wealth.
"So let a handful of centuries pass and
look at the globe again. The biggest land
mass is split into three continents by a com-
plicated central sea. East of it, a wide river
no longer meanders through swamps but
flows in a distinct channel across a fertile
geometry of fields and ditches. On the glittering surface boats and barges move upstream and down to unload their cargoes
beside the cubes, cones and cylinders of
the first city. A great house with a tower
stands in the city centre. On the summit,
high above the hazes of the river, the secretaries of the sky use the turning dome

of heaven as a clock of light where sun, moon and galaxies tell the time to dig, reap and store. Under the tower the wealth of the state, the sacred grain surplus, is banked: sacred because a sack of it can keep a family alive for a month. This grain is stored life. Those who own it can command others. The great house belongs to modern men like ourselves, men, not skilful in growing and making things, but in managing those who do. There is a market beside the great house from which tracks radiate far across plain and forest. These tracks are beaten by tribesmen bringing fleeces, hides and whatever else can be exchanged for the life-giving grain. In time of famine they will sell their children for it. In time of war they can sell enemies captured in battle. The wealth of the city makes warfare profitable because the city managers know how to use cheap labour. More trees are felled, new canals widen the cultivated land. The city is growing.

"It grows because it is a living body, its arteries are the rivers and canals, its limbs are the trade routes grappling goods and men into its stomach, the market. We, whose state is an organization linking the cities of many lands, cannot know what sacred places the first cities seemed. Luckily the librarian of Babylon has described how they looked to a visiting tribesman:

He sees something he has never seen, or has not seen . . . in such plenitude. He sees the day and cypresses and marble. He sees a whole that is complex and yet without disorder; he sees a city, an organism composed of statues, temples, gardens, dwellings, stairways, urns, capitals, of regular and open spaces. None of these artifacts impresses him (I know) as beautiful; they move him as we might be moved today by a complex machine of whose purpose we are ignorant but in whose design we intuit an immortal intelligence.

"Immortal intelligence, yes. That undying intelligence lives in the great house which is the brain of the city, which is the first home of institutional knowledge and modern government. In a few centuries it will divide into law court, university, temple, treasury, stock exchange and arsenal."

"Here here!" shouted Weems unexpectedly, and there was some scattered applause.
"Bugger this," muttered Odin. "He's talked for ten minutes and only just reached the topic."
"I find these large vague statements very soothing," said Powys. "Like being in school again."

"But all tribesmen are not servile adorers of wealth [said Monboddo]. Many have skill and greed of their own. The lords of the first cities may have fallen before nomads driving the first wheeled chariots. No matter! The new masters of the grain may only keep it with help from the clever ones who rule land and time by rod and calendar, and can count and tax what others make. The great riverine cultures (soon there are five of them) absorb wave after wave of conquerors, who add to the power of the managers by giving them horsemen for companions. So the growth of cities speeds up. Their trade routes interlock and grapple, they compete with each other. Iron swords and ploughshares are forged, metals command the wealth of the grain. The seaside cities arise with their merchant and pirate navies."

"He's getting faster," whispered Powys. "He's covered twelve civilizations in six sentences."

"Men increase. Wealth increases.
War increases. Nowadays, when strong
governments agree *there must not be* another big war, we can still applaud the
old battles and invasions which blended
the skills of conquerors and conquered.
The are no villains in history. Pessimists
point to Attila and Tamerlane, but these
active men liquidated unprofitable states
which *needed* a destroyer to release their
assets. Wherever wealth has been used for
mere self-maintenance it has always inspired vigorous people to grasp and fling
it into the service of that onrushing history
which the modern state commands. Pale
pink people like myself have least reason
to point the scorning finger. Poets tell us
that for two millennia Europe was boister-
ous with energies released by the liquida-
tion of Asiatic Troy. I quote the famous
Lancastrian epic:

"Since the siege and assault was ceaséd
                              at Troy,
The burgh broken and burned to
                    brands and ashes,
It was Aeneas the Able and his high
                              kind
That since despoiled provinces and
                    patrons became
Wellnigh of all the wealth in the West
                              Isles;
For rich Romulus to Rome riches he
                              swipes,
With great bobbaunce that burgh he
                    builds upon first,
And names with his own name as now
                    it hath;
Ticius in Tuscany townships founds,
Langbeard in Lombardy lifts up homes,
And far over the French flood Felix
                              Brutus,
On many banks full broad Britain he
                    builds with his winnings,

> Where war and wreck and wonder
> By turns have waxed therein,
> And oft both bliss and blunder
> Have had their innings.

"Bliss and blunder. The flow of
wealth around the globe has involved
much of both, but wealth itself has continued to grow because it is always served
by the winners."

"Pale pink people," muttered Odin broodingly. "Pale pink
people."
"I don't think the blackies and brownies are much amused,"
said Powys. "Are you all right, Lanark?"
Monboddo's strong quiet voice purred on like a stupefying
wind.

". . . so north Africa becomes a desert, with several useful consequences. . . ."
"After the clean camaraderie of the
steam bath-house, the new recruits notice
that their parents stink. . . ."
". . . but machinists only work effi-
ciently in a climate of hope, so slavery is
replaced by debt and money becomes a
promise to pay printed by the government. . . ."
". . . by the twentieth century,
wealth has engrossed the whole globe,
which now revolves in a tightening net
of thought and transport woven round it
by trade and science. The world is enclosed in a single living city, but its brain
centres, the governments, do not notice
this. Two world wars are fought in thirty
years, wars the more bitter because they
are between different parts of the same
system. It would wrong the slaughtered
millions to say these wars did no good.
Old machines, old ideas were replaced at
unusual speed. Science, business and government quickly became richer than ever
before. We must thank the dead for that."

Monboddo glanced at Weems, who stood up and said solemnly,
"This is surely a good time to remember the dead. There are
hardly any lands where men have not died this century fighting
for what they thought best. I invite all delegates to stand with
me for two minutes and remember the friends, relations and
countrymen who suffered to make us what we are."

"Bloody farce," muttered Odin, gripping Lanark under the
elbow to help him rise.

"Soon be over," whispered Powys, helping at the other side.
The whole great circle gradually rose to their feet except the
black bloc, who stayed obstinately seated. There was silence
for a while; than a distant trumpet sounded outside the tent
and everyone sat murmuringly down.

"What's the point of this speech?" said Odin. "It's too Marxian
for the Corporate Wealth gang and too approving for the Marx-
ists."

"He's trying to please everyone," said Powys.

"You can only do that with vague platitudes. He's like all
these Huns—too clever for his own good."

"I thought he came from Languedoc," said Powys.

> "As I reach our present dangerous
> time [said Monboddo, sighing], I fear I
> have angered almost everyone here by a
> perhaps too cynical view of history. I have
> described it as a growing and spreading
> of wealth. Two styles of government com-
> mand the modern world. One works to
> reconcile the different companies which
> employ their people, the other employs
> the people themselves. Defenders of the
> first style think great wealth the reward
> and necessary tool of those who serve man-
> kind best; to the rest it is a method by
> which strong people bully weak ones. Can
> I define wealth in a way which lets both
> sides agree with me? Easily.
> "At the start of my talk I said wealth
> was a surplus of men. I now say a wealthy
> state is one which orders its surplus men
> into great enterprises. In the past extra
> men were used to invade neighbours,
> plant colonies and destroy competitors.
> But the liquidation of unprofitable states

by warfare is not practical now. We all
know it, which is why this assembly has
been a success: *not* because I have been
a specially good chairman but because you,
the delegates of states big and small, have
agreed to order onrushing history, onrushing wealth, onrushing *men* by majority de-
cisions reached through open and honest
debate."

Weems started clapping again, but Monboddo talked vehe-
mently over him.

"Believe me, this splendid logicalness
has been achieved only just in time! More
men have been born this century than in
all the ages of history and prehistory pre-
ceding. Our man surplus has never been
so vast. If this human wealth is not governed it will collapse—in places it is already collapsing—into poverty, anarchy,
disaster. Let me say at once that I do not
fear wars between any government represented here today, nor do I fear revolution. The presence of that great revolutionary hero, Chairman Fu of the People's
Republic of Xanadu, shows that revolu-
tions are perfectly able to create strong
governments. What we must unite to prevent are half-baked revolts which might
give desperadoes access to those doomsday machines and bottled plagues which
stable governments are creating, not to
use, but to prevent themselves from being
bullied by equals. No land today lacks desperadoes, brave greedy ignorant men who
can no longer be sent to work in less busy
parts of the world and are too ambitious
to join a regular police force. No modern
state lacks irresponsible intellectuals, the
enemies of strong government everywhere. Both types seem anxious to break
the world down into tiny republics of the
prehistoric kind, where the voice of the
dull and cranky would sound as loud as

the wise and skilful. But a reversion to barbarism cannot help us. The world can only be saved by a great enterprise in which stable governments use the skills of institutional knowledge with the full backing of corporate wealth. Council, institute and creature everywhere must work together.

"The fuel supply of the present planet is almost exhausted. The food supply is already insufficient. Our deserts have grown too vast, our seas are overfished. We need a new supply of energy, for energy is food as well as fuel. At present, dead matter is turned into nourishment by farming, and by the consumption of uneducated people by clever ones. This arrangement is a failure because it is inefficient; it also puts clever people into a dependent position. Luckily our experts will soon be able to turn dead matter directly into food in our industrial laboratories— *if we give them access to sufficient energy.*

"Where can this energy be found? Ladies and gentlemen, it is all around us, it streams from the sun, gleams from the stars and sings harmoniously in every sphere. Yes, Mr. Kodac! It is time for me to admit that sending ships into space is not just an adventure but a necessity. That greater outer space is not, we now know, a horrid vacuum but a treasure house which can be endlessly, infinitely plundered—if we combine to do it. Once again the secretaries of the sky will be our leaders. We must build them a high new platform, a city floating in space where the clever and adventurous of every land, working in a clean, nearly weightless atmosphere, will reflect heat and sunlight down to the powerhouses of the world.

"It has been suggested we call this enterprise New Frontier or Dynostar. I suggest the Laputa Project. . . ."

Monboddo's speech had hypnotized Lanark. He listened open-mouthed, nodding in the pauses. Whenever he understood a sentence it seemed to say everything was inevitable and therefore right. Yet his body grew less and less easy; his head buzzed; when Monboddo said "a high new platform, a city floating in space," he seemed to hear another voice, harsh and incredulous, say, "The man's a lunatic."
Even so, he was appalled to find himself standing and shouting **"EXEXEXEXEXEXEX"** at the top of his voice. Powys and Odin gripped his wrists, but he wrenched them free and yelled, **"EXCUSE ME! EXCUSE ME** but Lord Monboddo lied when he said all the delegates agreed to manage things through open, honest debates! Or else he has been lied to by other people."

There was silence. Lanark watched Monboddo watching him woodenly. Weems stood up and said quietly, "As host of this gathering I apologize to Lord Monboddo and the other delegates for . . . for Provost Lanark's hysterical outburst. He is notorious for his lack of control in civilized company. I also demand that Provost Lanark take back these words."
"I'm sorry I said them," said Lanark, "but Lord Monboddo has deliberately or ignorantly told us a lie. I pissed off a bridge, but I should not have been locked up before I had spoken for Unthank! Unthank is being destroyed with no open agreement at all, jobs and homes are being destroyed, we've begun hating each other, the Merovicnic Discontinuity is threatened—"
He was deafened by a babel of laughter and talk. A row of black-clad men stood behind Weems and Lanark saw two of them walk around the tent toward him. His legs trembled so much that he sat down. Voices were shouting for silence somewhere on his left. Silence fell. He saw Multan of Zimbabwe standing up, smiling at Monboddo, who said shortly, "Speak, by all means."
Multan looked round the table then said, "The Unthank delegate says this assembly has not held free and open debates. That's not news to the black bloc. Is it news to anybody?" He chuckled and shrugged. "Everybody knows three or four big boys run the whole show. The rest of us don't complain, why should we? Words by themselves are no good. When we get organized big, we'll complain and you'll listen. You'll have to listen. So this Lanark is very foolish to speak like he does. But he tells the truth. So on this side of the table we watch what happens. We laugh because it don't matter to us

how you claw each other. But we watch closely what happens, all the same."

He sat down. Monboddo sighed and scratched his head. At last he said, "I will answer the Zimbabwe delegate first. He has told us, with admirable modesty, that he and his friends are not yet able to share the work of the council but will do so when they can. That is very good news; may the day come soon. The Unthank delegate's case is less clear. I gather the police arrested him in the circumstances where his exalted rank was not apparent. He has missed our debates, but what can I do? I leave Provan one decimal hour from now. I can grant him a brief personal interview. I can promise that anything he says will be recorded in the assembly minutes for everyone to read. It is all I can offer. Is it sufficient?"

Lanark felt everyone watching him and wanted to hide his face again. He glanced over his shoulder and shivered at the sight of two black-suited men. One nodded and winked. It was Wilkins. Monboddo said loudly, "If you wish this interview, my secretaries will escort you to a convenient place. Otherwise the matter must be dropped. Answer, please, there is not much time."

Lanark nodded. He stood and walked from the tent between the secretaries, feeling old and defeated.

CHAPTER 44. End

As they crossed the wide dim floor Wilkins said cheerily, "That was great fun; you scared the shits out of old M."
The other man said, "These intellectuals have no staying power."
"Lanark has been around for a long, long time," said Wilkins, "I think he deserves a three-syllable name, don't you?"
"Oh, he certainly deserves it," said the other man. "There's nothing wrong with a two-syllable name, I'm called Uxbridge, but Lanark has earned something more melodious. Like Blairdardie."
"Rutherglen, Garscaden," said Wilkins.
"Gargunnock, Carmunnock, Auchenshuggle," said the other man.
"Auchenshuggle has four syllables," said Wilkins.

They went through a narrow door, climbed a dingy stair and crossed a small office into a slightly larger office. It was lit by a neon tube and the walls were hidden by metal filing cabinets, some piled on others. There was a metal desk in the corner. Without much surprise Lanark saw Monboddo sitting behind it with hands clasped patiently on the waistcoat over his stomach. "Bilocation," said Monboddo. "I would be nothing if I did not duplicate. Sit down."
Wilkins placed a straight wooden chair before the desk and Lanark sat.
"Wilkins, Uxbridge, go away. Miss Thing will record us," said Monboddo. Lanark saw a girl exactly like Miss Maheen sitting between two filing cabinets. Wilkins and Uxbridge left. Monboddo tilted his chair back, looked at the ceiling and sighed. He said, "At last the Common Man confronts the Powerful

Lord of this World. Except that you are not very common and I am not very powerful. We can change nothing, you and I. But talk to me. Talk to me."

"I am here to speak for the people of Unthank."

"Yes. You wish to tell me they have too few jobs and homes and social services so stupidity, cruelty, disease and crime are increasing among them. I know that. There are many such places in the world, and soon there will be more. Governments cannot help them much."

"Yet governments can fire great structures into space!"

"Yes. It is profitable."

"For whom? Why can't wealth be used to help folk here and now?"

"It is, but we can only help people by giving less than we take away from them. We enlarge the oasis by increasing the desert. That is the science of time and housekeeping. Some call it economics."

"Are you telling me that men lack the decency and skill to be good to each other?"

"Not at all! Men have always possessed that decency and skill. In small, isolated societies they have even practised it. But it is a sad fact of human nature that in large numbers we can only organize against each other."

"You are a liar!" cried Lanark. "We have no nature. Our nations are not built instinctively by our bodies, like beehives; they are works of art, like ships, carpets and gardens. The possible shapes of them are endless. It is bad habits, not bad nature, which makes us repeat the dull old shapes of poverty and war. Only greedy people who profit by these things believe they are *natural.*"

"Your flood of language is delicious," said Ozenfant, yawning slightly, "and can have no possible effect upon human behaviour. By the way, it was not clever of you to get Multan speaking for you. He is no enemy of the council, he is a weak member plotting to become strong. If he succeeds his aim will be my aim: to manage things as smoothly as possible. His only enemies will be people like you—the babies."

"I am not a baby."

"You are. Your deafness to reasoned argument, your indifference to decent custom and personal dignity, a selfishness so huge and instinctive that it cannot even notice itself, all make you the nearest thing to an adult baby I have ever encountered. And now you may retaliate by calling me as many foul names as you please. Nobody will know. Miss Thing cannot hear what is irrelevant to the business of the council."

Lanark said coldly, "You want me to lose my temper."

"Yes indeed," said Monboddo, nodding. "But only to cut short a useless argument. You suffer from the oldest delusion in politics. You think you can change the world by talking to a leader. Leaders are the effects, not the causes of changes. I *cannot* give prosperity to people whom my rich supporters cannot exploit."

Lanark put his elbows on his knees and propped his face between his hands. After a while he said, "I don't care what happens to most people. All of us over eighteen have been warped into deserving what happens to us. But if your *reason* shows that civilization can only continue by damaging the brains and hearts of most children, then . . . your reason and civilization are false and will destroy themselves."

"Perhaps," said Monboddo, yawning, "but I think we can make them last our time. What have you recorded, Miss Thing? Tell us, please."

The secretary parted her lips and a monotonous voice slid out between them:

> *"Greater Unthank Addendum to General Assembly Minutes: Provost Lanark referred to Unthank's serious employment, housing, health and pollution problems. Chairman Monboddo related them to the supranational crisis in these areas and intimated that the solution of such problems must await the primary solution of the worldwide energy famine. Provost Lanark called for a more urgent approach to local difficulties insofar as they affect the 0–18 spectrum. Chairman Monboddo suggested the outcome of difficulties in this spectrum was less disastrous than Provost Lanark feared."*

Miss Thing's mouth clicked shut. Monboddo slapped his brow and said, "Cryptonite! I forgot the Cryptonite deposits. Put them in, Miss Thing; it will let us end on a cheerful note." Miss Thing opened her mouth again.

> *"Chairman Monboddo suggested the outcome of difficulties in this spectrum would be less disastrous socially than Provost Lanark feared as the development by Cortexin of the Unthank*

*mineral resources was well on the way to putting
prosperity within the grasp of everyone."*

Lanark stood up and wrung his hands. He cried out, "I am useless. I should never have come here, I did no good to anyone, not to Sandy, Rima or anyone. I need to go home."

"Home?" said Monboddo, raising an eyebrow.

"Unthank. It may be bad but the badness is obvious, not gilded with lies like here."

"You are severe. But I will help you. Open the bolthole, Miss Thing."

There was a grey woollen rug in front of the desk. Miss Thing knelt and pulled it back, uncovering a round steel plate sunk in the linoleum. She put a thumb and forefinger into two small openings at the centre and lifted it easily out, though it was two feet across and four inches thick. "The way home," said Monboddo. "Look inside. You will recognize the interior of a familiar aircraft."

He stood up and rested, hands in pockets, on a corner of the desk. Lanark stooped and stared for a long time into the round hole. There was a cavity under it lined with blue silk. Monboddo said, "You do not trust me. But you will climb inside because you are too reckless to linger. Am I right?"

"You're wrong," said Lanark, sighing. "I will climb inside because I'm too tired to linger."

He stepped into the cavity, sat down and straightened his legs. The space lengthened and narrowed to fit him. He lay staring up at a circle of cream-coloured ceiling surrounded by blackness. He heard Monboddo murmur "Bon voyage," and a round black shape slid sideways across the circle of ceiling and eclipsed it with a low clang. Then the space he lay in dropped.

The drop was a long down-rushing swoop stopped by a jarring jerk. Then came another drop. With an indrawn scream he knew he was going down the great gullet again. The tiny office, the great round table, Provan, Greater Unthank, Alexander, cathedral, Rima, Zone, council corridors, institute had been a brief rest from the horror of endless falling. Monboddo had tricked him back into it. He screamed with hatred. He pissed with panic. He writhed and his face came out into a rush of milky mist. He was plunging downward in the bird-machine. The panic changed. He was the mind of this bird, an old bird

in poor repair. Each wingstroke tore out feathers he needed
for landing and the land was far below. He kept falling as
far as he dared, then levelling in a thrash of pinions which
thinned and flew back like darts. His bald breast and sides
were freezing in the fall. The misty air thinned to black and
the black map of a city lay below, the streets dotted lines of
light. Bits of the map were on fire. A big red flower of flame
drew him down to it. He saw a flaming glass tower, a square
of statues, engines and seething heads; he heard roaring and
sirens, tried to level and crashed sideways on cracking wings
through sparks, heat and choking smoke where a great dim
column swung at him, missed, swung away and swung back
like a mace to strike him down.

He woke, sore and bandaged, in bed with a tube running
into his arm. He lay there dreaming and dozing and hardly
thinking at all. He assumed he was in the institute again but
the ward had windows with darkness outside them, and the
beds were packed together with hardly a foot of space between.
The patients were all very old. All cleaning and some nursing
was done by those fit enough to walk, for there was a very
small staff. The light fittings were peculiar. Electric globes hung
from the ceiling by slim rods which were parallel to each other
but slanted toward a corner of the ward. When a nurse took
the tube from his arm and changed the bandages he said,
"Is the hospital sloping?"
"So you've found your tongue at last."
"Is the hospital sloping?"
"If that was all, we'd be laughing."
The meals were mainly beans and this pleased him, though
he couldn't remember why. The doctor was a hurried, haggard,
unshaven man in a dirty smock. He said, "Have you any friends,
old man?"
"I used to have."
"Where can we contact them?"
"They used to hang around the cathedral."
"Were you one of Smollet's mob?"
"I knew Ritchie-Smollet, yes. I knew Sludden too."
"Best not to mention that, Sludden is far from popular at pres-
ent. But we'll find if Smollet can take you. We have to evacuate
this place, there's going to be another shock. What's your
name?"
"Lanark."

"A common name in these parts. We had a provost called that once. He wasn't much good."

Lanark slept and wakened to screams and shouting. He was sweating and sticky. The air was very hot and the ward was empty except for a bed in a far corner; an old woman sat in it crying, "They shouldn't leave us here, it isn't right." A soldier came in, looking carefully round, avoided the old woman's eye and edged toward Lanark between the empty beds. He was a tall man with a sullen, handsome, slightly baby-ish face and did not seem to be carrying a weapon. His only insignia was a badge on his beret shaped like a hand with an eye in the palm. He stood looking down at Lanark, then sat on the edge of the bed and said, after a moment, "Hullo, Dad."

Lanark whispered "Sandy?" and smiled and touched his hand. He felt very happy. The soldier said, "We've got to get out of here. The foundation is cracked."

He opened the bedside locker, took out trousers, jacket and shoes and helped Lanark into them, saying, "I wish you'd kept in touch with us."

"I didn't know how."

"You could have written or phoned."

"I never seemed to have time. Yet I did no good, Sandy. I changed nothing."

"Of course you changed nothing. The world is only improved by people who do ordinary jobs and refuse to be bullied. No-body can persuade owners to share with makers when makers won't shift for themselves."

"I could never understand politics. How do you live, Sandy?"

"I report for movers and menders."

"What kind of work is that?"

"We have to hurry, Dad. Are you able to stand?"

Lanark managed to stand, though his knees trembled. The old woman in the corner bed wailed, "Son, could you help me too, son?"

"Wait here! Help is coming!" shouted Alexander fiercely. He took Lanark's right arm over his shoulder, gripped him round the waist and moved him toward the door, cursing below his breath. They were labouring uphill for the slope of the floor was against them. The screams and yelling grew louder. Alexander halted and said, "Listen, you used to be a sentimental man in some ways, so shut your eyes when you get out of here. Some things are happening which we just can't help."

"Anything you say son," said Lanark, closing his eyes. The arm round his waist gave such a strong feeling of happiness and safety that he started chuckling.

He was helped down many stairs amid loud crying and across a space where his ankles brushed past fingertips and then, though the air was no cooler, an uproar of voices and running feet suggested they were outside. He opened his eyes. The sight threw him off balance and he lost more balance trying to recover it. Alexander held him up, saying, "Steady, Dad." A great loose crowd, much of it children shepherded by women, slid and stumbled down a hillside toward a wide-open gate. But the hillside was a city square. The slanting lamp-standards lighting the scene, the slanting buildings on each side, the slanting spire of the nearby cathedral showed the whole landscape was tilted like a board.

"What happened?" cried Lanark.

"Subsidence," said Alexander, carrying him with the crowd. "There's going to be another soon, a bad one. Hurry."

Whenever Lanark's feet touched the ground he felt a vibration like a continuous electric shock. It seemed to strengthen his legs. He began moving almost briskly, chuckling and saying, "I like this."

"Jesus Christ," muttered Alexander.

"Do I sound senile, Sandy? I'm not. This gate leads to the graveyard, the Necropolis, doesn't it?"

"We'll be safer away from the buildings."

"I know this graveyard well, Sandy. So did your mother. I could tell you a lot about it. This bridge we're coming to, for instance, had a tributary of the river flowing under it once."

"Shut up and keep *moving,* Dad."

In the dim cemetery folk crouched on the grass plots or dispersed up the many little paths. From the height of the hill a loudspeaker was telling people to keep clear of high monuments. Alexander said, "Rima should be up at the top, can you go on?"

"Yes, yes!" said Lanark excitedly. "Yes, we must all get to the top, there's going to be a flood, a huge immense deluge."

"Don't be stupid, Dad."

"I'm not stupid. Someone told me everything would end in a deluge; he was very very definite about it. Yes, we must go as high as possible, if only for the view."

As they climbed the steep little paths Lanark felt more and

more energetic and cheerful. He tried to skip a little.

"Are you married, Sandy?"

"Steady, Dad, I wish you'd call me by my full name. No, I'm not married. I've a daughter, if that's any consolation."

"It is! It is! Will she be at the top of the hill too?"

"No, she's in a safer place than this, thank goodness. Do you hear the guns?"

There was a distant snapping sound.

"How can men fight like that at a time like this?" said Lanark, his voice squeaky with indignation.

"The Corquantal Galaxy are trying to liquidate their Unthank plant but Makers, Movers and Menders backed Defence Command in supporting the One-Wagers against them, so the council rump have sent in the Cocquigrues."

"I understand none of that. What are Cocquigrues?"

"I'll tell you when there's time."

Buildings burned in the city below. The glossy walls of the tower blocks reflected flickering glares upon a small knot of people between the monuments and the summit. Lanark couldn't see them clearly because tears came to his eyes. It struck him that Rima must be an old woman now and the thought was an unexpected pain. He muttered "Must sit" and settled on the edge of a granite slab. The vibration through it irritated his backside. He made out a nearby knot of men wearing armbands and stooping over an old-fashioned radio transmitter. Beside them a stout woman in a black dress waved to Alexander, then came over and laid a hand on Lanark's shoulder. He gazed up, astonished, into her large-eyed, large-nosed face with small straight childishly serious mouth. Though a little weary, and the glossy hair slightly streaked with grey, this seemed exactly the face he had first seen in the Elite Café. He said, "You aren't Rima?"

She laughed and said, "You always found it hard to recognize me. You've grown old, Lanark, but I knew you at once."

Lanark smiled and said, "You've grown fat."

"She's pregnant," said Alexander glumly. "At *her* age."

"You don't know my age," said Rima sharply and added, "I'm sorry I can't introduce you to Horace, Lanark, but he refuses to meet you. He's an idiot sometimes."

"Who is Horace?"

Alexander said dourly, "Someone who doesn't want to meet you. And a rotten wireless operator."

Lanark stood up. The vibration in the ground had become a strong, almost audible throbbing and Rima said tensely, "I'm frightened, Alex, don't be nasty to me."

The throbbing stopped. In a great quietness the hot air seemed to scald the skin. Lanark felt so heavy that he crashed on his knees to the ground, then so light that he rose in the air. When he came down again the ground was not where he expected. He lay listening to rumbling and shouting and looked at the firelit pinnacle of an obelisk; it leaned so far over him that he knew it must 'crack or topple. He got heavy, then light again, and this time only his head left the ground and fell back with a thump which dazed him slightly. When he next saw the obelisk it pointed perfectly upright and the glow on it was very strong.

"Tell me what's happening, please," said Rima. She lay curled on the ground with her hands over her eyes. Everybody lay on the ground except Alexander, who knelt beside the radio transmitter earnestly turning knobs.

"The ground is level again," said Lanark, getting up, "and the fire is spreading."

"Is it horrible?"

"It's wonderful. It's universal. You should look."

Behind the burning building was a great band of ruddy light with clouds rising into it from collapsed and collapsing roofs. There were no other lights. "First the fire, then the flood!" cried Lanark exultingly, "Well, I have had an interesting life."

"You're as selfish as ever!" shrieked Rima.

"Be quiet, I'm trying to contact Defence Command," said Alexander.

"Nothing can be defended now, I hear the water coming," said Lanark. There was a faraway rushing mingled with faint squeals. He hobbled between two monuments to the edge of a slope and gazed eagerly down, holding himself erect by a branch of a twisty thorn tree.

A blast of cold wind freshened the air. The rushing grew to surges and gurglings and up the low road between Necropolis and cathedral sped a white foam followed by ripples and plunging waves with gulls swooping and crying over them. He laughed aloud, following the flood with his mind's eye back to the river it flowed from, a full river widening to the ocean. His cheek was touched by something moving in the wind, a black twig with pointed little pink and grey-green buds. The colours of things seemed to be brightening although the fiery light over the roofs had paled to silver streaked with delicate rose. A long silver line marked the horizon. Dim roof-tops against it grew solid in the increasing light. The broken buildings were fewer than he had thought. Beyond them a long faint bank of cloud became clear hills, not walling the city in but receding, edge behind pearl-grey edge of farmland and woodland gently rising to a faraway ridge of moor. The darkness overheard shifted and broke in the wind becoming clouds with blue air between. He looked sideways and saw the sun coming up golden behind a laurel bush, light blinking, space dancing among the shifting leaves. Drunk with spacious-ness he turned every way, gazing with wide-open mouth and eyes as light created colours, clouds, distances and solid, graspa-ble things close at hand. Among all this light the flaming build-ings seemed small blazes which would soon burn out. With only mild disappointment he saw the flood ebbing back down the slope of the road.

Rima came beside him and said teasingly, "Wrong again, Lanark."

He nodded, sighed, and said, "Rima, did you ever love me?" She laughed, held him and kissed his cheek. She said, "Of course I did, even though you kept driving me away so nastily and so often. They've started shooting again."

They stood awhile listening to the snapping and crackings. She said, "Defence command have called Alex over to maintenance. It's very urgent, but he says he'll come back for you as soon as he can. You're to stay here and not worry if he's late."

"Good."

"I'm sorry you can't come with me, but Horace is an idiot sometimes. Why should a young man like him be jealous of you?"

"I don't know."

She laughed, kissed his cheek and went away.

After a while he hobbled back to the space between the monuments and sat once again on the edge of the granite slab. He was tired and chilly but perfectly content to wait. There was nobody about, but after a while he heard the crunch of a foot on gravel. A figure approached him wearing the black and white clothes and carrying the silver-tipped staff of a cham-berlain. Lanark had trouble focusing on the face under the wig: sometimes it seemed to be Munro, sometimes Gloopy. He said, "Munro? Gloopy?"

"Correct sir," said the figure, bowing respectfully. "We have been sent to bestow on you an extraordinary privilege."

"Who sent you?" said Lanark peevishly. "Institute or council? I dislike both."

"Knowledge and government are dissolving. I now represent the ministry of earth."

"Everything keeps getting renamed. I've stopped caring. Don't try to explain."

The figure bowed again and said, "You will die tomorrow at seven minutes after noon."

The words were almost drowned by a squawking gull turning in the sky overhead, but Lanark understood them perfectly. Like a mother's fall in a narrow lobby, like a policeman's hand on his shoulder, he had known or expected this all his life. A roaring like a terrified crowd filled his ears; he whispered, "Death is not a privilege."

"The privilege is knowing when."

"But I . . . I seem to remember passing through several deaths."

"They were rehearsals. After the next death nothing personal will remain of you."

"Will it hurt?"

"Not much. Just now there is no feeling in your left arm; you can't move it. In a moment it will get better again, but at five minutes after noon tomorrow your whole body will become like that. For two minutes you will be able to see and think but not move or speak. That will be the worst time. You will be dead when it stops."

Lanark scowled with self-pity and annoyance. The chamberlain said, respectfully "Have you a complaint?"

"I ought to have more love before I die. I've not had enough."

"That is everyone's complaint. You can appeal against the death sentence if you have something better to do."

"If you're hinting that I should go in for more adventures, no thank you, I don't want them. But how will my son—how will the *world* manage when I'm not here?"

The chamberlain shrugged and spread his hands.

"Well go away, go away," said Lanark more kindly. "You can tell the earth I would have preferred a less common end, like being struck by lightning. But I'm prepared to take death as it comes."

The chamberlain vanished. Lanark forgot him, propped his chin on his hands and sat a long time watching the moving clouds. He was a slightly worried, ordinary old man but glad to see the light in the sky.

I STARTED MAKING MAPS WHEN I WAS SMALL
SHOWING PLACE, RESOURCES, WHERE THE ENEMY
AND WHERE LOVE LAY. I DID NOT KNOW
TIME ADDS TO LAND. EVENTS DRIFT CONTINUALLY DOWN,
EFFACING LANDMARKS, RAISING THE LEVEL, LIKE SNOW.

I HAVE GROWN UP. MY MAPS ARE OUT OF DATE.
THE LAND LIES OVER ME NOW.
I CANNOT MOVE. IT IS TIME TO GO.

GOODBYE

TAILPIECE: How *Lanark* Grew

Hullo again. When Canongate published *Lanark* in 1981 I was 45 and thought the book would become famous, when I was dead. A London publisher told me *Lanark* might get a cult following in the USA and would do less well in Britain. But since 1981 it has been steadily reprinted here, and I have often been asked the following questions.

Q What is your background?

A If background means surroundings: first 25 years were lived in Riddrie, east Glasgow, a well-maintained district of stone-fronted corporation tenements and semi-detached villas. Our neighbours were a nurse, postman, printer and tobacconist, so I was a bit of a snob. I took it for granted that Britain was mainly owned and ruled by Riddrie people – people like my dad who knew Glasgow's deputy town clerk (he also lived in Riddrie) and others who seemed important men but not more important than my dad. If background means family: it was hardworking, well-read and very sober. My English grandad was a Northampton foreman shoemaker who came north because the southern employers blacklisted him for trade-union activities. My Scottish grandad was an industrial blacksmith and congregational elder. My dad fought in the First World War, which made an agnostic Socialist of him. He received a stomach wound that got him a small government pension, worked a cardboard-box cutting machine in a factory that survived the 1930s depression of trade, and in 1931 married Amy Fleming, a shop assistant in a Glasgow department store. She was a good housewife and efficient mother who liked music and had sung in the Glasgow Orpheus Choir. Dad hiked and climbed mountains for a hobby, and did voluntary secretarial work for the Camping Club of Great Britain and the

Scottish Youth Hostel Association. Mum had fewer ways of enjoying herself after marriage and I now realise wanted more from
life, though she seldom grumbled. So they were a typical couple.
I had a younger sister I bullied and fought with until we started
living in separate houses. Then she became one of my best friends.

Q What was childhood like?

A Apart from the attacks of asthma and eczema, mostly painless
but frequently boring. My parents' main wish for me was that I
go to university. They wanted me to get a professional job, you
see, because professional people are not so likely to lose their
income during a depression. To enter university I had to pass
exams in Latin and mathematics which I hated. So half my school
experience was passed in activities which felt to my brain like
a meal of sawdust to the mouth. And of course there was
homework. My father wanted to relieve the drudgery of learning
by taking me cycling and climbing, but I hated enjoying myself
in his shadow, and preferred the escapist worlds of comics and
films and books: books most of all. Riddrie had a good library. I
had a natural preference for all sorts of escapist crap, but when I
had read all there was of that there was nothing left but good
stuff: and myth and legend, and travel, biography and history.
I regarded a well-stocked public library as the pinnacle of
democratic socialism. That a good dull place like Riddrie had one
was proof that the world was essentially well organized. I realize
I am talking here about my life from 11 years onward, after the
Second World War. During it, with evacuation in 1939 to a farm
in Auchterarder (an experience I used in *The Oracle's Prologue*) in
the mining town of Stonehouse, Lanarkshire (which I used in
1982 Janine, my second novel) and Wetherby in Yorkshire, life
was not under the almost total jurisdiction of the Scottish Education system with my parents' full support, so not at all dull.

Q When did you realize you were an artist?

A I did not realize it. Like all infants who were allowed
materials to draw with, I did, and nobody suggested I stop. At
school I was even encouraged to do it. And my parents (like many
parents in those days) expected their children to have a party
piece – a song or poem they would perform at domestic

gatherings. The poems I recited were very poor A A Milne stuff. I found it possible to write verses which struck me as equally good, if not better, because they were mine. My father typed them for me, and the puerile little stories which I sent to children's magazines and children's radio competitions. When I was eleven I read a four-minute programme of my own compositions on Scottish BBC children's hour. But I was eight or nine years old when it occurred to me that I would one day write a story which would get printed in a book. This gave me a feeling of deliriously joyful power.

Q What sort of things did you draw when you were a child?

A Space ships, monsters, maps of imaginary planets and kingdoms, the settings for stories of romantic and violent adventure, which I told my sister when we walked to school together. She was the first audience I could really depend on in the crucial years between seven and eleven. If you have read *Lanark* you will notice how much of Book 1 – the first half of the Thaw section – draws upon my childhood. It does not show how much help and sympathy my mum, dad and sister gave me. I took it for granted as something natural and ordinary because so did they. When I came to use the material of my childhood in that novel what I remembered were our quarrels – they were more dramatic than the support I took for granted.

Q When and why did you want to make a story of your life?

A Surely everyone wants to be a hero or heroine? I'm sure all children do, probably when they stop being babies and find they have very little power over the world, apart from the power they imagine having. Books contained worlds I could grasp and manage through day-dreaming. The complete plays of Bernard Shaw and Henrik Ibsen stood on the middle shelf of a bookcase in my parents' bedroom beside Carlyle's *French Revolution*, Macaulay's essays, *The History of the Working Classes in Scotland* and *Our Noble Families* by Tom Johnson, a Thinkers Library volume called *Humanity's Gain from Unbelief*, an anthology of extracts for atheists called *Lift up Your Heads*, a large blue-grey bound volume with *The Miracle of Life* stamped in gold on the spine. This contained essays on the Dawn of Life, What Evolution Means,

Life that has Vanished, Evolutions as the Clock Ticks, The
Animal Kingdom, The Plant Kingdom, Man's Family Tree,
Races of Mankind, The Human Machine at Work, Psychology
through the Ages, Discoverers of Life's Secrets. The 476 pages
(excluding the index) were half given to black-and-white
photographs and diagrams. The middle shelf also held Shaw's
Quintessence of Ibsenism and *The Adventures of a Black Girl in Search
of God*, and I believe the last was the first adult narrative brought
to my attention, though I cannot remember it. I remember first
reading it with pleasure and excitement in my middle teens, but
years later my father told me he had read it to me when I was wee
– perhaps four years old. The story presents an evolutionary view
of the human faith through the quest of a black girl through the
African bush. Converted to Christianity by an English missionary she sets out to find God, not doubting he can be found on
earth, and encounters in various clearings the gods of Moses, Job
and Isaiah, then meeting Ecclesiastes the Preacher, Jesus,
Mahomet, the founders of the Christian sects, an expedition of
scientific rationalists, Voltaire the sceptic and George Bernard
Shaw the socialist, who teach her that God should not be
searched for but worked for, by cultivating the small piece of
world in our power as intelligently and unselfishly as possible.

The moral of this story is as high as human wisdom has
reached, but I cannot have grasped it then. My father told me
that I kept asking, "Will the next god be the *real* one Daddy?"
No doubt I would have liked the black girl to have at last met
the universal maker like my father: vaster, of course, but with an
equally vital sense of my importance. I am glad he did not teach
me to believe in that, for I would have had to unlearn it. But my
first encounter with this book was in a pre-history I have forgotten or
suppressed, though I returned to it later. It was a beautifully
made book with crisp clear black woodcuts decorating covers,
with title-page and text in a style reminiscent of Eric Gill. Like
the text it convincingly blended the mundane and exotic.

This was all on the middle shelf of our Riddrie bedroom
bookcase. The shelf above was blocked by the orange-red spines
of Left Wing Book Club, four-fifths of it being the collected
works of Lenin in English: dense text with no pictures or conversations in it at all. The bottom shelf was exactly filled by the
Harmsworth Encyclopaedia, because the bookcase had been sold
along with the Encyclopaedia by the publisher, who owned the

Daily Record in which they were first advertised. This contained many pictures, mostly grey monochrome photographs, but each alphabetical section had a complex line drawing in front, a crowded landscape in which an enthroned figure representing Ancient History (for example) was surrounded by orders of Architecture, an Astronomical telescope, glimpses of Australia and the Antarctic with Amundsen, and an Armadillo and Aardvark rooting around a discarded Anchor. I gathered that these volumes contained explanations of everything there is and had been, with lives of everyone important. The six syllables of the name EN-CY-CLO-PAED-I-A seemed to sum up these thick brown books which summed up the universe, so saying it gave me a sense of power confirmed by the pleasure this gave my parents. But the four colour plates showing flags of all nations and heraldic coats-of-arms gave an undiluted pleasure which was purely sensuous. I was fascinated by the crisp oblongs and lozenges holding blues, reds, yellows, greens, blacks and whites combining in patterns more vivid and easily seen than anywhere else, apart from our Christmas decorations.

Healthy children exercise their imaginations by playing games together. I was not healthy. My imagination was mainly exercised in solitary fantasies fed by films and pictures and books. From these I sometimes got the feeling that life could be glorious, a feeling often inspired by sexual episodes in books and not always the best episodes. I felt it in *1984* when Winston saves the girl he detests from stumbling in a corridor in the ministry of Truth, and finds after she has given him a note saying, "I love you"; also when David Copperfield gets the courage to propose to Agnes, who then tells him she has always loved him. Also in *Peer Gynt*, when his mother Aase and fiancée Solveig save him from The Great Boig by ringing the church bells and that vast foggy enclosing force dissolves saying, "He is too strong for us – he has women behind him." I also felt it in the climax of *The Portrait of the Artist as a Young Man* when Stephen Dedalus sees the young bare-legged girl paddling on the beach, and she accepts the worship of his glance, and with a heartfelt "Holy God!" he turns and walks toward the sunset knowing he will be an artist, which is the greatest sort of priest. Also in Joyce Cary's *The Horse's Mouth* when Gulley Jimson, fatally injured in the destruction of his mural painting, is carried off laughing in the ambulance because he knows he was doing his best work right up to the end.

And Joyce Cary's novel brought me to the books of William
Blake because Gulley Jimson kept quoting him. The Glasgow
Mitchell Library had facsimiles and originals – and Blake's work
in verse and picture and prose struck me then and strikes me
now as true, beautiful and good. The airy freedom of his
naked figures felt like liberation. So did the elaborately clothed,
slightly perverse figures of Aubrey Beardsley. And in case this all
sounds too high-minded I was terribly stimulated by the highly
coloured American comics which first came to Britain in the
late 1940s when I was in my early teens. They showed
Wonderwoman, Sheena the Jungle Girl and other females with
figures and faces like glamorous film-stars of that time, but
wearing much less clothing, and since the representation of
normal sexual practice was forbidden by the USA moral code
their adventures involved them in capture and bondage instead.
Such fantasies compensated for my own sexual timidity.

Q This spate of information about the fiction you enjoyed
suggests a terrible lack of interest in the life around you.

A Not lack of interest but lack of anticipation. I misled you if I
suggested I had no friends of my own. I had several, especially
one I called Coulter in the novel. We went on discursive walks
and sometimes bicycle rides together. But I could not take part in
the sports he liked (running, and watching football) and nights
out at the Dennistoun Palais. His accounts of his social adventures fascinated me like stories in books I read. I had no social
skill apart from *tête-à-têtes* and haranguing people at the school
literary and debating society – the skills of Adolf Hitler. I wanted
to be part of it, wanted to be an exciting, welcomed person in
other people's lives – especially in the lives of girls who attracted
me. Nothing like that seemed possible till I got to Glasgow
School of Art in 1952, a few months after my mother died. All
that is described as I remember it in *Lanark*. Memory is an
editing process which inevitably exaggerates some episodes,
suppresses others and arranges events in neater orders, but
nobody assumes that of their own memory. I don't.

Q So how autobiographical is *Lanark*?

A Book 1, the first half of the *Thaw* section, is very like my life until 17½ years, though much more miserable, as I explained. Also the hostel for munition workers which my dad managed during from about 1941 to '44 was in Wetherby, Yorkshire. I shifted it to the Scottish west highlands to preserve some national unity and bring in some references to Scotland's Calvinist past, though the Wee Free clergyman is sheer invention. I have never met such a man. The second half of the *Thaw* book is true to friends I made at art school and some of my dealings with the staff, for I filled notebooks while there with details to be used in my Portrait of the Artist as a Young Glaswegian. But unlike James Joyce's portrait I intended my artist to end tragically –

Q Why?

A Young artists couldn't make livings by painting easel or murals in 1950s Scotland. Nearly all art students became teachers, apart from a few who got into industry or advertising or became housewives. I supposed I would have to survive by some kind of compromise like that, but I had no intention of letting Thaw do so. Which is why I made him dourer, more single-minded than I am. His inability to attract women, and sexual frustration would also help push him towards madness. The episode with the prostitute, by the way, was sheer invention. It struck me as the sort of thing that would likely happen if I went with a prostitute. So I never did. In 1954 I was so sure of my *Thaw* story that, instead of taking a summer holiday job like most art students, I got dad's permission to stay at home and write it. Having rapidly filled notebooks with ideas and descriptions I felt able to finish a novel in ten weeks. At the end of that time I had written what is now chapter 12, *The War Begins*, and the hallucinatory episode ending chapter 29, *The Way Out*. I had found I did not want to write in the gushing emotional voice of a diary, but in a calm unemphatic voice readers would trust. This is not my normal reading voice. To make it a normal written voice I had to continually revise

Q But where did *Lanark* come from?

A From Franz Kafka. I had read *The Trial* and *The Castle* and *Amerika* by then, and an introduction by Edwin Muir explaining

these books were like modern Pilgrim's Progresses. The cities in
them seemed very like 1950s Glasgow, an old industrial city
with a smoke-laden grey sky that often seemed to rest like a lid
on the north and south ranges of hills and shut out the stars at
night. I imagined a stranger arriving, making enquiries and
slowly finding he is in hell. I made notes for that book. I wrote a
description of a stranger arriving in a dark city, in a train on
which he is the only passenger. But the *Thaw* novel had to be
finished, I thought.

Then one day in Dennistoun public library I found Tillyard's
The English Epic and its Background, which I will not attempt to
describe in detail, but the lesson I took from it was this. The epic
genre can be prose as well as poetry and can combine all other
genres – convincing accounts of how men and women act in
common and uncommon domestic, political, legendary and
fabulous circumstances. Nothing less than an epic, I decided, was
worth writing, and was helped to the decision by remembering
how much I enjoyed works that mingled different genres;
childhood pantomime, *The Wizard of Oz* film, Hans Andersen's
stories, Amos Tutuola's *Palm-Wine Drunkard*, Hogg's *Confessions
of a Justified Sinner*, Ibsen's *Peer Gynt*, Kingsley's *Water Babies*,
Goethe's *Faust*, *Moby Dick*, Shaw's *Adventures of the Black Girl in
Search of God*, classical myths and some books of the bible. All
these mingle everyday doings with supernatural ones.

I now planned to put my journey through hell in the middle
of my Portrait of the Artist as a Frustrated Young Glaswegian. In
some chapter before Thaw went mad he would attend a drunken
party and meet an elderly gent like himself but thirty or forty
years older who would tell him a queer fantastic story, enjoyable
for its own sake. Only when the readers reached the end of *Thaw*
would they see the interior narrative was a continuation of it. The
design of the book now hung in my mind like a scaffolding put
up for the erection of a large castle, with a few towers (that is,
chapters) completed or partly complete. Most of what happened
to me before the novel was finished provided me with building
materials that I stored in notebooks until I could construct the
other towers and connecting walls.

For example, chapters 7 to 11 describe an institute, a
province of hell in which modern professional middle-class folk
are the devils. This derives from both other writers and my own
experience. The architecture of the place partly derives from

H.G. Wells's Selenite empire in *The First Men on the Moon* and 21st-century London in *The Sleeper Awakes*, but mostly from the afterlife hell in Wyndham Lewis's *Malign Fiesta*. This was part of a trilogy, *The Human Age*, later published as novels, but the last two books were first written as plays for the BBC Third Programme and broadcast several times around 1955. I heard one such broadcast while in Stobhill hospital then, an experience that also gave me material for chapter 26 – *Chaos* – which describes the experience from a patient's point of view. I had been sent there with what our family doctor called 'stasis asthmaticus', and which I ascribed to my quarrel with a very nice girl who only liked me as a friend, whereas I wanted her to be my (A) lover and (B – later of course) wife. In the institute chapters I describe it from a very poorly qualified doctor's viewpoint, and mingled atmospheres and details from Wyndham Lewis's hell, Stobhill hospital, the London underground railway system and the London BBC television centre. I experienced the last when I had plays produced or commissioned there in the middle and late 1960s. But chapters 7 to 11 were written in 1969 and '70, by which time Lanark's story was becoming greater than Thaw's, and I had decided to put the last inside the first.

That large change came about because in 1961 I married and, in September 1963 became a father. The most significant part of my life no longer seemed my eccentrically frustrated youth. The toils of later life which I shared with many other folk now looked as important.

Q Are you telling me that the fantastic and grotesque events in books 3 and 4 are also autobiographical? How can they be? Lanark becomes Lord Provost of Unthank. You were never a figure in the local politics of Glasgow.

A I know, but experience allowed me to generalise. A writer whose play has been chosen for a TV production is very like a politician chosen for an important position because he has made a speech that appeals to widespread sentiment. He then discovers he depends on a host of directors, producers, dramaturges and technicians to whom he is a temporary creature, of use in assist- ing their work if he does not tamper with the notions it suggests to *them*. The writer of what was once his script may feel good if the production is finally applauded: will certainly be blamed if it is not, but his part in the business may strike him as one that could have been done as well or better by someone with less or very different ideas. TV production taught me all about politics.

Q In what sort of order were the parts of the book completed?

A Book One was completed in its present form before my son was born. My wife and I were living on Social Security money then so I sent the completed part to Spenser Curtis Brown's literary agency because I felt the book good enough to stand alone, though I would have preferred to complete it in the big way I had planned. But Mr Curtis Brown rejected it so I did complete it as planned. By the mid-1970s I had completed book Three and linked it to Book One with my Oracle's Prologue. I had a good agent who liked my work by that time, Frances Head, a London lady. She showed it to three London publishers, who tried to persuade me to split the *Thaw* and *Lanark* narratives in two and make separate books of them. They said it would be dangerously expensive for them to risk publishing so big a first book by an unknown novelist. But my first marriage had collapsed in an amicable way, I had no need of money and was greedy for fame instead, so I refused them.

Books Two and Four were written side by side – I moved from completing a chapter in one to a chapter in the other with an increasing sense of running downhill. In 1975 and '76 I was carrying manuscripts around and working on them in all kinds of places. I remember waking up on the livingroom floor of my friend Angela Mullane's house after a party where I had fallen asleep for a usual Scottish reason, and resuming work there and then because it was a quiet morning and none of the other bodies on the floor were awake. I couldn't do that now. I was then a young fellow of forty or thereabouts.

At the end of July 1976 the whole book was completed, typed and posted to Quartet Ltd, the only London publisher Frances Head had been able to interest in it. She, alas, had died of lung cancer. Quartet books turned it down for the usual reason – it was too long for them to risk the high cost of printing. I sulked for half a year then posted it to Canongate, the only Scottish publishing firm I knew. Five or six months passed before I got an enthusiastic letter from Charles Wilde, the Canongate reader, saying the Scottish Arts Council would probably subsidise printing costs. Chapters had appeared in *Scottish International*, a short-lived but widely read literary magazine eight or nine years earlier, so north Britain was more ready for it than the south. I finally signed a contract with Canongate on the 20th of March 1978.

Q *Lanark* was published three years later. Why did it take so long?

A Canongate arranged a joint publication with Lippincott, an old well-established firm in the USA; but before the book was printed Lippincott got swallowed up by Harper & Row, another old well-established USA firm. This caused delay. Then American editors proof-read the book, decided my punctuation was inconsistent. I told them that I used punctuation marks to regulate the speed with which readers took in the text – some passages were to be read faster than others, so had fewer commas. There was more delay while I restored my text to its original state. However, the delays gave me time to complete the illustrative title pages and jacket designs.

Q Were you relieved when *Lanark* was finally off your hands?

A Yes. For a while before I held a copy I imagined it like a large paper brick of 600 pages, well bound, a thousand of them to be spread through Britain. I felt that each copy was my true body with my soul inside, and that the animal my friends called Alasdair Gray was a no-longer essential form of after-birth. I enjoyed that sensation. It was a safe feeling.

Q So you the time spent upon *Lanark* over so many years was time well spent?

A Not entirely. Spending half a lifetime turning your soul into printer's ink is a queer way to live. I'm amazed to recall the diaries I wrote when a student, often putting the words into the third person as a half-way stage to making them fictional prose. I'm sure healthy panthers and ducks enjoy better lives, but I would have done more harm if I'd been a banker, broker, advertising agent, arms manufacturer or drug dealer. There are worse as well as better folk in the world, so I don't hate myself.